Robert James Waller

SLOW WALTZ IN CEDAR BEND

THE BRIDGES OF MADISON COUNTY

ARROW

This edition published by Arrow in 1998
an imprint of The Ranodom House Group
20 Vauxhall Bridge Road, London SW1V 2SA

Papers used by Random House UK Ltd are
natural recyclable products made from wood
grown in sustainable forests. The manufacturing
process conform to the environment regulations
of the country of origin.

A catalogue record for this book is available from
the British Library

Printed in Australia by McPherson's Printing Pty Ltd

ISBN 0 099 27934 7

SLOW WALTZ IN CEDAR BEND

For high plumage and southern winds.

One

The *Trivandrum Mail* was on time. It came
out of the jungle and pounded into Villupuram Junction at 3:18 on a sweltry afternoon in south
India. When the whistle first sounded far and deep in
the countryside, people began pressing toward the
edge of the station platform. What could not walk
was carried or helped along—bedrolls and market
baskets, babies and old people.

Michael Tillman got to his feet from where he'd
been leaning against a sooty brick wall and slung a
tan knapsack over his left shoulder. A hundred people
were trying to get off the train. Twice that many
were simultaneously trying to get on, like two rivers
flowing in opposite directions. You pushed or were
left behind. A pregnant woman staggered in the
crush, and Michael took her arm, got her up the steps,

and swung himself into the second-class car as the train moved out.

Wheels turning, engine pulling hard, running at forty miles an hour through the edge of Villupuram. No place to sit, hardly a place to stand. Hanging on to the overhead luggage rack with one hand as the train curved out of brown hills and into green rice country, Michael slid the picture of Jellie Braden from his breast pocket, looked at it, reminding himself again of why he was doing this.

Bizarre. Strange. All of that. This curious rainbow of man and knapsack out of Iowa and into the belly of India in search of a woman. Jellie Braden . . . Jellie . . . belonging to another. But Michael Tillman wanted her. Wanted her more than his next breath, wanted her enough to travel the world looking for her. He kept thinking this whole affair was like songs you used to hear on late night radio.

How does it all begin? Who knows. And why? Same answer. The old Darwinian shuffle. Something primal, something way back and far down. Something whispering deep in the bones or genes, "That one." So it happened: a kitchen door in Iowa opened and likewise did Michael Tillman when Jellie walked through it in her fortieth year.

The dean's autumn reception for new faculty in 1980, that's when it was. Just back from India after his second Fulbright there and still jet-lagged, Michael slouched against the dean's refrigerator, tugging on his second beer of the afternoon. He looked past faces looking at him or what they took to be him and answered tedious questions about India, suffering the white noise of academic chatter in the spaces around him.

An accountant's wife had taken over the India interrogation. Michael gave her 38.7 percent of his attention, planning escape routes and taking a long-slow swallow of beer while she spoke.

"Didn't the poverty just bother you horribly?"

"What poverty?" He was thinking about Joseph Conrad now, being halfway through *Heart of Darkness* on his third reading of it.

"In India. It must be awful."

"No. I was in the south, and the people looked pretty well fed to me. You've been watching those television shows that concentrate on good Catholic sisters hobbling around in the guts of Calcutta." She jumped a little when he said "guts," as if it were a word she hadn't heard before or maybe didn't like to think about.

"Did you see any cobras?"

"Yes, the snake charmer in the marketplace had one in a basket. The snake's mouth was sewn shut to keep it from doing any damage."

"How did it eat?"

"It didn't. It eventually dies. Then the snake man goes out and finds another one and sews its mouth shut, too. That's the way it works."

"My God, that's cruel, even though I abhor snakes."

"Yeah, working conditions have gone downhill all over. On the other hand, it's pretty much like the university. We just use heavier thread, that's all."

The accountant's wife blinked at him in the way

some people do when they encounter lunacy and went on. "Did you see any of those naked men with white paint or whatever on their bodies? Isn't that strange?"

"No, I didn't see any. They're mostly up north, I guess. Benares, or Varanasi as they call it now, places like that. Whether it's strange or not, I can't say, depends on your worldview and career plans, I suppose."

"Jellie Braden's been to India, you know." The senior man in comparative economics leapfrogged the accountant's wife and had Michael's attention.

"Who?"

"Jim Braden's wife. He's the new guy in econometrics we hired away from Indiana." Michael heard a car door shutting in the driveway. The senior man turned and looked out the window. "Oh, here they come now. They're a delightful couple."

Braden? Braden . . . Braden . . . Braden? Ah, yes, Jim Braden. He'd interviewed him six months ago before going to India. Never met his wife. She'd been out with a realtor looking at housing during their recruiting visit. Michael felt like writing "Standard issue, greater than or equal to earnest and boring" on the evaluation form. But he didn't and wrote instead, "Jim Braden is a perfect fit," which amounted to the same thing.

James Lee Braden III came into the dean's kitchen, smiling, shaking hands, being introduced. Jellie Braden smiled, too, in her pale blue suit with a fitted jacket that came to just over her hips and a skirt reaching to midcalf, medium-heeled black boots below the hem. Subtle Jellie Braden.

But not subtle enough. It was all there. The cool

patrician face coming only from an upper-shelf gene pool, the night-black hair and good skin. A body the old French called *rondeur*, polite writers would call superb, and flesh magazines would lose control over. Gray eyes coming at you like an arrow in flight and a confidence with men indicating she knew what they could and could not do. Where she had learned those easy truths wasn't clear at first, but you didn't have to be around Jimmy Braden very long to know it wasn't from him.

The faculty and assorted others with short attention spans laid down India and took up repertoire number two, another set of standard questions. This time with the Bradens, leaving Michael slouched there against the fridge by himself, watching Jellie.

"How do you like Cedar Bend?"

"Are you all moved in now?"

"What courses are you teaching, Jim?"

"Jellie—what an *interesting* name."

The dean's wife came over. "Hello, Michael."

"Hi, Carolyn, what's up?" He and Carolyn had always got along well even though the ol' deanaroo secretly wished Michael would pack it up and go somewhere else, anywhere. He occupied a high salary line, mainly because he'd been at the university fifteen years, and Arthur Wilcox would have preferred something a little less expensive and a lot more manageable sitting in Michael's office.

But Carolyn generally looked him up at these affairs, and they'd talk a bit. The decline of romance was one of their favorite subjects. A few years earlier she'd gotten acceptably drunk at the Christmas bash and said, "Michael, you've got balls. The rest of 'em are eunuchs." He'd put his arms around her and whispered in her ear, "Merry Christmas, Carolyn." Over her shoulder Michael had seen the chairperson of accounting watching them. The Chair was holding a glass of nonalcoholic punch and had a green star pinned to his lapel with "Hi! I'm Larry—Happy Holidays" printed on it in red felt-tip. Michael had grinned at him.

For a while he'd called Carolyn "Deanette." She'd liked it well enough to have a T-shirt made up with that handle printed on the front and had worn it to the fall picnic where the faculty was supposed to play volleyball and get to know one another better. Arthur-the-dean had taken offense and wouldn't let her wear the shirt after that.

When she'd told Michael about the T-shirt ban, he'd said "Screw 'im."

Carolyn had laughed. "Fat chance. Arthur's Victorian to the core, all bundled up." When he'd heard that, Michael's faith in things working out all right had died another small death. Carolyn was fifty-three but still had fire in her belly, quite a lot of it, he suspected. And he thought it was a damn shame, not to mention the waste of a good woman. How the hell does it happen, he wondered, these mistakes in the matching?

He and Carolyn talked a few minutes. Michael was looking past her, looking at the back of Jellie Braden's head and wondering if her hair was as thick as it seemed to be, wondering how it would feel to grab a big handful of it and bend her over the dean's kitchen table right then and there. He somehow had a feeling she might laugh and bend willingly if he tried it.

Carolyn Wilcox followed the point of Michael's eyes and said, "Have you met Jellie Braden yet?"

"No, I haven't."

The deanette reached over and tugged on Jellie's sleeve, rescuing her from the fumes of vapidity in which she was swirling. Deans' wives are allowed to do that when they feel like it, and they do it regularly, leaving a small semicircle of people holding glasses in their hands and looking stupid as the object of their focus is torn away. It's a shot they ought to put in the yearbook.

Jellie Braden turned around. "Jellie, I'd like you to meet Michael Tillman. If there's anything incorrigible about this faculty, it's Michael. In fact, he's probably sole owner of that property."

Jellie held out her hand, and he took it. "What makes you incorrigible, Dr. Tillman?"

"Just Michael, if it's okay with you. I don't like titles." He grinned a little when he said it. She smiled at the casual way he discarded something it took him nine years in various medieval institutions to acquire. "Aside from that, I happen to believe I'm highly corrigible, it's only Carolyn and the rest who think otherwise."

Carolyn patted his arm and drifted away. Jellie Braden looked at him. "I recall Jimmy mentioning you when we were here for his interviews. Somebody on the faculty told him you were eccentric or something like that."

"Jaded, maybe. A lot of people mistake that for eccentricity."

"If I remember correctly, he came back from the interviews and said you're a regular idea factory. He brought it up again the other day and said he was looking forward to working with you. That doesn't sound very jaded to me."

Michael felt a little tight in the chest and needed breathing space. "Word is you've spent time in India."

"Yes, I have." As she spoke, he watched the gray eyes shift up and to the right, to another place, the way people do when they go on time-share, go somewhere else for a while. The way he did, often.

India. The idea of it always brought smells and glinting images rushing back to her for an instant, always the same smells and images—jasmine on Bengali night winds, dark hands across her breasts and along the curve of her back, the scent of a man as he pulled himself up and into her. And his words in those soft and transient moments,

. . . did I ever play this song before?
Not in any lifetime I remember.
. . . will I ever play this song again?
Not in any lifetime yet to come.

"I just got in from there," Michael said.

"First trip?" She came back from wherever she'd been and turned to set her glass on the kitchen table. "Second. I was there in 1976, also."

"You must like it." She smiled and tilted her

head. "I noticed the cigarette bulge in your shirt pocket. Is smoking allowed here?"

"Forget it. We can go outside and stomp 'em out on the dean's driveway, though. That pisses him off, so I usually do it at least once when I'm over here."

Someone with less a sense of herself than Jellie Braden would have sideslipped away from the invitation. Bad form and all that, particularly for the wife of a new faculty member. But Jellie tilted her head toward the door and said, "Let's do it." The kitchen was almost empty, since the dean was holding forth in his parlor, and attendance was required unless you had a note from your doctor.

They sat on the dean's back steps, where she bummed a cigarette from him. He asked, "When were you in India, and for how long?"

"Some time back. I spent three years there."

She was being casually imprecise, and he wondered about that. "What part?"

"Southeast, mostly. Pondicherry."

"I've heard of it, never been there. Old French city, isn't it?"

"Yes." She blew smoke out across the dean's azaleas and didn't say anything else.

"Like it?" he asked. "Dumb question. Must have if you stayed three years."

"It was up and down. Overall, pretty good. I went to do some work for my master's thesis in anthropology and kind of got caught up in India in general. Never finished the paper."

"That happens. India pretty much splits people into two categories, you love it or you can't stand it. I'm in the former group."

They were sitting only about a foot apart, and she looked over at him. "So am I."

"How'd you meet, you and Jim?"

"After I came back from India I wanted to hang around Bloomington even though I wasn't in school. I wangled a job as secretary in the economics department. Jimmy was a junior professor, just out of graduate school with his bright, shiny degree. He always was polite to me and wore expensive suits, wrote articles on esoteric topics I didn't understand but which I dutifully typed. I was pretty much lost and wandering back then. When he asked me to marry him, I couldn't think of any good reason not to, so I said yes."

Michael listened to what she said and how she said it. She married Jim Braden because she couldn't think of reasons not to. That was a strange way of putting it. Close to her like this, gray eyes steady on his, he upgraded his earlier idea about putting her on the dean's kitchen table. The new plan involved stripping her naked, taking off his own clothes, and flying in that shimmering state of affairs all the way to the Seychelles, first class. Upon arrival it would be a headlong and forever plunge into lubricious nirvana. He was quite certain Jellie Braden would look better than wonderful under a jungle waterfall with a red hibiscus in her hair.

"How long ago was that, when you got married?" As soon as he asked, a voice in his head groaned, "You dumb ass, Tillman, why'd you say that? It's more than you need to know and too damned forward—you just met the woman." He stood up and stomped out his cigarette on the dean's driveway. Anyplace else he field-stripped them and stuck the butts in his pocket, but not in the dean's driveway. Michael was like an old dog there, staking out his territory, making sure he left a little something behind for Arthur to sniff.

She walked over to her car and put hers out in the ashtray. "Jimmy'll complain like crazy when he sees that. He won't let me smoke at home when he's there. I'll get a lecture on our way out of here, and he'll spray the car with air freshener two minutes after we hit the driveway." She looked at him and chewed lightly on her lower lip. "Jimmy and I have been married ten years. I suppose we better go inside."

He started pulling off his tie. "You go ahead. I'm going back to my apartment and snuggle down with Joseph Conrad."

"Nice meeting you," Jellie Braden said.

"Same here. See you around."

She smiled. "Sure."

And Michael thought of a waterfall in the Seychelles that would be just perfect. Fifteen months later he rode the *Trivandrum Mail* into south India, toward places he'd never been, looking for her.

Two

igh summer 1953, a far place called Dakota and the wind hot and making your greasy clothes stick to your body. Michael Tillman was fifteen then, leaning under the hood of Elmore Nixon's car, banker Nixon of First National in Custer. T-shirt riding up his back and toes barely touching the cement, he listened to the big V-8's erratic turn, adjusted the carburetor, listened again as the engine smoothed out and settled down.

"Mikey, get tha' sonabitchin' Olds finished. We got three more to go yet." His father was staggering around, whiskey flask buried deep in the back pocket of gray-striped coveralls.

Outside at the pumps his mother was filling the tank of a grain truck and wiping her forehead with the back of her arm. July 27, 4 P.M. at Tillman's Texaco, a world of heavy smells and flaking paint in fading greens and peeling whites. Roar of traffic on Route 16 out in front; tourists with suitcases lashed to car tops, on their way to see the faces of Rushmore.

Straightening up, Michael removed the protective cloth from the Olds' fender and slammed the hood. He backed the car out of the service bay and parked it off to one side, stood there for a moment, wiping his hands on a cloth. A Lakota Sioux in rundown cowboy boots, short and sweating into his pockmarks, waited by the roadside for someone or something or some other time better than the one in which he lived.

Michael went to the pop cooler and pulled a Coke from where it lay buried in ice and water. He held the bottle against one cheek, then the other. Stuck it up inside his shirt and laid it against his chest, shuddered once as cold met hot. No rain for weeks, dust devils moving down the roadsides.

"Damnit, Mikey . . ."

His father's voice slurred and reverberated from inside the station. He put the unopened Coke back in the cooler.

Michael slid into another car and pulled it into the service bay. His mother's handwriting was on the work order, "lube & oil." The Chevy lifted on the rack with a whirring sigh, and he unscrewed the oil plug on lawyer Dengen's Bel-Air. While the used oil drained into a bucket he looked out at Route 16. One good road is enough, that's what he was thinking.

He walked over to the Vincent Black Shadow parked in the rear of the station, touched the handlebars. His father had taken in the big English motorcycle as payment for a repair bill and said it was

Michael's to keep if he'd fix it up and learn how to maintain it. He did and owned it, spiritually and physically, from that moment on. One good road—the Shadow could take him down that road if he learned all there was to know about valves and turning wheels and routes out of here. Michael was already practicing at night, running the Shadow at high speeds through the Black Hills even though he wasn't legally old enough to drive.

On winter nights when the Shadow waited for spring to come again, there was the jumpshot arching through the lights of small-town gymnasiums. People took notice of Ellis Tillman's boy, said he might be good enough to play college ball. When he scored fifty-three points against Deadwood his senior year, they were sure of it.

At pajama parties the high school girls giggled and talked about boys. They said Michael Tillman had sad brown eyes, lonely eyes, and grease on his hands that wouldn't come off. They said he was shy but had cute muscles and looked good in his basketball uniform. They said he had a nice smile when he showed it, but he'd probably end up running his father's gas station and never would get the grease off his hands. Sometimes he'd take one of them to a movie in Rapid City, but mostly he kept to himself. He worked at the station and fished the trout in summer, practiced his jumpshot in the city park until it became a thing of magic. The Shadow, the jumpshot, algebra and Euclid's geometry—they were all of the same elegant cloth, universes contained within themselves, and he was good at them. He wasn't quite so good with girls or rooms full of people or English classes where poetry was discussed until it didn't exist.

Rooms full of people he didn't care about. Poetry could be dealt with sometime. But he wondered about girls who would become women. Somewhere out in these places of the world was a woman with whom he would make love for the first time in his life. And what would that be like? To be with a woman? Not sure. Not sure, but wondering. Would she be pleased with him, and how would a boy-man know what to do? Not sure yet. A little shaky thinking of it and reading the copy of *What Boys and Girls Should Know About Each Other* his mother had discreetly placed on his bookshelf. Neither she nor his father ever mentioned the book. As with everything else, he figured he was on his own. Nobody was handing out anything to anyone as far as he could tell, except small paperback books that were never mentioned and seemed pretty unromantic in any case.

The jumpshot took Michael down roads where the Shadow couldn't go. On a December night in 1960, Ellis Tillman leaned close to his Zenith portable and adjusted the tuning, trying to pull in KFAB in Omaha, Nebraska. The announcer's voice came and went: "For . . . information . . . local Farm Bureau agent." Long way, weak signal. Twenty below zero in Custer at 9:14, wind chill minus forty-eight. More static. He swore at the radio, and Ruth Tillman looked up from across the kitchen table. "Ellis, it's only a basketball game, not the end of the world. Have they said anything more about Michael's knee?"

"No. He'll be okay. He's a tough kid." Ellis Tillman took a sip of Old Grand-Dad and bent close to the radio. He was proud of his boy.

The stars shifted or sunspots went away, and the announcer's voice came back in double time:

> The Big Red machine's rollin' now, on top of the Wichita State Shockers, eighty-three–seventy-eight, with just under four minutes to go. Tillman brings the ball up-court for the Shockers, still limping on the bad knee that took him out of action in the first half. Over to LaRoux, back to Tillman, half-court press by the Big Red. Tillman fakes left, drives right, double screen for him by LaRoux and Kentucky Williams. . . .

"Go get 'em, Mikey!" Ellis Tillman stamped his feet on yellow linoleum and pounded the chrome-legged table so hard the radio bounced. Ruth Tillman looked at her knitting and shook her head slowly back and forth, wondering about men and what drove them onward to such insanity.

Four hundred miles away in Lincoln, smell of sweat and popcorn and the crowd screaming and the coach signaling for what he called the Tillman Special and you're moving right and slamming your left elbow into the face of the bastard who's grabbing for your jersey and you're cutting hard for the double screen LaRoux and Kentucky are setting up and a camera flash bursts from the sideline and your right knee is swollen to half-again its normal size from blood in the tissues . . . and you've done this a million times before . . . more than that . . . and the power in your legs and shoulders and the grace and balletlike movement and you're high into the air, left hand cradling the ball over your head and right hand pushing it in a long and gentle arc toward an orange rim with silver metal showing where the orange paint has rubbed off from the friction of a zillion basketballs . . . and the ball clears the rim and slices the net just the way it used to in the backyard of your South Dakota home and the crowd screams louder and you land on a knee that crumples into nothing and you go to the floor with Kentucky Williams stumbling over you on his way back down the court . . .

and you lie there
and you know it's over
and you're relieved it is.
And four hundred miles northwest
your mother bows her head.

Two days later Ellis Tillman got his copy of the *Wichita Eagle* in the mail. He'd subscribed to it while Michael was playing ball and would drop the subscription now. On the sports page was the headline

SHOCKERS FALL TO NEBRASKA, 91–89

Tillman Hits 24,
Suffers Career-Ending Injury

He thought about cutting out the article and posting it in the gas station with the other clippings about

Mikey. But Ruth Tillman wouldn't hear of any such thing.

Michael's grades barely slipped him into graduate school, but once he was accepted, jt was straight, hard work. Brutal work—six years of it, including his dissertation. In Berkeley he grew a beard and fell in love for the first time. Her name was Nadia, she wore black stockings and long skirts and came from Philadelphia where her father was a union organizer. They lived together for two years in the sixties when Berkeley was becoming the center of all that counted, so they believed.

Nadia joined the Peace Corps and thought Michael should do the same. "Give something back, Michael," she said.

He'd been offered a fellowship for doctoral study and wanted to take it. "I'll give something back another way," he told her.

Michael shaved off his beard. Nadia packed and left. Disappointed, but not angry, and on to other things. "It's probably better this way," she told him. "You're an only child, and from what you've said about your life, and from what it's like living with you, I'm beginning to think only children are raised to be alone. At least you were." She softened, looked at him. "It's been good, Michael."

He smiled. "It *has* been good. I mean that, Nadia. You've taught me a lot about a lot of things. Stay in touch." He kissed her good-bye, watched two years of his life roll away on a Greyhound, and walked to the Department of Economics, where he handed in his letter accepting the fellowship. He went back to his apartment and could still smell the scent of Nadia, looked at her posters of Lenin and Einstein and Twain on the wall. He missed her already, but she was right: he liked being alone and had been trained for it. Only children understand it ultimately will come to that, and they live a life practicing for the moments when it happens.

Three

The *Trivandrum Mail* slowed down, halted, arms passing fruit and tea through the windows in exchange for rupees. Mosquitoes passing through the windows in exchange for blood. Sweat running down the curl of his spine, down his chest and face, Michael Tillman stared again at the picture of Jellie Braden. People in the fields working rice, bullocks hauling loads of wood down country roads, birds flying alongside the train for a short distance and then veering off. Whistle far up ahead as the engine plowed past another village.

A face looked over his shoulder. The man smiled and pointed at the photo of Jellie. "Very pretty. Nice lady?"

Michael said she was very nice. The dam crumbled, everyone within a radius of ten feet immediately wanted to see the photo. They handled it carefully, passing it from one to the other and nodding, looking up at Michael and smiling.

"Your lady?" one of them asked.

He'd never thought of her that way and paused before answering. Then he grinned—"Maybe, I'm not sure"—while the train rolled on through the late afternoon and into a purple evening.

Two hours into the ride a seat opened up. He started for it, then noticed the pregnant woman off to one side, the one he'd helped onto the train. He pointed to the seat. She nodded in thanks and sat down. Soon after he felt a tug on his sleeve. Two Indian men had jammed against each other, leaving a corner of their seat for Michael. He tossed his knapsack in the overhead rack and crouched on the space they'd created.

Talk began, mostly sign language, but progress was made. The men were farmers going home from market. They asked simple questions and discovered Michael's profession. Immediately he was honored in the way Indians honor teachers—respect, awe, gratitude. "The highest calling," one man said in heavily accented English, and the others agreed, smiling and nodding. Maybe he's right, Michael thought. It's easy to lose perspective and become cynical when you're close to a profession or a person for decades. You start focusing on the ugly parts, forgetting the overall beauty of what's up close to you.

He'd begun graduate study with soaring thoughts of becoming a scholar and a teacher, indeed the highest calling as far as he could tell. In his early twenties he'd imagined bright students he would lead through the intricacies of advanced economic theory, maybe a Nobel Prize out there if the scholarship was diligent. But in some way he'd never been able to define, graduate school and his early years as a professor had taken the dreams away from him. Something to do with the emphasis on method, with plodding data collection and analysis. Something to do with social scientists trying to operate like physicists, as if the roiling complexities of social reality could be handled in the same way as the study of nature. And something to do with students who cared only for job preparation, who demanded what they called "relevance" and had no real interest in the abstractions he found so lovely, so much like a clear, cold mountain stream running through his brain. "Good theory is the most practical thing you can study," he told them. They didn't believe him.

He gave a little speech at a College of Business and Economics faculty meeting. "We are interested, it seems, not in creating, but only in maintaining—maintaining our comfortable, enviable life-style. If the taxpayers ever discover what's really going on around here, they'll march on us. We're like the goddamned students and the students are like us dumb bastards: it's come down to cooperate and graduate."

Two heads out of 137 nodded in agreement, 135 wished the dean would get on with the meeting and talk about next year's salary prospects. Michael didn't make any more speeches after that.

So the dreams eroded. And Michael Tillman began to turn inward, to follow only what made sense to him. He was trying to get back the old feelings, the awe he'd once experienced in contemplating the great sweep of time and space, wondering about the peculiar evolutionary magic that had put him and not someone else here at this particular time in a universe still expanding.

People saw him as distant, and he was. People saw him as arrogant, but he wasn't, quite the opposite. He simply decided to go off by himself, go his own way. People mistake shyness and reclusiveness—both of those—for arrogance. It's a convenient label slapped on by those who see only the surface of things and nothing more. He understood as much and let them believe what they chose to believe.

As a teacher he was different, but effective. Good students liked him, the middling ones were afraid of him. The poorer students avoided his classes. He wasn't a kindly Mr. Chips, and never would be, yet he respected grit and determination, spending long hours with those who had trouble in his classes. And he reserved a special disdain for the talented ones who lazed through their student years.

"Do what he asks and you're okay, dead meat otherwise," the graduate students said. "He walks around barefoot in the classroom sometimes, but he knows what he's talking about."

The undergraduates wrote good things and bad things on his evaluations:

"Tests are too hard. Needs to understand young kids and parental pressure better."
"He's a little scary but gives me a lot of help outside the classroom. This is a *hard* course."
"His ideas have caused me to reevaluate my life."

"Seems arrogant at times, self-centered. Nobody can be as smart as he seems."

"I liked his aproach [*sic*]."

"Needs a haircut and sometimes takes the Lord's name in vain."

"Good in class but never seems to be around except for his office hours. I'm working at Kmart to pay off my Camaro and my schedule doesn't fit with his."

"Knows his stuff but lives in another world."

"Great teacher. One of the two best I've had."

Michael had come out of graduate school on the run. The twenty-six articles on his résumé got him tenure in 1970 and a full professorship in 1978, a week before his fortieth birthday. After that he raised his head and began looking around, trying to get the magic back. People still called and asked what he was doing on this or that subject. "Nothing," he'd tell them. "On to other things."

"Like what?" they'd ask.

He kept it vague, enigmatic, matching the drift of his own mind. "I'm fooling around with Jeremy Bentham's early work on the pleasure-pain calculus and its applications to problems of contemporary democracy."

That stopped them. There'd be a moment of silence down the long lines of Mother Bell. Then: "I see. Too bad you didn't keep working on the earlier material; I thought you were on to something with that."

It went along that way, a life of slightly unsettled contentment, all right in general but cut through with an aloneness he simultaneously treasured and disliked. He had his work and the Shadow. He had a woman or two he saw occasionally. And then came Jellie Braden. And then came the *Trivandrum Mail* running southward into traditional India, where the old ways endured.

The train pulled into Madurai at ten o'clock. Michael asked about a place to stay, and the conductor directed him to a small hotel just up the street from the station. "Very clean, very pleasant," he said. Michael trusted him.

When he went through the front door the action level cranked up. Most of the small Indian hotels are designed for people traveling in basic Indian ways, white faces being rare at their registration desks. The desk clerk was obviously pleased with Michael's choice of hotels, and three bellboys were assigned to take him to his room, even though he carried only a knapsack.

One of them ran ahead and slid six feet on the floor tile, stopping exactly at Michael's room and opening the door. Another spoke a little English and said the hotel restaurant was closed, but he would be happy to run down the street and get something.

Michael knew he could count on an omelet. He asked the bellboy to fetch one, along with some bread and tea and cheese or yogurt. Twenty-five minutes later the boy returned with tea, bread, yogurt, chutney, and a three-egg omelet. Just where the eggs came from was useless information at that point. Besides, it's an inquiry Michael never made in India, regardless of the circumstances.

After food, sleep. One of the boys knocked on Michael's door at first light, as requested. Michael cold-showered, had cereal and goat's milk along with toast and tea in the restaurant, then started looking for a car to take him on to a place called Thekkady in the western mountains. The hotel manager was happy to assist, and a white Premier, one of the small, ubiquitous, Indian-made sedans, pulled up in front of the hotel thirty minutes later.

"He has an all-India license," the manager said.

Michael wasn't sure about the significance of that but took it to be a good omen. The driver used a whisk broom to clean off the backseat, and they headed out on the trail of Jellie Braden.

The day after Michael first met Jellie at the dean's reception, somebody somewhere yanked an autumnal lever and the aging rocket ship called college lifted off. He had a Tuesday–Thursday teaching schedule but went in even though it was Monday and frittered around. He read mail that had come in his absence, posted his office hours, straightened out the schedules of a few students who couldn't get the classes they wanted. Word along the student grapevine was, "Tillman knows how to get around the bureaucracy, go see him if you need help."

He was still thinking about Jellie Braden. He hadn't reacted that strongly to a woman for a long time. Maybe never. No, not maybe . . . never. The physical attraction was there, and maybe something else, too. He'd spent a restless night thinking about primal things versus rectitude, with no conclusion having been reached.

He opened up on Tuesday with his standard lecture, "Complexity and the Boundaries of Human Policymaking," dazzling the seniors with a little fancy stuff out of combinatorial mathematics. A typical first class session, letting them know this was going to be serious business. Most of the faculty merely handed out syllabi and directions to the restrooms. But he'd walk in, look at the students, and say, "We begin with complex systems, an examination of our own limited intellects in a contest with unlimited possibilities."

After that he'd turn to the blackboard and grin to himself as he heard them digging out notebooks and pens they hadn't anticipated using the first day. Michael Tillman, classroom serial killer.

On Thursday he was keeping the office hours posted on his door:

> *Tillman*
> *2:00–4:00 Tues. & Thurs.*
> *By Appointment Otherwise*

Early in the semester traffic was light. The students were still drinking beer and hadn't really gotten into the books yet. Things usually picked up about three weeks farther on, right before the first examination. He was leaning back, feet on his desk, office door propped open with a book praising Reaganomics written by one of the faculty's supply-side economics. It was understood he chose his doorstops carefully and rotated them periodically, a kind of floor-level editorial on the times around him. Quiet rap of knuckles on the open door, and he looked up into gray eyes: Jellie Braden, in tight jeans, red sweater with a white shirt collar peeking out of it, well-traveled hiking boots. Black hair tucked up under a round, short-billed wool cap.

He hadn't fully appreciated her long legs on Sunday. The skirt and boots she'd worn to the dean's party had disguised her lower parts, though he would have guessed as much if he'd thought about it. An old green book bag was slung over her right shoulder.

"Hello, Michael Tillman. I was on my way to Jimmy's office and saw your door open."

He swung his feet off the desk, tossed the computer magazine over his shoulder, and said, "Hello yourself, Jellie Braden. Nice of you to stop by. Come in, sit down, the smoking lamp is lit in here."

"Okay. I have a few minutes before Jimmy's out of class." She gave the impression she didn't have anything better to do with a little downtime, but he didn't really think she meant it that way.

"Jellie, you look like what the admissions crowd calls a mature student, knapsack and all."

"I am exactly that. Well, a student, anyway. My maturity's an open question."

He was about to comment on what he saw as her rather obvious maturity but decided not to. "What are you taking?"

"A course in cultural traditions of the North American Plains Indians—Native Americans, as we know them now. Another one in archaeological field methods. I haven't been able to find a job yet, and I'll be damned if I'm going to lie around the house all day and watch the soaps. What are you teaching this semester?"

"A senior-level course in decision making and a graduate course in quantitative methods. Hot stuff, you ought to sign up for them."

"I thought you were an economist?"

"I still am, sort of. Got interested in more applied topics a few years ago. Age does that to you."

"It all sounds pretty grubby to me. Something to do with making money and screwing consumers, I'll bet."

Michael laughed. "Money, maybe. Screwing consumers, no."

"How do you separate the two? It always looks like the same thing to me."

"Good point. But I'd rather not think about it. I'm like the old A-bomb scientists; I just produce the knowledge, what the public chooses to do with it is not my responsibility. That's rubbish, of course, but it gets me by if I dare to reflect too much on what I'm doing."

"Well, at least you're honest about it. Don't you wear a suit and tie when you're teaching?"

"No, I used to when I first started. Damn chalk dust gets all over the good material. Besides, this climate's just too deucedly cold in the winter to dress very fancy. Somehow I never felt right wearing long johns underneath pinstripes. As the tailors say, the cloth doesn't hang properly. Jeans and sweaters work out okay. That also bothers the dean, but then just about everything I do bothers the dean, whether I'm trying to bother him or not." Michael tapped a pencil on the desk and grinned at her. "I once designed a uniform for the dean, but he didn't take to the idea."

Jellie grinned back. "Just what would a dean's uniform look like?"

"A jumpsuit plus face paint done in what I called 'manager's camouflage,' mottled tones of brown and gray to blend in with filing cabinets and other office equipment. I told him, 'Arthur, you'd be able to skulk around and do all kinds of secret things, check up on us to make sure we're not dancing through the first-floor lobby with garlands in our hair.' "

Jellie's grin twisted into a little crooked smile. "Exactly what did the dean say about your idea?"

"He didn't say anything. Just shook his head and walked away. That was after I went on to tell him how the uniform could be coupled with what I called the 'administrator's go-squat,' a modified duck walk that would keep him down at desktop level. I demonstrated the go-squat for him in the hall outside his office and guaranteed him he'd have the ultimate in close supervision if he'd adopt the uniform and the walk. Guess he didn't grasp the concept. Carolyn liked the idea, however."

Small talk, nothing talk. It went on from there. Jellie began dropping by his office once a week or so, and she and Michael whacked their way toward each other through the old thicket of ignorance separating strangers. Sometimes he had a partial erection just talking to her and was glad he wore his jeans snug, which kind of held events under control. He'd given up on organized religion years ago, but it's handy when you need it, and he said over and over to himself, "O Absolute, give me Jellie Braden; somehow You must do as much for a simple man." The words became a mantra that never left his mind.

At the fall picnic on a Sunday, Michael sat on one end of a teeter-totter in a park along the river, languidly watching the accounting department take on the marketing department as part of an exciting volleyball tournament organized by the dean and his secretary. His secretary liked Michael even less than the dean did, calling him impertinent. Michael thought about impertinence and factored in cigarette smoking, which the dean complained about. The result popped out: *Be gladdened in your heart you have tenure.* He was glad, and the sun was late-September pleasant.

The economists were anxiously waiting in the wings for their second crack at the marketeers, part of a double-elimination scheme designed by a sports fanatic in the operations research area. The genius had used some fairly high-powered mathematics to make up the pairings based on the departmental won-loss records from the last three picnics and had run off a four-color diagram on one of the Apples.

The dean shot up into the far reaches of delirium when he saw the printout and insisted everyone look at "Don's good work," as he called it (an extra two hundred for Don at salary time, Michael guessed). Michael thought it was using a sledgehammer to drive a tack and said so when the dean asked his opinion of Don's brilliance. What he said was, "I think Don-Don applied high thinking to low living."

Jesus, the faculty was out of shape. Flabby bodies

whacking a volleyball into the trees, stumbling around, falling down, the dean tooting on his whistle. He looked to see if the hospital emergency unit was standing by.

"Wanna teeter, Tillman-Michael?" Jellie was coming across the grass toward him, smiling. He'd seen her earlier from a distance. Anytime he was in the same physical area as Jellie his radar kicked in, and he was aware of her location at all times. She and Jim had arrived an hour earlier. Michael had come alone on the Black Shadow, goosing it a little as he passed the dean's car on his way into the park and waving to Carolyn when he went by. No *Deanette* T-shirt this year, and he felt bad for her. That's why he had a bookstore make him up a T-shirt reading *Possible Dean* and was wearing it.

"No, I have the totter end. You'll have to teeter. That's the easy part, anyway, and it's what I do during the week." He stood up a bit, lowering the other end of the seesaw. He outweighed her by about sixty pounds and scooted up the board to balance things out, then tossed her a beer out of the little six-pack cooler by his feet.

"How does Jim feel about his wife sharing an unsanded plank with another man?"

"Mostly he doesn't pay any attention to that sort of thing, but he can be jealous in a petulant way sometimes. And for no good reason, I might add. But he likes you and knows we're friends, so that's different. Anyway, he's totally focused on pounding the marketing department to smithereens in the next round of wretchedness over there."

She was luminous in the soft, slanting light of an

autumn afternoon. Her breasts rose and fell pleasantly beneath her cotton blouse as they teetered and tottered. Her jeans stretched tight across her hips and thighs where she straddled the board. Did the Absolute build in this much torment as a last delicious bit of private entertainment for Him or Her or Whatever? Michael Tillman wondered.

"No volleyball, Michael? You look like you're in good shape, and judging by the pathetic little war going on over there at the net, you'd be a dominant force."

He glanced toward the net and saw James Lee Braden III in his horn-rims, sweatshirt, and floppy khakis doing side-straddle hops as he warmed up for a second run at the marketeers. Braden III went into the dirt when he tripped over Dr. Patricia Sanchez's foot. Then he realized he hadn't answered Jellie's question and she was watching him watch her. He took a hit of beer and said, "Nope. I did my four miles on the road this morning at dawn. That's enough for one day. Besides, I might fall into Kipperman-the-accountant's stomach and not find my way out by class time Tuesday."

Jellie Braden laughed, and they went up and down on a September afternoon in Iowa.

Four

In the countryside west of Madurai the morning was sweet and clear, in the way India feels before the heat and dust come up. Especially sweet and clear, because if it all worked out, Jellie was four hours ahead in the high country of the Western Ghats. Maybe tomorrow wouldn't be as sweet and clear. Maybe he had no business doing this, following her. The old doubts again, bothering him for this whole trip. Forget it, push on. Jellie had her problems, whatever they were, and Michael had his —forty-three, sinking toward a time when it would be too late for this kind of thunder in his brain and body. If it came to war, it could be sorted out in the hills of India, as good a place as any. She could send him away, and he'd be no worse off than he was sitting back in Cedar Bend listening to gossip about Jimmy Braden's wife running off on some existential quest.

* * *

At Thanksgiving their first year in Cedar Bend, the Bradens invited Michael for dinner. They'd only been in town for three months, but Jimmy was set on having what he called "a major *do*." Jellie protested, saying they didn't know many people and somehow Thanksgiving had always seemed a special time for family and close friends. Her parents were coming from Syracuse, that was probably enough. But Jimmy made up a list, looked at it, and said if two-thirds of them came, it would be a respectable showing.

Jimmy's list was predictable, safe. He said, "I thought about inviting Michael Tillman, but I doubt if he'd come. He doesn't seem the type for Thanksgiving dinner. Then again, Michael's single and so is your friend, Ann Frazier, from sociology. They're both kind of different, maybe we can do a little matchmaking over turkey."

Jellie thought about it. She imagined Michael sitting at their dining room table. Strange and different Michael Tillman, big-shouldered and brown-eyed with brown hair longer than the approved length for a business school faculty member. A little something out of the ordinary. Sunburned in the face, almost a workingman's face, as if he'd be comfortable cashing his paycheck in a bar across the street from where he might have worked as a machinist. And his long, smooth fingers with the faintest imprint of grease even hard scrubbing couldn't remove.

A month before, she and Jimmy had been coming home from a local theater production. The night streets were wet from October rain, and suddenly

there was Michael beside them when they stopped for
a light. He sat on the Shadow, revving its engine. She
remembered the car radio was playing a song by Neil
Diamond, "Cracklin' Rosie," while Jimmy was telling her to find the public radio station devoting an
entire evening to Beethoven. It stuck in her mind, the
song playing at that moment. From that time on, she
could be anywhere and hear "Cracklin' Rosie," and
instantly she was back on the streets of Cedar Bend,
looking at Michael on the Shadow.

Jimmy had leaned out the window of the Buick
and said, "Hi, Michael."

Michael—yellow bandanna tied around his head,
leather jacket, boots, and jeans—turned and waved
to the Bradens, then looked straight ahead. When the
light changed he gunned the Shadow and was gone,
straddling that smooth black machine of his and disappearing into the countryside.

Jimmy said, "I think it's a bit chilly and wet to
be riding a motorcycle, don't you?"

But Jellie didn't hear him. She was watching the
Shadow's taillight moving away from her. And she
wanted to be riding with Michael Tillman, to be going out there where she had once traveled and was
now afraid to go again. She wanted to climb on that
black machine and feel the beat of its engine between
her legs and the roar of wind in her ears.

Admit it, she'd always had a taste for a peculiar
kind of man, the sort that seems ill designed for the
world in which they live (Jimmy is a whole other
story—those were her break-even years). Michael
Tillman was like that, she sensed, as if a great fist
had reached back and plunked a hard-drinking, hard-

cussing, nineteenth-century keelboatman into the 1980s, given him an intelligence out beyond where the rest of us live, and said, "Now, behave yourself," all the while being doubtful that he would. And he didn't.

Her taste in men probably had something to do with the genes arching forward from her great-great-grandmother, Elsa, who had been a radical feminist when it was considered improper if not immoral for a woman to think about such things, let alone speak and parade in the streets on behalf of them. Elsa Markham had left her husband, taken up with an equally radical socialist, and gone on the road as a warrior for women's rights and free love. The Markham family didn't talk much about Great-Great-Grandmother Elsa.

Jellie kept that side of herself hidden for a long time. Not totally suppressed, hidden, tucked way back where it couldn't get hold of her and disrupt the well-designed life her parents had drafted in clear terms for their two daughters. Jellie's older sister, Barbara, had shouldered arms and marched straight into that well-designed life. She got her degree in elementary education, married a successful insurance broker, and stayed in Syracuse. The Markhams were pleased with Barbara's choices, and the world was good.

In their late girlhoods, Barbara read *Little Women* and loved it. Jellie told her it was cloying. Jellie read *Madame Bovary* and loved it. Barbara told her it was trash. Then she ratted on Jellie and told Mother Markham that Jellie wanted to be Emma Bovary. Mother grabbed Jellie's copy of Flaubert and read it in one

sitting, concentrating on the passages Jellie had under-
lined. A lecture on virtue followed, but Jellie got out
of it by saying she didn't want to be like Emma at all
and that you could look at *Madame Bovary* as a kind
of primer on how *not* to live. What she really wanted
to say was Emma handled it all wrong by being loose
with money. A true romantic would have concentrated on the sex and let it go at that.

Given that Elsa Markham's restless ways had
somehow fluttered down to her, it was nearly inevitable Jellie's life would turn out as it did. Her India
experiences early on gave her some pause, however,
and Jimmy came along. She was in a space where she
needed to paddle flat water for a while, fatigued from
the emotional roll and toss high adventure brings with
it. Jimmy looked stable, and he was. Jimmy looked
comfortable, and he was. Jellie needed peace and
quiet. When he proposed she said yes for reasons she
wasn't sure of, but they had something to do with
stability and comfort and peace and quiet.

Jellie fought hard against the tug of Elsa's genes
for years; still, they wouldn't leave her alone. Inside
the good faculty wife with a degree in anthropology
was a keelboatman's woman who wanted to put her
bare breasts against Michael Tillman's face and feel
his mouth come onto them.

When Jimmy showed her his list of invitees for
Thanksgiving, she hesitated. Her first inclination was
to go for comfort and stability. But Elsa Markham
took hold of her arm, and Jellie scratched "M. Tillman" at the bottom. "I think that's a good idea. Ask
Michael and see what he says." She decided at that

moment to wear her red dress with the long puffy sleeves if he accepted their invitation.

Michael Tillman didn't celebrate holidays—any of them—but Thanksgiving at the Bradens was a chance to be around Jellie, and he couldn't pass it up. Jim had said there would be a few other people, but he and Jellie especially hoped Michael would come, and oh, by the way, bring a friend if you want.

He came in from his morning run, got his dog and cat fed and squared away, then read for a while. Around one o'clock he stood before his bedroom closet and pulled out a gray tweed jacket and a blue, button-down-collar shirt. Most of his ties had fallen onto the closet floor a thousand or so years ago and looked like it, the silk ones wrinkled and dusty. But a dark red wool number, decorated with *Save the Turtles* rampant on a field of the swimming reptiles, looked like a candidate for resuscitation with the help of a good brushing. He pulled out a pair of wrinkled charcoal slacks and held them up. Malachi, the border collie who was named after Michael's favorite professor in graduate school, put his head on his paws and made small, whining sounds. "No dice, huh, Malachi?"

Michael turned, showed the slacks to Casserole-the-cat, and asked, "Whaddya think, Cass?" She blinked, yawned, and headed for the living room. With that kind of poll results on the slacks, he shoved hangers around, located a pair of presentable jeans, and finished off this exercise in hesitant elegance with gray socks and the old reliable cordovan loafers.

He picked up the bottle of red he'd bought for the occasion and walked the six blocks to the two-story brick the Bradens had purchased. Three cars were parked outside, the Bradens' Buick was in the driveway. Jim answered the bell, impeccable—perfect as it gets—in a dark blue pinstripe, white collar–barred starched shirt with a yellow-and-black polka-dotted tie. At the bottom end were black, light-weight wingtips—banker's shoes. Crisp white hanky in his breast pocket. Michael had already guessed Jimmy Braden came from old money, and today he looked it.

"Hi, Michael. Jellie and I are pleased you could come. I think you probably know everyone here except for Jellie's parents, who flew in from Syracuse. Say, that's quite a tie!"

Michael hated entrance scenes. His blue-collar upbringing surged forward when he was paraded into a room full of people, and he'd get sort of stupid and uncomfortable almost to the point of appearing bellicose, which he really wasn't. His growing years didn't provide him with much experience in entrances, that's all.

A motley little outfit awaited him in the small living room: sociologist (female, unpartnered, acquaintance of Jellie's), accountant and wife ("Did you see any cobras?"), the overweight operations research guy with an equally heavy wife and crushing hand-shake (double-elimination volleyball genius). Patricia Sanchez was in the middle of the sofa, seated next to a guy she dated from the student services office. An older man he took to be Jellie's father sat on Pat's other side. It was stuffy warm, with a perfect fire

crackling away and everybody looking at him standing in the doorway to the living room. He took a
deep breath and wished he could light up, but there
wasn't a chance in hell of that.

Jimmy took him by the elbow. "I think everybody here knows Michael Tillman from my department." The voices reached toward Michael in ragged
unison. He gave them all a little wave and handed the
bottle of wine to Jimmy.

"Jellie and her mother are in the kitchen. Oh,
how clumsy of me, I nearly forgot you haven't met
Jellie's father, Mr. Markham."

Mr. Markham was somewhere over sixty, with
bright eyes and a firm hand. He grinned. Michael
grinned back and judged Leonard Markham to be all
right, as long as you didn't cross him.

Through an open door and down the hall he
could see Jellie in the kitchen. She looked up, waved,
and called, "Hi, Michael, come meet my mother."

He went back to the kitchen while the living
room went back to whatever conversations he'd interrupted. Jellie wiped her hands on a white apron that
had *HI!* and four tom turkeys with big, floppy red
combs printed on it. She kissed him on the cheek,
whispering, "I'm so glad you came," then turned him
to the gray-haired woman who was doing something
or other with giblet dressing. The kiss and the whisper
surprised him, but he chalked it up to holiday spirit.

"Mother, this is our friend, Michael Tillman."

Jellie got her looks from her mother. Eleanor
Markham was a knock-'em-dead lady about the same
age as her husband and with the same gray eyes as
Jellie's. "I'm glad to meet you, Michael. We're so

pleased Jellie and Jim have made such nice friends in the short time they've been here."

She turned to Jellie. "Michael's the one who rides a motorcycle, right?" Jellie nodded. "Where do you ride it, Michael? Very far?"

"Oh, here and there. Around town, up to the Great Lakes sometimes, Colorado if I'm really feeling sporty. It's an old buzzard, and you have to carry a full tool kit if you're going any distance at all."

"Don't you live in an apartment, Michael? Where do you keep the motorcycle during the winter?" Jellie was stirring gravy, looking over her shoulder at him.

"In my living room."

Jellie laughed. Eleanor Markham smiled and asked, "Why on earth do you keep it there?"

"Because it's too big for the john."

Both of them were laughing now. Michael was grinning, appreciating a nice groove as much as any jazz musician. "Besides, I can work on it there during cold weather, and if the walls start closing in on me, I sit on it and go 'vroom, vroom.' When I'm not using it, my cat likes to sleep on the seat. I live on the first floor of an old place, been living there for ten years. It's hard to find people in a college town who pay their rent on time, and I do, so the landlord puts up with me."

"Mother, of course Michael would keep his motorcycle in the living room. It all fits, and it's perfect . . . unlike this damn gravy that won't thicken up."

He could see they were busy, so he excused himself and ambled back to the living room, trying to adopt a veneer of sociability, which was just about impossible for Michael Tillman to carry off. The furnishings were typical and a little better than that—good postmodern prints, agreeable pottery pieces, an abstract bronze sculpture about eighteen inches high, and a black-and-white print of Edward Weston's famous portrait of a cabbage, which cost somebody real bucks. A few new chairs, a few old ones. A Mozart quintet came from a system in the den.

He looked back once at Jellie, who was still fretting over the gravy, and tried to articulate in his mind what he'd seen on her face. A blend, maybe, of contentment and weariness, of being happy where she was and yet wishing she was somewhere else. The sense that she was running a long race she believed she was supposed to run but would rather not have been running at all.

"Come over here, Michael." Pat Sanchez reached out for his hand. He'd always liked Pat. She'd fought her way out of the Los Angeles barrios, got her doctorate at Texas, and joined the faculty about ten years before. They'd done a couple of papers together and ended up naked and laughing and drinking margaritas on her bed when they'd finished the first one late on a Friday night. After that they'd gone out a few times, then let go of it by mutual, but unspoken, consent. The mathematics of transportation networks evidently were not enough on which to sustain a loving relationship.

She introduced him to her friend, who had recently become vice-president of student services, but the friend already knew Michael from their days on the Student Conduct Committee. He had a therapeutic way about him, characteristic of those who devote their lives to dealing with the pleasures of dormitory havoc and other garbage the university continued to tolerate. He shook Michael's hand and said, "I remember you. You're the one who was in favor of expelling anybody who so much as thought about writing on the walls. What was it you said? . . . I used to quote you as an example of the kind of approach that just doesn't work with today's students."

Michael sighed inside himself, then thought about sticking the sweet fellow's head up his ass or in the fireplace, depending on whether he decided the coagulated brain ought to be quick-frozen or hard-boiled, but let it go and leaned toward him, whispering, "I remember almost exactly what I said. It went something like this: 'We're running a university, not a success center or an asylum for those with pounding glands. Cheats are cheats, destructive teenage drunks are just that, and we ought to throw the injurious little bastards all the way back to their mother's tit and let 'em suck on it or boot their asses right down the street to the cops and press charges.' That's what I said. I also said I couldn't stand all the transactional bullshit you people seem to believe in. That was after someone from counseling services called me a fascist."

Sweet Fellow, the veep, turned red while Pat lay back against the sofa cushions, trying to suppress her laughter and failing, and that cooled him down. Michael was glad she was there. He'd shot his mouth off at a little member of the central administration who didn't know what it was like in the gullies of the world, and it could have ruined Thanksgiving at the Bradens, which was the last thing he wanted to happen.

"Oh, Michael, will you never be tamed?" Pat was still laughing, holding her stomach.

At that moment Jimmy Braden came out of the kitchen, daintily ringing a small silver bell. "Ladies and gentlemen, dinner is served."

The crowd straggled off toward the dining room. Michael brought up the rear, wondering what the seating arrangements were and whether they'd be such that he could look at Jellie now and then, preferably often. After all, that's what he'd come for, not to deal with smart-ass little brats from the administration building.

Place cards were on the table, but he decided to let everyone else find their seats and then sort through the residual. The seat assignments gave the appearance of having come out of a random-number generator. But he knew Jellie too well to doubt there was an overall plan designed to get certain people away from their wives and dates and husbands and next to certain other people. Sort of a turkey-centered mixer. Michael watched people seat themselves, the chairs dwindling down to a precious few. Jellie caught his eye and pointed to the second place down from the head of the table, near the kitchen. He walked over and looked at the name card, which had *Possible Dean* printed on it in Jellie's handwriting. The card at the place next to his read *Jellie*.

James Lee Braden III carved, Jellie's mother poured, Jellie ran back and forth to the kitchen, and everyone else talked nonsense. Michael sat there watching Jellie move, feeling, for the first time, something beyond hibiscus and a waterfall in the Seychelles, thinking that maybe the old Darwinian shuffle had some steps to it he hadn't known about before. The physical attraction he felt for her was somehow being melded with deeper and quieter feelings of a higher order, a turn of events he hadn't counted on. And he became a little sad then in a way he couldn't grasp. Sad for her, for him, for Jimmy, and for where this might all lead or probably wouldn't. The voice of the Absolute sounded less certain, the mantra was beginning to waver. Some things were better left alone, he thought. He, and perhaps Jellie, if he was reading her correctly, were mucking around in a dangerous place where they had no business going, a place that was not as harmless as it first appeared. And, for a moment, he wanted to run, to ride the Shadow somewhere, anywhere. Anywhere that had a warm sun and simple ways.

The great turkey dance went on for nearly two hours. Wine and more wine, food and more food. Eleanor Markham told a funny story about Jellie's growing years, and everybody laughed, especially Jellie.

The female sociologist on his right rattled on about her life and times, touching his arm occasionally when she made what she considered a significant point. That left him feeling cramped and a little aggravated, since he was bound by the circumstances to be polite and couldn't look at Jellie out of the corner of his eye while he was talking with this expert on women's contributions to early American frontier life.

Somebody mentioned the afternoon football game between Dallas and Seattle. The sports fanatic from operations research moved into the opening and began citing yardage gained by various running backs, along with other related junk serving only to clutter up people's minds and keep them from thinking about anything that really matters. Jellie's mother was filling her in on what her old high school friends were doing now.

Jimmy was carving—he never ceased carving, it was his life-way. Jellie's father was talking to the vice-president of student services about fishing for brook trout in Connecticut. And the sociologist on Michael's right was asking him if he ever attended the lecture-concert series, saying she always seemed to go alone and didn't like going alone. He said he didn't go because, as far as he could tell, it was always the same person on the bill—a "scintillating new" (usually pubescent) Korean violinist who flawlessly executed memorized scores. The sociologist was all right, though, lonely in the way most of us were or are, and Michael continued to feign interest in lectures, concerts, and frontier women, once or twice feeling Jellie's hip against his shoulder when she got up to make a food run to the kitchen.

The operations researcher was still talking about the game coming on in less than forty-five minutes and said he hoped nobody would mind if he watched it. Several others said (not directly, of course) they also wanted to see young black men from the coasts have at one another on the plains of Texas, so that was settled. The sociologist straightened her glasses and said quietly to Michael, "All this attention given to athletics is just another capitalist plot to keep the masses occupied, don't you think?"

He really didn't want to think about it. He didn't

want to think about anything except the next touch of Jellie's hip against his shoulder. But he nodded and said, "You're probably right. On the other hand, it beats having the proletariat out there stealing hubcaps or sniffing bicycle seats." She turned her attention to the accountant's wife a moment later.

During a pause while the jock expert was wetting his throat and summoning up more good *Sports Illustrated* wisdom to tell everyone, Jim Braden said, "Michael, you used to be an athlete, didn't you? That's what somebody told me."

Jellie followed up. "Michael, is that true? You've been holding out on us."

Trapped. He hoped the subject would pass, but it didn't. Jellie's father pushed it along. "What did you play, Michael?" The operations researcher, who wouldn't know how to pull on a jockstrap if it was required of him, had a hunk of turkey halfway into his mouth and was obviously in a state of complete surprise, since Michael seldom mentioned his athletic history.

Everyone was looking at him, particularly the sociologist, as if she'd suddenly discovered the real reason why he didn't attend the lecture-concert series and why he seemed a little barbarous overall. There was nowhere to go. He would have continued to look for a way out, but Jellie said, "Tell us about it, Michael." She seemed genuinely interested, and he couldn't refuse Jellie.

He took a drink of wine and began. "The short version is this: I grew up in a small town in South Dakota—"

The accountant's wife interrupted him. "Where was that?"

"Custer . . . just outside of Rapid City in the Black Hills."

"It's pretty out there, isn't it?" With a mind like chaff in a high wind, she was now into travelogues.

The sociologist came out of her corner with a hard leftist jab: "It's where we stole the Native Americans' land in the nineteenth century."

"Yes, it's very pretty," Michael said, looking at the accountant's wife. "Though unfortunately my parents' small house sat on land stolen from the Lakota Sioux." He waited a moment for additional questions about the Black Hills. There were none.

"By the time I got to eighth grade I was totally bored with school and small-town life in general. So I started shooting baskets in the city park. Then my father helped me put up a basket in the backyard of our house. He took a real interest in the whole affair and installed a yard light so I could practice in the evenings. I seemed to have a knack for the jumpshot and got pretty good at it. My high school coach had graduated from Wichita State and sent them films of two or three of my better games. They offered me a scholarship, which was about the only way I was going to get to college. I played there for three and a half years until I banged up my knee pretty bad. That's it." He took another drink of wine and waited for the assemblage to move on to matters of greater importance, but they wouldn't let it go.

"What position did you play, Michael?"

"Guard."

"What are you, about six three?"

"Six two, in my socks."

"Were you an All-American or anything?"

"I made the All-Missouri Valley Conference Team my junior year."

Jellie put her hand on his and squeezed it. "Michael, you were a star, then!"

He couldn't tell if she was being genuine or mildly sarcastic. He hoped it was the latter and decided it was, with just a little bit of the former mixed in. "I never thought of it that way. I was just earning room and board, books and tuition."

"I'll bet your parents were very proud of you. Ever think about turning pro?" The operations researcher had found a real live veteran of wars that mean nothing, right at the Thanksgiving table.

"My dad pasted pictures of me from the *Wichita Eagle* all over Tillman's Texaco. My mother was more concerned about my grades. She always thought athletics was a pretty dumb way for people to spend their time."

The operations researcher had batted only one for two and was troubled by that. He plainly wondered how any mother could not love her son enough to applaud his exploits in short pants under the lights of several hundred gymnasiums during his formative years and felt sorry for Michael, believing he'd been deprived of maternal affection.

"As for becoming a professional, I had no interest, plus my first step wasn't quick enough for the big leagues. The phone from the pros never rang, and I wouldn't have answered it if it had."

"Don't you miss playing, Michael?" Jellie's mother was looking at him.

"No, I don't, Mrs. Markham. I truly don't. In fact, I couldn't wait for it to be over so I could get on with my life. Somewhere around my sophomore year in college I discovered I didn't like playing basketball and never really had. I just liked fooling around with the art and physics of the long-range jumpshot. It was a boy's tool for a boy's game, and I haven't touched a basketball in twenty years."

Jelly said, "That's an interesting point of view . . . the art and physics of the long-range jumpshot is all that really mattered. Michael, you ought to do an article on that sometime."

If Jellie had put her hand back on his at that moment, he'd have written an essay about now-fading jumpshots on the linen tablecloth with a turkey bone. But she didn't and changed the conversation by listing the selection of desserts available. Michael went for sour cream raisin pie. Jellie had made it from her grandmother's recipe, and it was a knockout.

Over coffee and brandy, someone asked Jellie about her name and where it came from. Her parents laughed, and Jellie pointed at both of them. It fell to her mother to tell the story.

"When Jellie was about seven years old, she went through a plump stage. Her father started calling her his 'little bowl of Jelly.' The neighborhood children picked it up and teased her by calling her Jelly-Belly and Jellyroll and Jellybean and just about everything else you could imagine. She used to come in from playing with tears streaming down her face. As soon as that began happening, Leonard quit calling her Jelly and felt bad he'd ever started the whole business. But the kids wouldn't drop it."

Jellie came on line. "Mom bailed me out, though. She convinced me that my nickname was spelled with an *i-e* on the end instead of a *y* and that it was really a French name pronounced with a soft *J*—JahLAY— even though we kept the American pronunciation. I liked that idea and began to take pride in my new name. It stuck with me, and I've used it ever since."

"Then what's your real name?"

For God's sake, Michael thought, looking at the accountant who had been dumb enough to ask the question. Leave it alone. If she wanted you to know, she'd already have mentioned it.

"I never tell." Jellie laughed. "Jimmy, everyone needs more brandy. I'll get some more coffee." That gave the fans time to pull on their jockstraps, backward, of course, and get the television cooking: "Third-and-six on the Dallas five. Heeerrre's the pitch-out. . . ."

The sociologist had papers to grade, Pat Sanchez and her date decided on a walk. Jellie and her mother were cleaning up in the kitchen. Michael went outside for a smoke, and when he returned the rest of them, except Jellie and her parents, were watching the game. Michael sat at the dining room table with Leonard Markham and asked about fishing for brook trout, saying he used to do a little trout fishing in the Black Hills. Mr. Markham knew how to talk about what interested him, giving Michael the right amount of information without getting boring. He'd have made a good teacher instead of the paper box manufacturer he was, Michael thought. He liked Leonard Markham.

Later, Jellie and her mother joined them at the table, Jellie sitting across from Michael. This is what he'd come for, the chance simply to look at Jellie Markham Braden on a cold autumn day in 1980. He was careful, though, because once or twice her mother caught him staring at Jellie in a way not related to the conversation. And mothers know about the secret thoughts of men, particularly when those thoughts concern the daughters of the mothers.

Struggling for something to talk about, Michael brought up India and watched Eleanor Markham's face go dark—just a little, but still there—when he mentioned it. Jellie quickly turned the conversation in a different direction. That was the second time he'd picked up something strange about her India days. Something that made her reluctant to go into it other than acknowledging she'd been to India and stayed for three years.

Michael could only tolerate being in Jellie's general vicinity for relatively short periods of time back then. His feelings toward her were just too overpowering, escalating in intensity minute by minute, and he was half-afraid he'd blurt out something obvious and stupid, some unseemly remark tipping off her husband or somebody else, including Jellie, about the way he felt. He wanted to be able to see her, be around her as often as he could, without feeling any more surreptitious than he already did. So about six o'clock he excused himself under the pretense of going home to feed his animals.

Jellie wrapped her arms around herself and shivered on the front steps when she said good-bye to him. "Thank you for coming, Michael. I know these affairs aren't your style, but I wanted my parents to meet you. You're a different sort than they normally come into contact with. . . . I didn't say that quite right. I didn't mean to imply you're a curiosity piece, just that you're different. My dad said to me a few minutes ago, 'I like that Michael Tillman; he's got some fiber to him.' I knew he'd like you."

Michael understood what she meant. "I like him, too, Jellie. Thank you for inviting me, I had a nice time." He couldn't help looking hard at her once more before leaving. He just couldn't help it, wanting to put his arms around her and say, "Don't go back in the house. Come home with me, I'll kiss your mouth and your breasts and what surely is your soft, round belly and tear you to pieces and put you back together again. Afterwards we'll go down the road, far away, doesn't matter where."

Jellie set her gray eyes on Michael's for maybe five seconds, her face almost serious. A different look than she'd ever given him before, as if she were half seeing into his thoughts. She said nothing, just looked at him, then dropped her eyes and smiled a little before opening the door and going back inside.

A year later he was west of Madurai and pushing hard into southwest India looking for her. The driver spoke only a few words of English, so it was a quiet ride except for the ceaseless roar of wind through the open windows. Fifty miles out the driver stopped, went over to a roadside shrine, and left some coins.

"Bad spirits," he said, getting in. "Evil." He shifted gears, looking back at the shrine.

In Virudunagar the driver had breakfast and the car had a flat tire. Apparently the donation at the shrine had been insufficient. The spare was shot, so it took a major expedition through the streets until a garage was located. After the obligatory haggling over price, the tire was hauled to the shop and cold-patched. That'll be good for another sixty miles, Michael thought. Their stop in Virudunagar had taken nearly two hours.

Michael leaned back on the red vinyl car seat and looked at villages and farm country going by. Near Rajapalaiyam the driver slowed and halted on a bridge over a wide, shallow river. A woman ahead of them was driving a flock of geese across the bridge. On the sandbars below, other women, their skirts hiked up, were doing laundry, waving clothing over their heads and slapping it hard against rocks.

The geese were almost across, moving slowly. Too slowly for the driver. He honked. The woman pushing the geese along turned, giving them a nasty look. Only rich folks rode in cars, and she was having none of it. The beat of life in village India is in adagio time. Only rich folks from somewhere else are in a hurry.

A woman came toward them across the bridge. She wore a torn red sari of the cheapest cloth, toe rings on her brown feet, and carried a load of sticks on her head. One arm was raised to balance the load, the other swung beside her, bracelets jingling. She was stunning. Beautiful by any standards anywhere.

The way Bardot looked in her salad days. She glanced through the car window at Michael, and he smiled, couldn't help smiling. He thought she might smile back. She looked as if she might for a moment, but then turned her head and stared straight down the road as she moved past the car.

He leaned forward and saw the Western Ghats rising up far ahead. Somewhere in those mountains was Jellie, near a place called Thekkady, or at least she was supposed to be there. And what she was doing there he didn't know and still wasn't sure he wanted to find out.

An hour more and they were into the foothills, climbing slowly and carefully around hairpin curves, waiting for huge, roaring Indian tour buses demanding the road and giving no quarter. Cooler now. Three thousand feet, maybe, pine trees right outside the car windows. Michael didn't know Jellie had walked this same road in terror fifteen years earlier. She had called herself by another name then.

Five

Following her first Thanksgiving in Cedar Bend, Jellie didn't stop at Michael's office for nearly two weeks. Her pattern had been to come by for coffee and a smoke at least once a week, and he decided he'd really screwed it up, that Jellie and maybe other people were beginning to see how he felt and she'd decided to quash anything and everything of that sort right at the front end.

When Jimmy Braden called and asked if they could talk for a few minutes, he was sure Jellie had said something to him. He sat there waiting for the blows, waiting for Jimmy to say Jellie was uncomfortable with the way he looked at her and that she wouldn't be stopping by anymore, let alone sending invitations to subsequent Thanksgiving dinners.

But Jimmy didn't want that. In some ways the news was worse. He was going to teach in London for the spring semester, and Jellie was going with him. He'd applied for a visiting professorship the previous year and cut a deal with Arthur on his way in, allowing him to do the London job if it came through. His application had been lost in the British bureaucracy. But finally it had worked out at the last minute. Now Jimmy was looking for faculty members who would shift their teaching loads around to cover his absence.

Michael had a tight gut just thinking about Jellie being out of his sight for that long, thinking about her black hair blowing in winds coming off the North Sea, about her laughing and going to the theater and never thinking of him, though there was no particular reason she should. Selfish stuff, he knew that, but he recovered and said he'd pick up Jimmy's intro-level course in econometrics or find a graduate student who could do it. Jimmy promised to reciprocate some time, and Michael had no doubt he would.

"Thanks a lot, Michael. That fixes everything up. We're leaving in ten days, right after the semester is over, be back in August. We're going to travel during the summer."

Jellie in Scotland, Jellie along the hedgerows, Jellie in Paris . . . Jellie where he couldn't see her. An hour later she rapped on Michael's door. "Hi, motorcycle man. How's the war?"

"The war is being won, Jellie. I'm whipping the students up the hills of December, and victory is mine, or will be in less than two weeks." She stood in the doorway instead of coming in and flopping down on a chair the way she usually did.

"Sorry I haven't been by to say hello. I've been

getting ready for my final exams, and Jim said he told you about the London trip. God, what a mess, finding a house sitter on short notice, getting bills paid and things set up at the bank. I've been running for days with no letup. What are you going to do over the holidays? Any big plans?"

"No, not much at all. It's too damn cold to crank up the bike and ride it someplace. I'll probably try to finish the paper I'm doing on comparing complex structures so I can present it at the fall meetings. Get my trimonthly haircut, spend a few days with my mother out in Custer over Christmas. Other than that, watch the snow fall, I guess, and listen to the Miles Davis tapes I ordered while I spruce up my lectures for the class I'll be covering for Jim. My notes in that area are a little yellowed. It'll go by pretty fast, it always does." He wanted to say he'd be thinking about her every other minute, but he didn't.

"Sounds pretty low key. No special Christmas wishes?"

He looked at the ceiling for a moment, struggling, trying to pull himself up and out of a self-indulgent funk. Michael had wishes all right, but nothing he could talk about. He recovered and leaned back in his chair, fingers locked behind his head, forcing a little grin. "Well, sometime I'd like a leather belt with *Orville* tooled on the back. Used to be a guy in Custer had one, and I thought it was pretty neat when I was a kid."

Jellie grinned back. "Only you, Michael, of all the people I know, would say something like that. God, it's almost surreal."

"Well, life is surreal, Jellie. Except for Orville.

He didn't dwell on those things, just drove his grain truck and whistled a lot."

"I think Orville had it all worked out. I'd like to hear more about him, but I've got to run. I'll try to stop in before we leave. Take care, Michael, and say hello to Orville if you see him. Ask if he'll write a self-help book for the rest of the world."

He watched her jeans as she left and walked down the hall, then got to his feet and went to the door so he could watch her a little while longer. She looked back once, as if she knew he'd be standing there and fluttered her hand in a final wave as she turned the corner, heading for the office of solid, steady James Braden.

Michael ran into her the following week in a small shopping area near the campus. They had coffee at Beano's, sitting in a back booth in midafternoon. Her exams were over and preparations for London were well along, so she was a little calmer and seemed in no hurry this time. She was wearing one of her standard winter outfits: jeans, long-sleeved undershirt beneath a flannel shirt, down vest.

He leaned against the wall, one foot on the seat of the booth, and glanced at all the old posters of campus events plastered on the walls. The undergraduates—those who were finished with exams and some who weren't—were drinking beer. Two men, gay activists from the philosophy department, were playing chess at a table next to them.

Jellie asked if he had any suggestions for London restaurants. He told her, except for a day here and there on his way through, his experience with London was mostly limited to making connections at Heathrow and he didn't know the city well. Michael's tastes ran to societies less well organized than those in the West, and most of his traveling had been in southeast Asia. He didn't mention the women in Bangkok with their long hair and compliant ways. He glanced at his watch and said he had to give his last final examination in twenty-two minutes, starting to make departure motions.

"Michael, I'll miss our talks over coffee, and I'll miss *you*, truly I will."

He looked at her for a long while. For the first time he really didn't care what she or anyone else thought about him looking at her in a certain way.

She took a deep breath and started to say something, then paused for a moment before continuing, as if she were trying to decide whether or not to speak at all. "I don't want to get deeply into this now, but . . ." She hesitated.

His hands were shaking for reasons he wasn't sure of, and he held them under the table where she couldn't see them. He could feel a small tic in a cheek muscle, just below his left eye. In the spaces of a man's life there are moments when things shift into some other gear. He sensed that was happening now.

"What are you talking about, Jellie? What don't you want to get into?"

"What I'm trying to say . . . is that . . . that I'm not going to just miss you. I'm going to *miss* you. I know more than you may think I know about how you feel about some things . . . how I feel . . . Oh, good God, I'm making a muddle of this. . . ."

He got his hands quieted down and reached for

one of hers. She put it out to meet him halfway. He laid his other hand on the little bundle forming on the table. "C'mon, Jellie, say what you've got to say. I want to hear it, whatever it is."

"Michael, it all sounds a little presumptuous, what I'm trying to get across. If I'm wrong, please forget I ever said it. Promise?"

"I promise."

She added her other hand to the stack on the table and stared at them, cleared her throat. "Behind all the laughter and light talk we share with each other, there's something else going on, isn't there?"

He stayed quiet, looked at her. She had the stage, and he wasn't about to climb up on it right at the moment. He wanted her to finish what she had to say, to let it run wherever it was going. Good or bad, it was time for that. A waitress going into the kitchen dropped a stack of dishes, and every head in Beano's, except two, turned to see the disaster. He could see the second hand on his watch going by. Fifteen minutes until his examination on the other side of campus.

"Damnit . . . isn't there? There's something else going on between us, isn't there?" She squeezed his hands in both of hers and rapped them lightly on the table.

He nodded.

"It's been there since we first met at the dean's reception in late August, hasn't it?"

He nodded again and talked straight: "You walked through the door and something started to hum inside me. The hum has now escalated into a symphonic scream I can't turn off."

"Oh, Michael . . . Michael." She looked away

from him, at the wall, then at the ceiling. Twelve minutes to exam time. He didn't move. The last fly of a summer past, surviving on the largesse of Beano's, landed on his coffee cup and walked an endless path around the rim.

"My mother saw it at Thanksgiving, something about the way you were looking at me, and I guess the way I looked back. No, that's not being honest enough—I was looking back at you the way you were looking at me. When we were doing dishes in the kitchen, she mentioned it to me and said, 'Be careful, Jellie, be *very* careful.' "

Two forty-seven. Beano's was clearing out as about half the crowd hustled off to the three o'clock exams. "Michael, maybe this will all settle down while I'm gone. It just has to, doesn't it?"

He said nothing, shrugging his shoulders, smiling at her.

She stood, pulling on her parka and mumbling, "I feel like a schoolgirl." She looked down at him. "I'm glad I said what I said, Michael. And I'm glad you said what you said and for the way you've handled it the past few months. You like to think you're a little rough around the edges, but you're actually pretty smooth. You're a damn fine man, Michael Tillman, attractive and kind and everything else—isn't there a woman out there somewhere for you? I mean someone other than . . ." She left off the *me*—couldn't bring herself to say it, though he wished she had said it—and let her voice circle down to nothing.

"I understand what you mean. Who knows? All I know now is how I feel about you." He picked up his coat and started sliding out of the booth, disoriented, thinking the distance to next August could only be measured in light-years.

She bent over and kissed him on the cheek. "Ride easy. I'll send you a card." And she was gone then, working her way through the tables and out the front door of Beano's.

He left two bucks on the table and began an easy run through the campus, feet on the sidewalk, mind and heart somewhere else. Across the creek, along the duck pond, and only one minute late into a room where he would ask of students what they knew.

Six

The Bradens lifted off for England on December 20, the day Michael finished grading final exams. Depression over Jellie's leaving was momentarily lightened by several strong performances in both the decision-making and quantitative methods courses. He expected good work from the graduate students, but the undergraduates overcame their senior blues and rose to the task, surprising and pleasing him.

The old Shadow crouched in the living room, waiting for the turn of wrenches and better weather. Michael stacked exam papers on its seat and cranked up the computer, which shared the desk with greasy tools and unwashed coffee cups. A few taps on the keys and the GradeCalc program came up. In went the scores, GradeCalc churned away for thirty seconds, and out came final distributions, normal curves, standard deviations, and all that other good stuff, most of which he ignored in his grading.

Two hours later, the final grade sheets with one whole cover page of instructions that would make a computer blink—instructions he didn't read and hadn't read for all fifteen years of teaching and apparently didn't need to read since nobody ever complained—were filled in and signed. He had twenty minutes to drop off the grades before the registrar shut down at four-thirty. Coat on, over to the campus, turn in the grades.

Done. Free, for a month. Fifteen years of doing this, another twenty to go unless the dean could prove professional incompetence, which he couldn't, or charged Michael with moral turpitude, which he wouldn't, because the entire university except for the accounting department would be out on its ear if those standards were enforced. Stay away from the coeds in your classes—that was the main rule for survival, put down with no punches pulled by the former dean, an old guy who had hired Michael fresh out of graduate school. Way before sexual harassment started flashing in the front of everyone's mind, the old dean had a famous lecture he gave to young faculty members, the males, that is. The essence of it went something like this:

> Gentlemen, I know you're all adults, but let me remind you about a few matters. A lot of these young women are traditional midwestern girls, and they expect to take you home to meet Mother and Father on the weekend following bedroom activity, with

wedding announcements to be mailed soon after. Forget about the air of sophistication they seem to exude. The coeds are big trouble, I mean *big* trouble. The undergraduate males are a bunch of donkeys, mostly, and you're going to look sleek and worldly to the coeds, and they're going to look pretty good to you. Some of them will sit in the front row in short skirts with paradise twinkling at you. You'll have plenty of opportunities for good times between the sheets—it's a goddamn cafeteria out there—but forget it, at least until they're no longer in any of your classes, and I would strongly recommend you stay away from them altogether. I have problems enough without sobbing young women sitting in my office and claiming you discriminated against them in your grading because of some kind of confusion involving preconjugal folderol. In other words, cause me that kind of grief and I'll kick your butts down the academic mountain and see you never work in this business again.

It was a lecture on how to avoid trouble, not develop sensitivity toward females. Michael was sure the latter issue never crossed the old dean's mind, given the faculty was 99 percent male.

Having said that much, the dean told them the famous story that had been part of the university saga for twenty-five years. Seems one of the Russian teachers was in his office when a coed came in to see him.

He motioned for her to sit down and said he'd be with her in a moment, all the while intently finishing some piece of work he had on his desk. When he looked up, she was standing there in the buff with the office door shut. The issues were a little complicated, but the nub of it was this: Give me a passing grade or I'll scream.

You want cool under pressure? You want big *cojónes*? The professor of Russian had them both, in spades. He could have been a neurosurgeon or a space commando. He got up, threw open the door, and walked forthwith into the hall, where he pointed in at the young woman and shouted in heavily accented English, "Get out of my office. Now!" Passersby were treated to a reasonably decent glimpse of a reasonably good, young female body (that's part of the saga, anyway, though Michael noticed that as the story was carried forward and repeated, her physical attributes approached Amazonian proportions, her body filling out and improving with age, as it were).

He'd always wondered just what lesson should be drawn from the tale, since it never had been clear whether or not the young woman and the Russian had anything going on the side. But, having told it, the dean shooed the junior faculty out of his office and left them with the following two guidelines for not letting their moral turpitude drift: Keep your pants zipped and your office door open.

About two-thirds of those receiving the lecture followed the dean's advice. The other one-third cut a swath like a combine through the waving fields of coed grain and apparently suffered little for it, partly because those peering out from glass houses have no interest in chucking accusatory rocks at others. Michael left the coeds alone, simply because he didn't find them attractive. Too young, too naive, and what the hell do you say to them in the morning? "Who do you have for Western civ?" C'mon.

So the grades were in, and Michael was unfettered until January 17, when he'd do it all over again. Down the halls of the administration building he went, admiring the waxed oak floors, inhaling the vapors of incompetent power radiating from the walls and oozing from under darkened doors like smoke from a burning village where truth and beauty had once been found. The temporary lightness he'd felt after finishing a good set of exams was dissipating as he thought about Jellie Braden. He was getting angry at her for going to England, for just bloody taking off and leaving him there to mourn her absence.

Irrational? Of course it was irrational. He had no right to anything other than what he already had when it came to her, which was nothing. She's sitting in Kennedy now, he thought, waiting for TWA to take her lovely body and equally lovely soul onto nine months of new experiences and different people. Maybe she was right, maybe her absence would do it, get him cooled off and refocused on something other than her.

Then he started to waffle: "Come back, come back, Jellie Braden. I need to look at you one more time, just one. I want to continue the conversation we started. I want to hear more of how you feel about me and for us to get the air cleared." But the mail doesn't come on Sundays, and James Lee Braden III had taken his wife on to foreign pleasures, leaving Michael Tillman foundering in his wake.

As he passed by the provost's office, a janitor had the door propped open while emptying wastebaskets. Michael glanced inside. Clarice Berenson, the provost's secretary, stared at a computer screen. The office was empty except for her.

They went back a ways, Clarice and Michael. She'd come home to Cedar Bend from New York when her gynecologist husband dumped her for a psychiatric nurse. After the bad scene with her former husband she had a negative attitude toward men overall. But she and Michael got together occasionally, and they flew pretty close to the sun when they were rolling.

Clarice was into serious opera and worked part-time on an M.A. in Spanish, and that along with her job kept her busy. But now and then she liked to shake it real hard. That's where Michael came in, and their schedules seemed to work in perfect sync when it came to getting crazy.

Clarice looked up, grinning. "Well, it's the campus rebel with no apparent cause. How you doin', Michael?"

"Not bad. Just turned in my grades and resting on my oars. How about you, Clarice?"

"Since the provost-sir flew off to Los Angeles about two hours ago, things have picked up quite a bit. I'm just shutting down. Want to have a beer?"

"Better than that, how about beer and dinner?"

"Now you're talking, Michael. We could even

take it up another level and go jump around at Beano's tonight. Bobby's Blues Band is playing there, starting at nine. It'll be end-of-the-semester nuts, but that suits me just fine."

"You're on. But first I need to clean up a bit. Say, about seven? Go down to Rossetti's for pasta, then over to Beano's for the fun?"

"Perfect. I'll pick you up, I think it's my turn to drive."

"Okay, see you in a little while."

Michael started drinking beer when he got home. Sat on the Shadow with a Beck's dark in his hand and John Coltrane on the tape deck. Malachi stood up and put his paws on Michael's leg. He rubbed Malachi's ears while the music played, thinking about Jellie Braden flying through the darkness away from him. But those kinds of thoughts weren't fair to Clarice, he decided, and two more beers got him away from his loneliness and into the evening . . . kind of.

Clarice was not Jellie Braden when it came to looks. On the other hand, that was also a little unfair, since to Michael's way of thinking nobody compared with Jellie along that dimension. But Clarice had that same indefinable quality we lump under "class," and she was more than just presentable. And, just as important, she was not on her way to London.

Clarice knocked on his door at ten to seven while he was pulling on a white cotton turtleneck that worked pretty well with faded jeans. She came in and got a beer from the fridge. He padded around barefoot, looking for a clean pair of boot socks. When he carried his boots out to the living room, Clarice was perched on the Shadow, wearing a maize-colored sweater and forest green corduroys tapering down just above her dainty tassel loafers.

"Lookin' good, Clarice, real good." He said it and he meant it, with three bottles of beer propelling the warmth of the compliment even further than he might have taken it otherwise.

"Thank you, Professor Tillman. How's the winter repair job on the bike coming along? I see you have the chain off and hanging over the back of a chair."

"Aw, the old guy is in need of constant attention these days. Parts are getting just about impossible to find, but the mail-order catalogs keep him going. If I have to, I'll start running off my own parts at a machine shop somewhere. He and I are together for life."

"Well, I'm glad somebody is." The divorce still hurt, Clarice never tried to pretend otherwise around him. "Any big trips planned for the summer?" She tilted back her dark blond head, took a drink of beer, and gave him a lickerish grin. They both knew what was coming down before the night was over.

"Thought I might ride up along Lake Superior. I haven't been there for a while. It's kind of pretty and not too crowded if you stay away from the big holidays. Wanna go with me?" He wasn't sure why he made the offer. He usually preferred traveling alone, but he was feeling deserted and left behind, and Clarice was looking especially good that night. He liked Clarice a lot.

She knew his travel habits and looked surprised, little quizzical smile on her face. "Maybe . . . when are you going?"

"I can go just about anytime, since I don't teach summer school anymore. If you're interested, we can work it out to your schedule. Ready to rumble?"

The spaghetti was good. They took their time over dinner, drinking a bottle of wine and talking before plunging into the maelstrom that was Beano's around nine-thirty. Bobby had the Blues Band cooking: "Put on your high-heeled sneakers, Mama, and your wiglet on your head/Put on your high-heeled . . ." Drummer, lead guitar, bass, Bobby singing and playing harmonica. And, of course, Molly Never (that's what she claims her parents named her) absolutely screaming on electric violin, legs apart, black heels and black stockings, black miniskirt, purple blouse. She looked like a funky Peter Pan who had been around the darker side of life. The band hit 115 decibels and headed up from there.

Bobby'd had this same band for twelve years, and they operated with a hard, disciplined precision. He shouted over the microphone, "Here's a song made famous by three black girls from Memphis, now to be sung by three white boys from small towns in the Midwest. That's why you pay Beano's exorbitant cover charge, to hear that kind of shit, right?" The crowd roared.

Clarice and Michael stood off to the side, waiting for a table to open up, which could take hours. She was screaming at him, him at her, as they tried to talk over the searing lead guitar of one Doppler Donovan, who wore a cowboy hat on his head and military-issue, jungle-style combat boots on his feet. Bobby had gone into a honky version of a Chuck Berry skip as he slid into his harp solo, amplifier cord looking as if it were coming out of his mouth where he held a small microphone against the harmonica.

Michael looked over at the booth where he and Jellie had sat a week ago. It was occupied now by two couples engaged in a pairwise beer-chugging contest. Her words floated through the smoke and the noise of Beano's: "There's something else going on between us, isn't there, Michael?"

Clarice slipped her arm around his waist and hugged him, bouncing up and down to the beat. She wanted to dance, and she'd eventually get him out there. But Michael wasn't comfortable on dance floors, never had been, so he was waiting for the second round of beer drinking to override the spaghetti and give him courage.

A student staggered up, towing a platinum blonde wearing greased-on jeans and a black leather jacket. Ghastly beer breath washed Michael's cheeks as the student shouted over the music, "Great class, Dr. Tillman, absolutely great. How'd I do?"

Michael didn't post grades, particularly in Beano's. But what the hell, beer breath had done all right, and it was party time. He held up one of Beano's custom napkins and pointed to the *B* on it, grinning.

The student threw both arms over his head in joy and spun back onto the dance floor, where he went into a ponylike boogaloo, pawing the air. Five minutes later he sent the waitress over with two draws for Michael and Clarice. It was semester's end, and they were all burying the dead and praising the living, so the atmosphere was celebrative, sort of like a New Orleans funeral at ten thousand watts. Doppler Donovan led the band into something called the "Drake Neighborhood Slide," and Clarice pulled Michael out on the dance floor.

The evening closed as he knew it would—warm, libidinous, and thoroughly satisfying. He and Clarice were good in bed together, and before it was over she was kneeling on the bed, palms and breasts and face pasted against the wall, with him behind her licking the perspiration off her shoulders and doing several other things that pleased her greatly, as she constantly and fervently emphasized while all of this was under way: "Yes, Michael . . . god*damnit*, yes, yes, *yes!*"

Seven

$\mathcal{J}$ellie from a distance. The ambiguity of those months she was in England was hard on him. His running shoes slushed along the streets of Cedar Bend, and ice clung to his hair where it stuck out beneath his blue stocking cap. The faculty and students were suspended in a climatic purgatory somewhere between the lights of Christmas and the warming of the earth in April. Gray muck draped like a shroud over Bingley Hall, ceiling lights bright and cold. Wind from the Canadian prairies smacked the building's north side and howled through the corridors when an outside door was opened. Unlike wine, or the coed of legend who removed her duds in a Russian professor's office, a midwestern winter does not improve with age.

Thinking almost constantly about Jellie, Michael

pushed the students hard and even held an extra three-hour class on a Sunday afternoon, promising them time off for good behavior later in the semester. He knew he'd begin to lose them and himself when the warm came again, so they were getting the hard stuff out of the way early. They hammered onward. By February's close he was thinking of calling for mass, campuswide psychotherapy to counter the late winter blahs. But they hung on, as ancient sailors in pounding seas clung to the mainmast and with the same faith in better times to come.

Then over the bare trees fluttered the first sign of hope in the form of colorful travel brochures pinned to hallway bulletin boards. The words and pictures promised sun and sand, tonic and tans, and, somewhat more slyly, fast times amid the palms of Florida or the south Texas coast. The classroom buzz as they waited for the bell ran to snow conditions in Colorado and who was driving which twelve people to South Padre Island in an old Dodge van.

By that time Michael had frightened the lower 20 percent of the class into filing drop slips. Those remaining were a group of battle-scarred veterans, deserving of a short rest before he bullwhacked them up the slopes of learning toward victory, and maybe graduation. The inevitable questions came: "Professor Tillman, is it all right if I miss your Thursday class before spring break? A bunch of us are going to Daytona Beach, and we want to leave Wednesday night."

He looked at the nice young woman who asked the question—it was a different one every spring, but they all ran together after a while—and said, "Why do you think I dragged you in here for an extra three hours on a Sunday afternoon? Yes, you may leave early, but get the notes for my dazzling lecture on matrix transposition from someone, because I'm not going to repeat it after you get back." He grinned at her. "Now get out of my hair and leave me alone. I have serious work to do in saving a world having no interest in being saved."

Friday came, beginning of spring break. Gusty March winds late in the month, minivans and station wagons filled with impatient spouses lined up outside the building, motors running, waiting for classes to end. The library was nearly empty, except for graduate students catching up on their work and junior professors slogging their way toward a tenure decision. By the time Michael got out of Bingley at five, the campus was quiet.

At home he leaned back in his chair and stared at a Polaroid picture of Jellie pinned to a piece of corkboard above his desk. She looked out at him, standing by a stone wall in Ireland, in her hiking clothes, hair tucked under her round tweed hat with the little bill, leather bag over her left shoulder. She'd mailed him a card saying hello and not much else in late January. The photo came a month later, accompanied by a neutral-sounding note in her small, neat handwriting:

2/21

Hi, Michael.

We took a long weekend and came over to Ireland to scout things out for a more extended trip this

> *summer. I hope your spring is going well. Crave our coffee talks and miss you.*
>
> *Jellie*

He noticed she didn't underline "miss" in the way she had said it in Beano's just before she left. Maybe that was looking too hard for what didn't exist. Jellie wasn't coy, and what she said about getting cooled down might be working—for her, at least. For Michael, it wasn't, and the picture only made matters worse. He sat there and stared at it for hours, thinking and wanting. He just didn't see how he could go on living his life without Jellie Braden next to him all the time. Five months to go, and she'd be back. He couldn't wait for her to return and never wanted to see her again, all at the same time. He kept trying to conjure up ways to defend his psyche against the assaults she made on it without even trying, but he failed and sat there waiting for August.

And it came eventually, August has a way of doing that. The summer had passed in kind of a quiet haze. One of those periodic budget crises took hold of the university, the provost's office went into a frenzy, and Clarice had to delay her vacation until autumn. For some reason Michael didn't feel like going up to Lake Superior and instead took the Shadow on a long run into the pretty back roads of the Smokies, enjoying the steady hum between his legs of a machine he'd rebuilt twenty times since his father had given it to him.

He jogged through the streets of Cedar Bend at

first light before the heat settled in, staying in shape, beating back the years, though it was getting harder to do. Slowly he could feel his legs going, and on rainy days the old knee injury flashed little twinges of pain as a reminder of his boyhood follies. Sometimes he went by the Bradens' two-story brick. Quite often he did that. Running, then stopping for a moment, looking at the front steps where he and Jellie had stood the previous Thanksgiving, remembering the subtle, unspoken signals they'd both sent that night without being sure the other was receiving them.

In June he wrote a piece on the role of tax incentives in attacking large-scale social problems. *The Atlantic* surprised him by taking it, sending a check for $1,200. He knocked out a heavy-duty, academic version of the article for the *Journal of Social Issues*, and that one had wings, too, with the following spring projected as the publication date. Michael knew his department head would dismiss the first as catering to popular taste and the second as not having sufficient stature in the field of economics, though it was an okay journal in its own niche. But he didn't much care anymore what members of the administration thought about his work, so none of that bothered him.

By mid-August he was wired tight. East of him a 747 would be loading at Heathrow one of these days, Jellie settling onto her seat with a book, Jimmy Braden running around the cabin looking for a pillow and blanket. She'd once said Jimmy was a master at sleeping on airplanes but absolutely panicked and couldn't sleep at all without his pillow and blanket. So rounding up his bedroom gear was always his first chore after boarding. Michael could picture Jellie in her demure, wire-rimmed reading glasses, glancing at a book, then out the window as the big plane lifted off and brought her back toward Cedar Bend.

Classes started in less than a week, and Michael was in his office fussing around, hoping he might see Jimmy Braden, which would be his signal Jellie had returned. The phone rang.

"Hello, Michael, how are you?" Her voice was warm, soft, the diction clear and crisp as always, except when she was sitting in Beano's talking to a man about secret things she felt and thought he might also feel.

"Jellie—are you back or what?" He noticed his voice shook just a little, and he didn't like it. American males have their standards, after all.

"Yes, we got in late last night. Jimmy's still sleeping, but I'm all fouled up timewise, so I've been up since four o'clock wandering around. Did you get the picture I sent?"

"I did indeed. Thank you. You looked well and happy." He didn't say anything about hanging it on his wall. This was an intricate dance along the halls of ambiguity, and Michael was feeling his way, not wanting to open up things too rapidly.

"Yes, I am feeling well. I ran into one of my old friends from India on the tube in London. She got me back into yoga, and it does wonders for my body *and* my mind."

Oh, Jellie, Jellie, he was thinking, don't say anything about your body. Give a poor man space to breathe, space to be less wicked than you already have made him in his impure thoughts.

"Michael, any chance we might meet somewhere? I'd like to talk, but I don't want to come to your office since I suspect Jimmy will be up at the university as soon as he comes to."

"Sure, anyplace. You name it."

"How about the bar at the Ramada out by the shopping center?"

"Fine. When?"

"What time is it now?"

He looked at his watch. "Twenty to eleven."

Silence on the other end for a few seconds. "Would eleven push you too hard? I'd like to be gone when Jimmy wakes up so I don't have to think up some reason for going out."

"No, that's fine. I have the Shadow tied down outside the building. Eleven, then?"

"Yes . . . Michael?"

"I'm here." Too cool, being way too cool.

"I'm looking forward to seeing you."

"Me too, Jellie. See you in twenty minutes."

It was only a ten-minute ride out to the Ramada, so he went down to the mailboxes, collected a pile of book advertisements and a very pleasant invitation from *The Atlantic* editor to send some more pieces. That got him thinking for a moment: maybe he could hack it as a free-lance writer. Not enough in that to keep him going, probably, but he could take early retirement, annuitize his retirement fund, and maybe pick up ten or fifteen grand a year just by fiddling around with his word processor.

There was also a letter from the University of California Department of Economics inviting all of its Ph.D. alumni to a reception at the winter meetings in Las Vegas. The usual, Michael got it every year.

But he never went, even though he was grateful for the degree and sent them money when they asked for it.

He pulled the Shadow out into traffic getting heavier as the students returned for the fall semester and rolled down Thirty-second Street, bumping into Route 81 about ten blocks farther on. The highway ran a winding route through one of the nicer sections of Cedar Bend, and he leaned the Shadow into the curves, noticing a slight valve tick needing attention.

Jellie was already seated when he got there. It was dark in the lounge, and he couldn't see her at first, partly because she was back in one of the corner booths off to his right.

"Michael, over here."

Jellie. After all these months, there she was and calling out to him. Black hair gathered high, big-hooped silver earrings, light yellow summer dress with sandals. Walking toward her, feeling clumsy, estranged from her. She held out her hand, Michael took it and slid in beside her. She kissed him on the cheek, then, butterfly-quick, leaned back and looked at him. He was gone again, over the hill just seeing her, hands sweating and heart valves ticking like the Black Shadow.

"You're all suntanned, Michael. You look great, just wonderful, and no preschool haircut yet."

"Nah, I've been putting it off. I hate going to barbers, something to do with loss of manhood, maybe. More likely because, when I was about four years old, the only barber in Custer threatened to cut off my ears if I didn't sit still while he was working on me."

She laughed. "Really? Did that really happen?"

"Yes, it did. My childhood was one long charge through the brambles of anxiety after that. You look wonderful, too, Jellie. I've thought about you a lot."

She looked down, then up at Michael, then down again. The bartender came around the bar and over to where they sat, lighted a small candle on the table-top, and asked what she could get for them. Jellie ordered a club soda with lime. Michael asked for a St. Pauli Girl, which the bartender didn't have, so he settled on a Miller's.

While they waited for their drinks, Jellie asked him about his spring and summer. He told her about the two articles, and her eyes widened when he mentioned *The Atlantic*. "Hey, that's the big time. Congratulations."

The bartender came back. Jellie insisted on paying the check, so he let her.

Michael held up his beer, and she touched her glass to his. "What shall we drink to, Michael?"

"How about survival. If not that, retirement."

"Michael, you're just the same." Her chastisement was gentle. "How about we drink to a nice summer day and your success in writing."

"And to your safe return," he said.

"How's the Shadow running?"

"Good, overall. It's a perpetual battle, but good. I took it down into Tennessee this summer, but didn't stay long. The Smokies are a nightmare; they're thinking of limiting the number of tourists that can visit there. Then I rode it out to Custer and stayed a week with my mother."

"How is she?"

"Old, and getting more fragile every day. I'm afraid we're not more than two years away from a nursing home or something along those lines."

Jellie didn't say anything for a while. He drank his beer, she drank her club soda and lime. He took out his cigarettes and offered her one. She refused. "I've stopped smoking. Something about yoga that leads to that, not sure what it is."

He nodded and flipped open the Zippo, lit his, and leaned back against the padded booth. She slid over farther so she could turn and look straight at him.

Michael was tired of the dancing. "Where are we, Jellie, the two of us? It's been a long nine months for me." After he said it he wished he'd moved into this a little slower. Typical male fashion—no foreplay.

She didn't say anything for a moment. He'd forgotten just how gray her eyes were until she kept them on his for at least ten seconds.

"I've done a lot of thinking, Michael." Those were bad-news words, he could tell. Something in the words themselves, something in the way she said them. What they felt for each other didn't require thinking. It required acting, not thinking. The happiness from seeing her again started draining down and out of him.

She paused, then went on. "I had the words all ready to say, but it's much harder than I thought it would be. I'd convinced myself the way I felt about you was a kind of girlish infatuation with a different sort of man than I'd ever encountered before, or at least not for a long time. But with you here looking at me with those good brown eyes, your hair drifting over your shirt collar and all, it's more difficult . . . a lot more difficult."

"Say it, Jellie. I already know what's coming."

"I suppose you do, and I'm going to say what I have to say before I get to the point I can't say it. We've got to cut this clean before real trouble starts." He was prepared for it, but that didn't stop the harpoon from entering his chest and going out the other side. "Jimmy asked me several times in the days before we left for England if there was anything wrong with me. He said I was acting a little strange. It was you, Michael—no, *us.* I was thinking about us, fantasizing about things I don't even want to mention."

"That's all right, Jellie, I've had the same kind of images in my mind since the day I first saw you. Mine would just blow you away if I started talking about them."

"Women have those thoughts, too. Let me go on. In ways you'll never know, and I don't want to talk about, I owe Jimmy a lot. Look, we both know Jimmy. He's a little goofy in certain ways, but he's very kind to me.

"Jimmy was crushed when the best schools wouldn't accept him for his doctorate. His grades were good, but only because he worked so hard. God, his parents just hammered and hammered at him about the whole idea of success. But Jimmy does not have a truly fine intellect. He knows that and has come to terms with it, though it bothers him because of the world in which he's chosen to earn a living, a world where he's constantly reminded of his limitations just by being around people like you, Michael."

"Oh, hell, Jellie . . ." He started to do a foot shuffle into something resembling modesty, a little dance called the South Dakota backstep. But she'd have none of it and interrupted him.

"Michael Tillman, don't play the country boy with me, please. It's not becoming, and I know better. You scare Jimmy. He knows he's not in your league. He could write all his life and never get an article accepted by the journals in which you've published. I don't mean to imply you don't work hard, I know you do, in spite of the casual way you seem to operate. And Jimmy likes you. He likes you a lot, and he's appreciative of the good ideas you give him. If he ever makes full professor, you'll be responsible for it in good part."

"Jimmy's all right, Jellie. He's a lot different than me, but I respect him for the way he keeps his head down and the numbers crunching. I couldn't do that."

He lit another Merit and took a drink of his beer. This was turning into something a little unpleasant, and he didn't want that to happen with Jellie. She was floating off, getting loyalty and Jimmy's shortcomings and her own emotions all tangled up. Chewing on him in small ways as a means of protecting herself from her own feelings.

"Jellie, let me try and say what I think you're telling me. You feel good things for Jimmy, among them at least a kind of love, I'm sure. You're a loving person. And you feel a gratefulness toward him for something I don't know about and won't ask about. Though I have a feeling India works into it some-how—I figure you'd tell me if you wanted me to know, even though it wouldn't affect how I feel about you no matter what it is. And you want to make sure our feelings for each other don't go any further than just that—feelings. Have I got it right?"

She nodded, tears in her eyes.

He had momentum and kept rolling. "Here's the bottom line, Jellie Markham Braden: I'm in love with you, truly and powerfully in love. I guess I knew it when you walked in the dean's kitchen a year ago in your blue suit and black boots, knew it when we sat on the back steps that day. Christ, teeter-totters in the park. Do you have any idea of how much I've wanted you, all of you, everything that makes you up, tangible and otherwise? The whole works, that's what I want. As much as I can get in the years I have left, and I'm no youngster anymore. Do you understand that, Jellie, how deeply I feel?"

"Michael . . . don't." She reached in her purse, took out a handkerchief, and put it against her eyes for a moment. The bartender was not insensitive; she had a feel for what was going on and turned up the television to cover their conversation. Michael nodded at her in thanks, and she gave him a little wave.

He put his hand on Jellie's neck, the first time he'd ever touched her in that way. Her skin felt exactly as he'd known it would, and the sensation ran up his arm, went down somewhere inside of him, and made a low, sad sound for all the times he'd never feel it again. "It's okay, Jellie. We'll make it work. We'll put some bandages on the cuts and promise not to look under them ever again. I'm not sure I can stay in the same town with you, but I'll try. Really, I'll try, Jellie. Maybe we can eventually work it out so we can have coffee at Beano's now and then. Maybe it'll spiral down and we can do that."

She stuffed her hanky back in her purse and reached out for his left hand, holding it tight in both of hers. "You're right, Michael, in everything you said. Damnit, I know why people get frustrated with you sometimes and are secretly afraid of you. Your mind is like a rifle bullet when you decide to let it run full tilt, and that's scary. Carolyn, the dean's wife, said that about you the first day I met you. She said, 'Michael Tillman frightens the hell out of Arthur, and Arthur retaliates in mean little ways.' The dean was going to turn you down for full professor on those grounds alone, even though you'd done twice as much work as it took to qualify. Carolyn told him, 'Arthur, you pull that piece of crap on Michael and you'll see me waving from the first train out of Cedar Bend.' "

Now they had Carolyn and Arthur into it. Jellie kept wandering away from the subject, but he understood why. There was a door closing behind them, and she wanted to keep it open all the while she was pulling it shut.

"Jellie, let's let it rest where it is. You know where to find me. Come by if you feel you can. Hell, I just like to be around you, to look at you, to smell your perfume when I get close, which I haven't done nearly enough."

"I don't think so. There's something about being in each other's presence that's just too strong for me— for both of us. I came off the plane clear-headed and ready to tell you exactly how I felt and what I was

going to do, now here I am turning into mud pie.
I've got to get my life organized again. I'm going to
take another class this fall, so I'll be on campus three
days a week. If I feel okay about it, I'll stop by to see
you. If I don't, and I probably won't, it's not because
I'm not thinking about you. You understand that,
don't you?"

"Yes. I understand, Jellie. I don't like it, but I
understand. And I'll be thinking about you, too.
That's all I ever seem to do anymore."

As they left the Ramada bar, Jellie pulled a small
package from her purse and handed it to him. "I
forgot to give you this."

He tore open the wrapping. Inside was a belt
made of English bridle leather with *Orville* hand-
tooled on the back.

Michael took the Shadow out of town and let it
go all the way to Des Moines, where he turned around
and came back into Cedar Bend through one of those
soft August twilights. Going home past the campus,
he could hear the marching band practicing, getting
ready for the first football game. They were playing
some old song from some old movie. Michael Tillman couldn't remember the name of either the song
or the movie, because he was thinking about Jellie
Braden and wondering how he was going to get
through the years ahead without her.

The lights in Bingley Hall flickered on, and the
race to December got under way. Jimmy Braden
came by Michael's office for new ideas, and the football team was doing well. On those Saturdays when
the team was playing at home, the streets were packed

with Cadillacs and Lincolns, driven by overweight men who wrote out large checks to the athletic department and whose daughters were in the best sororities.

Michael paced the classroom, tossing a piece of chalk up and down in his right hand. "Consider, for a moment, the nature of systemic problems, the elements of a puzzling issue and the subtle, intricate relationships among those elements. What we must do is learn how to overcome what I long ago began to call the Archimedean Dilemma." He always hesitated at this point and looked out at the class. "Who, by the way, was Archimedes?" They all focused on their notebooks, pretending to be doing something.

He pushed and prodded, and finally a young man (bad complexion, front row) said hesitantly, "Wasn't he some kind of scientist or something?"

Michael gave them a two-minute capsule on the life and times of the Greek mathematician. After that, he picked up the thread of the lecture again. "Archimedes said, 'Give me a lever and a place to stand, and I will move the world.' That's what structural modeling is all about, finding a lever, a place to stand, an angle of entry into complexity." He paused, thinking of Jellie, while the students wrote in their notebooks and wondered if he would ask about Archimedes on the first examination.

During the second week of school he was looking out the window while covering a fine point in Boolean algebra, looking at nothing except the quaver of now turning leaves in the wind of September, and saw her. At first it didn't register, since he was working hard at getting the students to appreciate the intellectual leavings of one George Boole, the nineteenth-century mathematician who took formal logic up about fifty notches. But the long-legged walk and tweed cap finally got his attention—Jellie. He stopped talking, he wasn't sure how long, and watched her wind along a sidewalk, knapsack over her shoulder. Jellie from a distance, always from a distance. When she moved out of sight, he turned back to the class. They were all looking at him in a strange kind of way. His face, maybe, or his body. They saw something, in his eyes or the momentary sag of his shoulders, and they knew they hadn't seen it before. Michael glanced at the wall clock. Five minutes to go. "That'll be all for today," he said. As he scraped up lecture notes from the desk in front, they filed out, some of them giving him sidelong glances and talking to one another. A young woman whispered, "Did you see how he looked? What happened to him all of a sudden?"

Michael hadn't realized how much it showed. Jellie was right in believing they had to stay apart. Aside from protecting themselves from each other, people would start to pick up on how they felt, even if they were merely in the same room together. He'd been looking at advertisements for faculty positions in the *Chronicle*, but at his salary and rank it would be difficult to make a move. Besides, with his mother's health declining, he felt a responsibility to stay in the middle of the country and not be too far from her. Still there might be something somewhere that met his requirements and took him away from the town where Jellie Braden lived.

It's hard to say where all this might have gone if it hadn't been for the ducks. Probably to the same place by a different route. The history of the situation is this: University presidents relish new buildings, so do Boards of Education. Bingley Hall was just fine— old, but with a patina of learning and struggle rubbed into its corridors and heavy in its air. Still, the president decided one of his premier colleges needed a new building. Presidents don't bequeath knowledge or grateful students to the world, they leave behind bricks and mortar. Whether those bricks and mortar are actually necessary is irrelevant. The important thing is to get money and build buildings carrying the names either of heavy donors to the university or members of the administration who served the university loyally, though not necessarily brilliantly. *The Arthur J. Wilcox College of Business and Economics*— you could see the lettering in the dean's rodentlike eyes as he scooted around Bingley Hall with rolled-up blueprints clutched in his sweaty paws. Fat chance.

The money could have been used for faculty salaries or student financial aid, but that's never in the cards. As the president was fond of saying, privately, of course, "It's much easier to get money for buildings than it is for faculty salaries." But, in spite of hard economic times in the state, the board floated a bond issue and ponied up $18 million for a new building. That had occurred the previous winter, and final construction plans were now being drawn.

Arthur posted emerging versions of the plans in the coffee room for everyone to slobber over. Michael was standing there looking at an updated set and noticed the location of the new building had been moved fifty yards from its original site. "They're going to put the sonuvabitch right over the duck pond," he said to no one in particular. The other faculty members present looked at him in a way that said, "So what?"

Michael went to see Arthur and explained to him the rather neat and profound role the pond played in the traditions of the campus. It wasn't much in terms of water area, elliptically shaped and maybe a hundred feet long by fifty feet wide. But it was home for little geezers with orange legs who looked at Michael when he walked by and went "Quack" when he grinned and said hello to them.

It was also a place for moonlight walks and tender thoughts, a place where ten thousand engagement rings had been slipped over shaking fingers through the years, not to mention various other assignations getting a little more carnal late at night. When Michael looked out his office window, he could see the ducks on their pond a block away, and often he had found solace in that when dealing with education gone berserk.

But guys like Arthur J. Wilcox have no appreciation for tradition, it's not tangible enough. Michael talked hard, but it didn't register. Arthur just kept saying, "But, Michael, we need a new building."

"What about the ducks?" Michael was angry. "Where will they go? Are we going to build a new eighteen-million-dollar pond for them, too?"

Arthur didn't understand ducks, either. You could see it on his face. That and the plain wish Michael would just go away and leave him alone with his blueprints.

Michael was pretty sure he wouldn't have raised as much hell about the duck pond as he did if he hadn't been half-crazed with sorting out his feelings in those days, trying to push Jellie far back and out of his mind and failing in that attempt. He worked his way up through the provost, who didn't understand ducks any better than Arthur. Stomping past Clarice's desk on his way out of the provost's office, he turned around, then talked with her for a moment.

Next he made an appointment to see the president. Michael laid out his case: Move the building, keep the duck pond. The prez was smooth. Years of dealing with demented faculty and recalcitrant alumni who stapled their checkbooks shut when they saw him coming had provided him with a sheen and style worthy of the very best (or worst, depending on your point of view) slithering public relations man.

"Professor Tillman, I do understand your concerns. Tradition is important, I agree with you. But in evolving times we must sometimes cast off our old traditions and establish new ones. I like ducks, too. In fact, I'm a member of Ducks Unlimited and go duck hunting every fall."

Michael was wondering if, in addition to professional incompetence and moral degradation, presidential dismemberment was sufficient cause for loss of tenure.

One of the best students Michael ever had went on to law school and stayed in Cedar Bend after graduating. Michael called him. "Gene, what can be done to prevent these clowns from pouring cement over ducks and tradition?"

Gene always had a soft spot for radical causes, so he looked into it. He called back in two days, flat out saying the building couldn't be halted by legal

chicanery. Something to do with state law and a
Board of Education master plan for masterful buildings and a master race.

"Screw 'em, Gene. I'm going to plant myself
right in the middle of that pond and make 'em drag
me out with chains."

"Michael, I'll defend you free of charge if you
do it. But you're going to lose. You'll be better off
spending your time looking for another home for the
ducks."

Knowing bureaucrats hate bad publicity more
than anything else, Michael wrote a long article for
the university newspaper, making what he thought
was a powerful and eloquent plea to save the duck
pond. That started a fair amount of debate over the
whole affair, which drove Arthur dotty.

Arthur went completely out of his mind when
the longhairs from the Student Socialist Brigade made
up signs reading "Save the Ducks" and began
marching around Bingley Hall in their Birkenstocks.
Recruiters from the Fortune 500 who were on campus
interviewing savvy students told Arthur they were
looking for good corporate citizens, not radicals. He
took them over to the faculty club for cocktails and
reassured them this was merely one of those periodic
outbreaks coming down to us as a result of universi-
ties being too lenient in the sixties and it would soon
be over. Afterward he took the recruiters to his office,
unrolled his blueprints, and showed them all the wonderful space the new building would have for interview rooms. They liked that a lot better.

The university newspaper was flooded for a few
days with letters pro and con. One of the bookstores

printed up T-shirts with the logo *Ducks, Not Cement* and sold them for twelve dollars each, proving once again capitalism can profit even from the concerns of its enemies. Michael was surprised to see Jellie write a letter to the newspaper in support of his position. It was a nice letter. And he knew it probably caused her trouble at home, since Jimmy had dropped by to talk with him about the issue and seemed utterly amazed, or perhaps bewildered, that Michael could get so worked up over eight or ten ducks.

But nobody except Michael cared very much. The longhairs marched, Arthur fretted, and the earth-moving machinery was carted into position on the back of big, muddy trucks. Gambling on having a mild winter, the contractors would begin digging on the following Monday. Michael was sure the tame ducks wouldn't know how to handle the filling of their pond and contacted the Humane Society. He and the society put a notice in the paper saying anyone who wanted to help in getting the ducks moved should show up early Saturday morning and be pre-pared to get wet.

Light frost lay upon the grass of autumn when Michael rode the Shadow through early light and parked it by the pond. While he sat on the bike, taking one last look at tradition and little geezers who slap-slapped about on orange legs and flat feet, he noticed someone walking down the road toward the pond. Jellie. Jellie in the morning, Jellie at the duck pond. She wore old jeans and her hiking boots, a heavy sweater and a red stocking cap with *Grownup* printed on the front. Her hair was in a ponytail, and she was smiling as she walked toward him.

"Hello, Michael. I came to help you find the ducks a new home."

He cared for her more at that moment than ever before.

"Jellie . . . thanks for coming. It's going to be something of a mess, I'm afraid. But the little folks need somewhere to go."

She walked over to him, wrapped both her arms around one of his, and leaned against the Shadow, putting her head against his shoulder. The physical contact was unnerving and surprised him, but he thought, Maybe we're going to work it out and be friends, nothing more. He only thought that for a moment. Being merely Jellie's friend and nothing more was impossible for him.

The Humane Society troops pulled in, a professor from the biology department riding along with them. He had cages and a net that could be fired out over the pond with small rockets, which took him about twenty minutes to get set up. Jellie didn't say much, Michael didn't say much, watching the professor and his helpers from the Humane Society, all of whom wore chest-high rubber waders. They strung the rocket net along the shore while the ducks woke up and swam around in circles, alarmed and telling everyone who would listen about how they felt.

Jellie and Michael walked over near the water where the professor was crouched, making adjustments on his apparatus. He straightened up and said, "Ready." Everyone stood back while he threw bread crumbs onto the water. Alarm is one thing, bread crumbs are something else, and the ducks swam toward them, quacking. When the ducks came within range the biologist fired his rockets, which scared hell out of the ducks. But the net arched across the pond, went down past the face of a rising sun and over ten frightened ducks.

The biologist waded into the water, motioning for the Humane Society to follow him. They got around on the pond side of the net, gently pushing the net and ducks toward shore. The professor obviously had done this before. He glanced up at Jellie and Michael. "We'll hand you the ducks. You two can put them in the cages, very carefully, if you please." So saying, he rolled up his sleeves and began reaching under the net, which now formed a small semicircle near the shore. It was all very crisp, easier than Michael had thought it would be. He and Jellie put the ducks in cages, Jellie petting them and talking in a low, sweet voice as she handled the terrified birds.

The operation took less than ten minutes. The biologist rolled up his net while Michael and Jellie carried three cages to the Humane Society truck and put them in the back. A woman in a tan shirt with a *Humane Society of the United States* patch on it said, "We're taking them out to Heron Lake north of town. You know where that is?"

Michael nodded. "I'll follow you on my bike." He looked over at Jellie. "Want to come? There's room in the truck, or you can ride with me."

She turned to the woman from the Humane Society. "We'll meet you out there." At that moment, Michael felt as if some kind of decision beyond transportation had been made.

He kicked the Shadow's starter and helped Jellie climb on behind him. She'd never been on a motorcycle before, so he gave her a twenty-second lecture on where to rest her feet and how to lean with him in the curves. She wrapped her arms around his waist and said, "This is fun, Michael," as he pulled out behind the truck.

The campus was quiet early on a Saturday, air warming rapidly, prodded on by a fat, red sun. The Shadow rolled smoothly down the streets of Cedar Bend and out into the countryside through tunnels of red and yellow leaves. Jellie's arms tightened around Michael. He could feel her body tucked against his lower back and rear. They could be far into Minnesota by evening if he just let the Shadow run on toward wherever the highway went.

They swung into the state park entrance, still following the Humane Society truck and its little cargo. Through the park and on to Heron Lake, lying cool and flat on a windless morning. The ducks were shown the water and knew what to do with it, waddling out of their cages and paddling around, looking for food. The biologist said, "It'll take them a while to adjust. With all the people at the university handing out grub, they're not used to foraging on their own. But I'll check on them every few days. Eventually they'll get accustomed to life out here. Portions of the lake stay open during winter."

This was the way it was meant to be, Michael was thinking as they rode back into town. Jellie and he, and the Shadow, and bright autumn mornings with the road out in front of them. Instead he was taking her home to James Lee Braden III, who probably had tickets for the football game that afternoon.

He glanced at his watch—eight-fifteen—it was going to be a long day and a long life.

Jellie was trying to say something, but Michael couldn't hear her over the wind and sound of the engine. He eased off the Shadow, letting it slow down and coast, and tilted his head back toward her. She put her fingers on the side of his neck, speaking in a soft voice, right into his ear: "Michael, can we go to your apartment?" He turned his head for an instant and looked into the gray eyes. She was half smiling, half not smiling. A strange, warm, loving look.

He nodded and began to shake a little. She laid her cheek against his back and put her hand under his jacket and inside his shirt, moving it slowly back and forth over his chest and stomach. The Shadow took him toward home, as it had taken him there so many times over the years. And it took him and Jellie Braden toward a future he'd long ago decided would never come. When they got off the Shadow at his apartment, smoke from burning leaves was drifting through the neighborhood. In the distance voices were singing the university fight song at a morning pep rally.

He held the door for her and they went inside, into the world of a man who lived alone and stayed mostly to himself. Dishes in the sink, a pair of jeans on the floor, streaks on the windows. Small kitchen, large living room, bedroom off through another door. In a corner of the living room nearest the kitchen was a scarred maple table where he took his meals. The three chairs around the table were each of a different kind and Goodwill rough. Plain, ceramic salt and pepper shakers sat on the table next to a stack of paper napkins.

Near the table and along the wall was his work area. His desk was a nine-foot unfinished door laid across sawhorses. Brick-and-board bookcases flanked the desk, with one long board running over the top of it, holding reference books. In the middle of the desk was a computer, turned on and with words typed across the screen, cursor blinking. The far end of the desk held a stack of audio equipment, tapes in desultory piles on and next to the equipment.

Jellie took off her stocking cap and laid her coat over the back of a chair. As she looked around, it struck her that she knew very little about Michael Tillman. More than that, she'd never been completely alone with him. "I think I need a drink," she said. "Do you have anything with alcohol in it?"

"Beer, wine, and maybe"—he opened a cupboard door and looked inside—"a little whiskey." He took out the whiskey bottle and held it up. It was a third full. Clarice sometimes preferred whiskey when the nights were long and wild and getting wilder.

"About two fingers of the Jack Daniel's over ice with a little water"—Jellie took a deep breath—"should do it."

Michael stood for a moment, holding the whiskey bottle, looking at her. "You okay?"

"Yes." She smiled and brushed loose strands of hair back from her face. "About eighty percent, at least."

"I could take you home if you want."

She shook her head, small silver earrings from

her early days in India moving as she did it. "Let's try the Jack Daniel's first."

He owned four glasses. All of them were in the sink, dirty. He washed one and pulled an ice cube tray from the refrigerator.

Jellie walked slowly past his desk, trailing her finger along the edge of it. Above the desk were notes and two snapshots. One of the pictures was her standing by a stone wall in Ireland. The other was a yellowed, curling, black-and-white shot of a young woman in a long dress and a bearded man in a dark turtleneck sweater, jeans, and sandals. She stared at the second photo and recognized the eyes. "Is that you?"

He looked up from the counter where he was fixing her drink. "Yes. A long time ago in Berkeley." He poured Jack Daniel's and handed the glass to her. "The woman's name was Nadia. She's an implacable feminist now—was starting to become one then, in fact—works for the National Council of Women. We exchange notes at Christmas."

Jellie didn't say anything. She read the words typed on the computer screen: *In this place I hear the quiet rasp of things as they used to be. I come at dawn, I come at nightfall, and all the hours in between. I come to hear the rustle of twilight robes and songs from the time of Gregory. I come because old things live here, things I understand without knowing why.*

"Is this something you're writing?" She sipped on her whiskey and pointed at the screen.

"Yeah, I keep fiddling around, thinking I might have a novel inside me." He set the bottle of beer he was drinking on the counter.

"Do you?"

"Maybe. It's harder than I thought it would be. Writing the academic stuff and essays, you're always bound to reality. So far I'm having trouble dealing with the freedom to make up anything I want to say. It's kind of strange—in fiction you get to tell lies and are applauded for it."

"Justifiable lies," she said. "I suppose that happens sometimes in real life, too."

"If you're a relativist it does. And maybe now and then if it's absolutely necessary to cushion someone from a world gone too harsh and bitter."

In the far corner of the room was an easel folded and leaning against a window. "Do you paint?" Jellie asked.

Michael grinned, shoved his hands in the pockets of his jeans. "I try. I know a guy named Wayne Regenson over in the art department. He and his wife periodically fight like hell. When that happens he drops by for a little male support, which I'm not very good at, but better than nothing, I suppose. In return he's been trying to teach me oil painting. It's coming real slow. Real, *real* slow. In some ways, though, it can be a lot like mathematics—true mathematics—the same feelings in your brain. The elegance of saying much with little, bringing together left-brained technique and right-brained shapes."

"Like the long-range jumpshot, too?"

He thought for a moment. "Yes, that too."

"Is this one of yours?" She was looking at an oil painting, framed and hanging on the wall. It was a group of black, vertical lines sprouting slashes of green and a ribbon of yellow winding away from the viewer, back into the vertical lines. Farther and farther the streak of yellow wound, disappearing then in a splash of red.

"Yes, it's the only one I can bear looking at. Actually I kind of like it."

"So do I. Does it have a title?"

"I call it *Butterfly Gone.*"

Jellie tipped her glass and took a serious drink of Jack Daniel's. She turned and looked at him, then out the window. In the hard, south light of November, he noticed for the first time the early lines of age coming to her face.

"This seems very strange, Michael. All our talks, our resolutions about right and wrong . . . all of that." The university band was marching down the street a block away, playing the fight song, *"We will go undaunted, hear our cry, hear our cry."* Jellie Braden watched the dark curling leaves of late autumn stir and begin to tumble across the grass as a light breeze came in from the west.

Michael always remembered how she had looked that morning in Cedar Bend, staring outside at the things of autumn. Still looking out the window, she'd reached up and taken the elastic band from her ponytail, shaking the thick black hair loose and long. She'd looked over at him then, the gray eyes soft and no longer like an arrow in flight, saying, "I'm a little shaky. It's been a long time since . . . well, a long time."

"When are you expected home?"

"I have the day. Jimmy's attending a reunion of his fraternity on campus. They're all going to the game and out to dinner after that. All that arm punching and male bonding was more than I could think about tolerating. Besides"—she smiled—"there were the ducks."

In midafternoon they heard the roar of the football crowd from the stadium. The sound of it came faintly over tapes of Cleo Laine ballads and sweet obscurities whispered in Tamil by Jellie Braden on an autumn afternoon in the high latitudes.

"If God lives at all, God lives in moments like these," a man had once said to her. And she had said that to Michael Tillman in English, looking up at him, touching his face with her hands, loving him and missing that other man and sometimes confusing the two of them even though she didn't want to on that afternoon.

Michael looked down at the pulse of blood in her throat, at her eyes widening as she arched her breasts and belly toward him, eyes looking first at him and then straight upward as India rolled within her and time went back to the high country of an older land where dark hands had moved over those same breasts and a voice had commanded her, "Wider now, Jellie, wider still, everything, Jellie. Give me all of you, and I'll give you back yourself when we have finished." And in the high country she had screamed aloud in some combination of fear and pleasure. And she had done that once more in a bed in Iowa, then turned the scream into a dwindling, involuntary cry for all the things she had once felt and now felt again with another strange man who lived in his own far places.

Michael had a sense that day she was feeling and doing things not attributable to her life with Jimmy Braden. It was obvious this was a woman who had gone before into sensual frontiers where he was sure Jimmy never ventured. Something about how nakedness did not bother her. Something about how she moved freely and uninhibited beneath him and with him, how she touched him with hands that were practiced and surprising in what they did. Something about the directness of her words when they first lay on the bed, still dressed, and she had pulled back from him, smiling. "I seem to remember it's necessary for me to take off my jeans if this is going to work out in the best possible way."

Later, with post–football game traffic moving along the streets outside, he fetched beers for them. When he came back into the bedroom Jellie was sitting on her knees, legs under her. She'd grinned at him, hair hanging in disarray above her breasts. He lay down beside her, and she touched his chest. "It was worth the wait," she said quietly. Malachi lay in the doorway, head on his paws, brown eyes turned up toward the bed. Casserole sat on the dresser and licked a paw.

Michael ran his hand slowly along Jellie's body. "*Now* it seems worth the wait. It didn't seem that way while waiting." He raised up on one elbow. "One of my many quirks is I get crazy hungry after making love. How's a toasted cheese sandwich sound? That's about all I have."

"Make three, and we'll each have one plus another to share." She leaned over and kissed him. "My secret passion is fried potatoes with a little onion mixed in. You got potatoes, motorcycle man, big fresh ones?" She smiled. "Out in the kitchen, I mean."

"I got potatoes, Jellie-Who-Sometimes-Talks-Raunchy-in-the-Afternoon. I also got onions and lotsa beer."

"We're in fat city. You cook the sandwiches, I'll handle potatoes. Deal?"

"Deal. Do we have to get dressed, though? I love seeing you naked."

"God, no. Given what I suspect—what I hope—will go on after we eat, that'd be wasted effort." She bounced off the bed. "On to the naked kitchen for naked lunch, then. Who said that, naked lunch? I should know. William . . ."

"Burroughs. Ol' wild and woolly William S. It's the title of one of his books."

"Get out the bread and show me the potatoes, Captain America. I'm starving, too."

Two weeks later she was gone. She'd had surges of guilt about Jimmy. So had Michael. Jellie cried once, thinking of it. "How can I be so callous and yet not care I'm being callous? I want you so much nothing matters, not guilt or anything like that."

But something had gone wrong in her marriage. It had been there for a long while, and the semester in England had underscored it, brought it into hard, sharp relief. Michael asked if that was merely rationalization to salve over what the two of them were doing.

She shook her head. "I keep thinking of the word *inertia*. Sometimes, I think people stay together because of inertia and not much else. I have the feeling Jimmy and I are riding a tired horse, but we just keep going on because we don't know what else to do.

Jimmy wants to be a university administrator, a dean or something, and I can't get very excited about that, about being a good little administrator's wife. I told him I want to finish my master's, go on for a Ph.D., and find a teaching position. He only said it would be difficult for both of us to find jobs we want at the same university. We had a couple of bad arguments about that in England."

Michael let her talk, let her work through all of the complicated things she was feeling. In some ways, Jellie was a traditional woman. In other ways, she was the new and emancipated woman, intent on finding her own way in the world. All of that was difficult enough to sort out by itself, and now he'd entered the situation and cluttered it up even more. Though, when Michael mentioned that, she was kind enough to say he was not part of the clutter. But he was.

Jellie had to go to Syracuse for Thanksgiving. Her parents had come out to Cedar Bend last year, so it was her turn to visit them. Jimmy's folks were coming up from Rhode Island. She and Michael spent the entire afternoon together the day before she left, and he picked up something a little different in her behavior, something that started to haunt him.

"Anything the matter, Jellie?"

She looked at him lovingly. There was no question about how she felt, as far as he could tell. "No, not really." He didn't push it, figuring it would pass.

Michael fiddled around over the long Thanksgiving weekend, counting the hours until Jellie would return. He fixed a tuna sandwich on turkey day and ate it while looking at the Polaroid of Jellie standing by a stone wall in Ireland. The computer keyboard was dusty, and the Shadow needed work, but he couldn't find any motivation to do anything except jog in the mornings and think about her.

On Sunday evening the department head called and asked if Michael could cover Jimmy's econometrics class the next day. Jimmy had been delayed in Syracuse, some kind of personal emergency was all the department head knew. Michael went crazy, paced the floor, pounded the walls, Malachi and Casserole watching him in a kind of wonder.

Monday night and still no word. He got the Markhams' phone number from information and dialed it. Eleanor Markham answered. Jesus, it would have to be Mother Markham. Michael used the pretense he was covering Jimmy's class and wanted some idea of how long he might be away. Shallow, transparent, but then he wasn't thinking very well.

Mrs. Markham was cool, very cool—brittle, in fact—and said Jimmy was on his way back to Cedar Bend. She had known something about Jellie and the motorcycle man a year ago. She knew a great deal more now, Michael had a hunch. She'd said *Jimmy* was on his way back. She hadn't used both their names or a plural pronoun, indicating both of them were returning. Michael was screaming inside and wanted to ask about Jellie, but he had the clear sensation Eleanor Markham had no interest in talking with him about anything.

He hung up and went absolutely wild in his head. The phone rang fifteen minutes later. It was Jimmy. He was back and wanted to come over. Michael said, "Yes, come right away, no problem, come as soon as you want to," obviously overplaying it, but Jimmy didn't have a feeling for that kind of stuff and missed it completely.

He rapped on Michael's door five minutes later. Michael knew there was serious business afoot, just by looking at him. No tie, rumpled clothing, hair askew. Not the Newport Jimmy Braden Michael had come to know.

"Michael, something terrible has happened, and I don't have anyone to talk to about it. I'm close to falling apart."

The voice inside Michael's head was shouting, "Jimmy Braden, you fey little bastard, what's going on? Where's Jellie?" It was screaming loud enough for Jimmy to hear, but he didn't because he wasn't listening. Jimmy merely sat on a kitchen chair, put his head in his hands, and cried. Michael brought himself down—level, brother—get level, stay level, and ask the right questions.

"Talk to me, Jimmy. What's happened? Does it have something to do with Jellie?"

He sobbed and moved his head up and down in the affirmative. Don't panic, get the information, get to the bottom, omit the extraneous junk and side issues. "Where's Jellie?"

Jimmy looked up, crying hard, and got it out: "She's gone to India."

"What?" Michael nearly shouted. "India? What the hell for? What's going on? Get straight and talk to me, Jimmy. I can't be of any help unless you do that. Why'd she go?"

"I don't know. We didn't have a fight or anything. Saturday morning Jellie just said she had some things to think about and was going to India. Christ, Michael, I begged her, groveled, said whatever it was could be worked out, but she wouldn't talk about it. She wasn't mean or cold, none of that, just far away from all of us, thinking about something. It was an awful scene, an absolute hell. Her parents were screaming, my parents were screaming, I was stumbling all over the place, and Jellie was packing her suitcase."

"Okay," Michael said. "We don't know *why* she went, but do you know *where* she went? She once mentioned a place called Pondicherry, in the southeast. Is that where she went?"

"I don't know."

Jimmy was sniffling again. Michael scrounged around for a box of tissues, couldn't find any, went in the john and brought out a new roll of toilet paper. Jimmy ripped off a wad and worked on his eyes with it, his voice thick and wet, phlegm in his throat. He blew his nose and said, "I tried to find out where she went, but the airlines won't give out that information on passengers. India's a huge place, so it's hard to say where she is, but, yes, she spent time in Pondicherry when she was there before."

Jimmy didn't drink coffee or beer. Michael poured him a glass of orange juice, lit a cigarette, and went over to the Shadow, straddling it, arms folded. He looked up at the wall and saw the picture of Jellie hanging there, decided it wasn't a good idea for Jimmy to see it displayed so prominently. When Jimmy went back to wiping his eyes, Michael took it down and slid it under some papers on the desk. Jimmy Braden sat bent over, elbows on his knees, at the same kitchen table where Michael had made love with his wife a week ago, scraping the salt and pepper shakers onto the floor as he laid her down. She was laughing then.

"When did she leave, Jimmy? What airline was she taking out of New York?"

"Saturday night. She left Saturday night. She took a flight out of Syracuse to Kennedy. Wouldn't even let me or anyone else go to the airport with her and wouldn't tell me what airline she was taking out of New York."

"Somehow none of this sounds like Jellie," Michael said. Smiling, warm, caring Jellie. It didn't sound like her at all.

"I know it doesn't. That's what makes it so strange, Michael. It seems so unlike her."

Or maybe it isn't, Michael thought. Maybe there are things about Jellie Braden none of us know, or at least that he and Jimmy didn't know.

"Jimmy, I'm going to ask you a question. You can choose whether or not to answer it. I don't have to know, but I've somehow gotten this sense Jellie doesn't like to talk about her India days. Did something happen to her over there?"

Jimmy looked up. "Michael, I can't say anything about that. I'd tell you if I could, but I just can't. I just can't. Please understand."

Michael appreciated him for feeling that way and sticking to it. It would have been easy at a time like this to spill out the whole story, but he didn't. Michael decided Jimmy Braden might be a better man than he'd given him credit for.

"All right, then let me ask this: Do you think whatever happened to her in India had anything to do with her going back there now?"

"I don't know. I can't imagine why, if she's told me the truth about her time in India. Like I said, I can't talk about it, but I guess I *can* say what occurred in India was over a long time ago, or at least I thought it was."

Michael needed time to think, be by himself and start working out the options. Yet he didn't want to let Jimmy go home alone in this condition.

"Jimmy, want me to arrange for someone to take your classes for a while, until you get yourself together again?"

"No, I need to be doing something. I've never been good at just sitting around and thinking, at intro-spection. I've got to get myself squared away some-how, and maybe getting back to school will help. Jellie just needs time to think, I'm sure."

Michael lowered his opinion of Jimmy by an amount greater than he'd raised it a moment ago. Jesus Christ, he thought, don't put up with this shit, man. Screw the university. Get on the first plane to India and start looking for your wife. Talk to her, try to sort it out. That was not the way of Jimmy Braden, though. He was going to lie back and take it, and hope.

But Jimmy Braden had never changed the oil in a banker's car when summer was high and the wind from the western lands was hot and made your greasy clothes stick to your body. He'd never stuck his head under the hood of an automobile and listened to the turn of an engine while his father staggered around with a flask in his pocket and yelled at him. And Jimmy Braden had never cut hard to the right and gone into the air with his knee swollen and twelve thousand crazed assholes screaming for and against him.

Jimmy had counted on the momentum of blood and wealth to carry him along. He'd never ridden in steerage, which made him inert when assertiveness was required—if there's no need to climb, then there's no reason to learn how to climb. That was Jimmy's way, and Michael understood it.

But it wasn't Michael's way. And, at that moment, he felt something deep and sad for Jimmy Braden. Inside of Jimmy, someplace, there had to be the old push from our times forty thousand years back, out on the grasslands, when the choice was either to fight for what was yours or have it taken by the malevolence around you. Civilization has its benefits, but it had robbed Jimmy and others like him of the basic instincts.

When things stabilized and Michael was reasonably sure the husband of Jellie Braden could make it through the night, he got him into his Buick and on the road. Jimmy said just talking about getting back to his work made him feel better, that at least he still had his work and maybe they could talk some more tomorrow.

He also blurted out a curious statement, saying he believed how he felt was mostly a matter of pride.

Some of the old ways from the grasslands evidently *were* still there, but he couldn't take the next step. Before Jimmy's car turned the corner, Michael was looking in the Yellow Pages for airline telephone numbers.

Eight

*I*f you want to get to India fast, you deal with Air India. It's the national airline and a good one. Every night at eight-thirty flight 102 lifts off from Kennedy and makes a two-hour stop in London the next day. Afterward it heads nonstop for either Delhi or Bombay, alternating between the two cities, depending on the day.

There are other options, some of them convoluted. Aeroflot can get you to Delhi, but you have to put up with a long layover in Moscow. Before it collapsed, Pan Am went to Delhi twice a week from New York via Frankfurt. Those were the major eastern routes, except for British Air, which Michael had never ridden out to India. The western routes can get even more circuitous—several different airlines and overnight layovers in Bangkok or Kuala Lumpur or Singapore.

After checking his atlas to make sure he knew where Pondicherry was located, Michael called Air India. It was booked solid for the next fourteen nights, with two seats available on December 11 and one on December 13, then solid again until after Christmas. Given the number of expatriates and former citizens out in the world, India has relatively sparse international air service, but the Indians all go home around Christmastime, and things get very tight from Thanksgiving forward.

He rummaged his bookshelves until he found a world airline guide three years out of date. British Airways showed a nonstop from Chicago to London and then a later flight straight out to Madras on the east coast. Pondicherry was about 150 kilometers south of Madras, on the Bay of Bengal. Michael wasn't worried about that leg; if he could make Madras, he could make Pondicherry. All he really was concerned about was getting to the Indian subcontinent. India has the best rail service in the world, in terms of number of trains going here and there. If not a train, then a bus. If not a bus, then a car and driver. If none of the above, he'd walk. It didn't matter. What mattered was Jellie Braden somewhere in the swirling crowds of India. If she wasn't in Pondicherry, he'd be in tough shape. She'd be almost impossible to track down if she decided just to lose herself out there. But, by God, he was going to try.

He called the British Airways 800 number. Yes, said the quite lovely, very British, very female voice at the reservations desk, that flight was still operating, but there were no openings for the next three weeks. Did Mr. Tillman want to be put on a waiting list?

Yes. He called Air India again and also had them put him on a waiting list, with the date open. Anytime, he told them. Anytime.

Things to do. His mother first. He called her, and they talked for a long while. He'd never missed spending Christmas with her in the last twenty years but told her he had to go to India right away and didn't know when he'd be back.

Her ears were failing her, but she heard something in the way he spoke, urgency, intensity. "Michael, don't tell me you've finally found a special lady for yourself? I've never heard your voice sound quite like it does now. Is that it?"

"Mom, the answer is maybe. That's all I can say. It's just real important I do this thing—go to India—but I hate to miss Christmas with you, if it comes to that."

"Michael, thank you for caring and for asking. I'm glad we've gotten to be with each other as much as we have over the years. Go to India and find this lady, whoever she is. Then bring her home so I can meet her. I still haven't given up hope on having grandchildren, you know."

"Mom, I promise I'll come out to Custer as soon as I'm back, though I'm not sure when that will be."

"Fly on, Michael. If this is your moment, take it. Stop talking to me and get to India."

The departmental secretary was a first-rate person who knew the systems and ways to get around them. Michael always gave her a bottle of wine at Christmas and sent her flowers at the end of the academic year. She agreed to fill out his final grade sheets and forge his signature on them. She didn't even ask why. He asked her not to say anything, and she said, "Don't worry, you and I understand each other. Wherever you're going in such a hurry and whatever you're going to do when you get there, I'd like to be a fly on the wall." She finished her words with a strange little knowing smile.

Jimmy Braden had come back on Monday night. On Tuesday Michael announced to his classes they were shutting down that day. Since he wouldn't be giving a final examination, he told them everyone got one-half a grade higher than what the scores in his grade book currently showed. To hell with it, once in a while you're entitled to be flaky. Hats flew in the air, and a young woman's voice came from far back in the classroom: "We love you, Professor Tillman. Merry Christmas." He gave one of the MBA students who lived upstairs in his building a hundred bucks to make sure Malachi and Casserole were well cared for.

Travel light. Real light. He'd booked a flight to New York, but no reservations beyond, and he might get hung up anywhere on his way to India. New York, Moscow or London, Cairo or Athens. Anywhere. It might take him a week or more to get to India. Jimmy Braden could sit in Cedar Bend and pray and mope all he wanted. Jimmy had already told his story to at least five other people, so he was getting lots of sympathy.

But Michael was going to India to find Jellie, and he was going now. There was a reason she pulled out, and he had a pretty strong feeling it had something to do with him. Maybe not, but that's how he guessed it. People get lost in India. That's why a lot of them go there. He had to find Jellie before she just drifted off and, for whatever reason, retreated to a mountain commune or ashram in the boondocks where he'd never find her.

Old L.L. Bean knapsack. Three shirts, only one of them clean. Wear the clean one, blue denim. Jeans, one pair on the body and another pair in the bag, and some khakis. Wear bush jacket en route. Navy blue cotton sweater. Shoes? Wear the old field boots, take sandals, too. He could buy clothes in India if he needed them; the *khurtas* and some pajamalike bottoms underneath worked just fine for him. Other essentials, including a good map of the India subcontinent he'd purchased on his last visit, showing railroad and domestic air routes. Small flashlight, old cotton hat with the wide brim.

Damn, no malaria pills. Take the risk. No, have physician call the drugstore, pick them up on the way to the airport, even though he should have started taking them a week ago. Working hard, throwing clothes around the bedroom, folding shirts, rolling up the jeans and khakis with underwear and socks inside the roll, Malachi and Casserole watching. Jam the old pair of sandals in the top, cinch it up. The knapsack bulged. He hefted it—not too bad. Anything else? Small canteen. It can be a long time between drinkable water supplies in India.

The taxi came at eight A.M. on Thursday morning, sixty hours after Jimmy had sat at Michael's kitchen table, bawling his guts out. It was bizarre all right. Jimmy Braden was lurching around Bingley Hall telling people, in so many words, about how

poorly Jellie had treated him, running off that way.
And Michael was on his way to find her, but Jimmy
didn't know that. A stop at the pharmacist's, another
at the bank. Three thousand in American Express
Cheques, $100 units. Five hundred in cash.

At the local airport, waiting for the commuter
jet to Chicago, Michael remembered a detail he hadn't
taken care of and called the departmental secretary.
After he cleaned up the detail, she said, "Michael, a
cable for you just came in, hand-delivered."

He thought for a moment. This was dicey if it
was from Jellie, which he had a feeling it might be.
"Betty, read it to me, and I'm swearing you to secrecy
ever after concerning the contents. Deal?"

"If I told everything I knew about what happens
around here, Bingley Hall would implode in the
world's largest cloud of dust. Besides, I have some
vague sense of what's going on. I've seen your face
change in the last few months. I saw you on your
motorcycle out near Heron Lake early one morning
not long ago, and I also saw who was riding behind
you. But I've never said anything, and I won't. Now,
I put that together with the weeping going on in
Jimmy Braden's office—all over the building, for that
matter—and it doesn't require a mathematical genius
like you to make it add up."

"Betty, Betty, Betty . . . you may end up being
one of the great loves of my life. Read me the cable."

"Okay, I'm opening the envelope. It says thirteen hundred hours. Let's see, that's . . ."

"That's one in the afternoon, Betty. What's the
date?"

"It's today's date. How can that be?"

"Time difference. It was sent about one-thirty A.M. this morning, our time. What's it say?"

"It says, 'M, Please try to understand. There are feelings so strong within me I need space and time to work them out. I'll be in touch sometime, I promise I will. J.' "

The hell with space and time, that's what Michael Tillman thought. Sometimes you let circumstances go their own direction, in the way Jimmy was doing, but sometimes you have to get in the middle of situations and manage them. He had a feeling Jellie was pretty confused, and he wasn't going to let her just wander off in a fog. If he screwed up her life by going to India to look for her, she'd have to live with it, and so would he. But he wasn't about to sit on his duff in Cedar Bend and hope for better days.

"Betty, where did the cable come from, what city?"

"Madras. Did I pronounce it right?"

"No, but that's okay. Everybody in the States gets it wrong. Betty, run the cable through your shredder, please."

"I will. Don't worry. And, Michael? . . ."

"Yes?"

"I'll be back here cheering for you. Go find her."

"Thanks, Betty. Do you prefer necklaces or bracelets?"

"You know that's not necessary. But I'd like a bracelet sometime from some exotic place, if you insist."

"Done. Good-bye, and thanks again. My plane is boarding."

" 'Bye, Michael. Good luck."

* * *

At O'Hare he called Air India and had British
Airways check to see if anything had opened up.
Nothing. "What if I go down to the gate and see if
there's a no-show?" he asked the woman running the
British Airways counter.

"You can try." She looked at his ticket. "Your
flight for New York leaves before ours departs for
London. If you wait for us, you'll miss your New
York flight."

"I'll chance it. I'm feeling lucky, somehow."

She shrugged and typed his name into the computer as a standby. "We're in the new United terminal, at the far end. Good luck."

He bought cigarettes and coffee, then went to the
United terminal. An hour and fifteen minutes until
British Airways 42 would leave for London. The passengers were lined up, long line winding back and
along the terminal wall. Baggage . . . he never could
understand why people carry so much. Huge suitcases
tied with ropes. Christmas presents, bedrolls, tired
kids with winter colds and runny noses tugging on
their parents' hands, crying.

The line moved slowly. Twenty-five minutes before departure. Then twenty. Only two people left to
check in. "Michael Tillman, Mr. Michael Tillman,
please come to the British Airways podium."

He was there in four seconds.

"Mr. Tillman, we have a seat for you on the
London flight departing in approximately fifteen minutes. However, we are not able to confirm a seat for
you on flight 34 to Madras. Do you still want to go
with us tonight?"

"Yes. I'll pay for the ticket with my Amex card."

Six hours later he was looking at Ireland down below in first light, and he thought of Jellie standing along a stone wall somewhere down there, having a Polaroid picture taken, which eventually hung on a wall in Iowa. Except the picture was now in the pocket of his bush jacket. If you're going to be a tracer of lost persons, a photo might be useful. He'd thought of that at the last moment and brought the photo with him.

Heathrow was chaotic, as usual. Michael passed up the transit lounge and went out into the main terminal, where he could look in the eyes of ticket agents. No problem. As the agent told him, people often book more than one flight under different names, and several cancellations had come in during the night.

"Do you wish to book a return flight from India, Mr. Tillman?"

He told her to put him down for January 12, a few days before the spring semester started. Indian officials strongly prefer you have a return ticket before a visa is issued. That's a precaution flowing partly from the old hippie days when Western kids went seeking truth and enlightenment and ended up being dope-smoking, social welfare problems for the Indian government.

Michael pulled out his Amex card, got the ticket, and located the tube into London. He told an official he needed a visa to India and was steered in the right direction. Three hours later he was back at Heathrow, through security, and sitting in the transit lounge. Five hours before his flight to Madras.

Time always moved pretty fast for Michael in big airports. He liked to watch people come and go, read a little, nap a little. After going into the restroom and washing his face, he bought a copy of the London *Times*, settled down on a chair, and put his feet on the knapsack. But he couldn't concentrate on the paper and fished the picture of Jellie out of his pocket. He sat there looking at it while the public address system summoned people to planes leaving for distant places. And somewhere out in those great spaces was a woman named Jellie Braden. She was out there, somewhere . . . somewhere.

Nine

In spite of his smart-lip comment to Jellie one time, Michael Tillman was not jaded. Maybe a little cynical, probably more than he had a right to be, but not jaded. Never had been. That's an advantage coming down from the kind of childhood he spent. You grow up not expecting too much, so when good things happen in your life you're amazed they happened at all. Long-haul travel was that way for Michael. When the pilot came on the intercom and said they were passing over Baghdad, he looked down from his window seat and saw a brown city in the desert forty thousand feet below.

He'd done that before on his first trip to India, thinking, Baghdad—I never thought I'd be flying over Baghdad. And he reached back like a mule skinner with a whip, pulling the memories forward, seeing himself working on the Shadow in his father's gas station thirty years before. Working on it and looking out at the highway and knowing the Vincent Black Shadow could take him down that road if he learned all there was to know about valves and turning wheels and highways running eastward.

When the plane was two hours out of Madras, Michael took his shaving kit out of the knapsack and went to one of the tiny restrooms. This kind of travel leaves a film on the body and mind, and he'd developed the custom of shaving and cleaning up before landing. Somehow that also cleaned up the mind a little.

The cabin was still dark, most people sleeping or trying to, a few reading lamps on. The flight attendants were talking quietly with one another in the midplane kitchen. He stuck his head in and asked for a cup of tea. They fixed him up, and he went back to his seat, steaming cup in hand, in good shape overall but with the special, taut feeling in his stomach he always got when approaching a distant place, particularly India.

He lifted the window shade and looked out. India coming up below, like a woman sprawled in the sun. Daylight, rugged brown hills, green splotches of jungle. The cabin lights came on, breakfast was announced. He didn't feel like eating much but puttered around with fruit and toast, knowing it might be a while before he ate again.

The plane came down over the jumbled spread of Madras, port city on the Bay of Bengal. Estimated population over four million. India treats such numbers casually, however, since the cities have a constant flow in and out, mostly in, of a wandering people.

India is on the move, that's the dominant impression Michael always had. Look anywhere in the country-side or in the cities, and there are people walking, riding bicycles, hanging off roaring buses or leaning out of train windows. Moving . . . moving . . . India.

He walked in from the plane past men holding military rifles. Long line at the desk for those with foreign passports. Michael settled himself. You don't hurry India. India has its own style, its own pace, and high-strung Westerners who demand all tasks be carried out with speed and crisp efficiency don't do very well there. Warm and humid, and Michael was glad to be traveling light. The brown face above a dark green uniform looked at his passport, checked the ninety-day visa, and pounded the stamp.

Customs was no problem since Michael wasn't carrying anything of value except cash and traveler's checks. But he was bringing in more than $1,000 U.S., and a form was required. India loved forms, though Michael had always been skeptical about where these forms eventually found a home. It was hard to believe that a currency official somewhere actually paid attention to the millions of handwritten documents gushing from the pens of travelers: "Hmmm, I see that Michael Tillman from Cedar Bend, USA, brought thirty-five hundred dollars with him on 2 December. We'll need to keep track of him in this country with nearly one billion people and a telephone system that, at best, wobbles along."

Outside the protection of a large Indian airport, no rules applied. Touts, hundreds of them, pushing whatever could be imagined. Maybe a few rupees could be bilked from the tall white guy with the knapsack. Except he looked a little roadwise, no luggage, looked like a hard traveler. It would be better to move on to someone with a little more fat. Thousands of people were milling around, coming and going, many of them simply hung on for the entertainment value provided by a major airport. The cops kept most of them outside the airport, where they pressed their faces against dusty glass and waited for passengers to exit.

A tourist desk in the lobby was actually open for business, which was a new twist. India was apparently working harder at getting gringos to come and leave some foreign exchange on their way through. On Michael's earlier visits, he had the clear sense nobody cared whether you came or didn't, whether you died in the customs line or went home.

The man at the desk spoke understandable English. Michael said he wanted to go to Pondicherry. The man told him it was a three-hour ride by car if the traffic was heavy and would be happy to arrange a car and driver for Michael. He quoted a price of $30 U.S. That sounded steep for India, and Michael said as much.

"Oooh, but you see, it is a six-hour round trip for the driver, since he must go to Pondicherry and come back empty. So you must pay for both ways."

Michael knew better. He knew the driver would hang around Pondicherry and maybe get a fare back to Madras. How about the guys outside with their cabs?

"Oooh, yes, sir, they will say they will take you for quite a lower price. But, sir, they are not quite reliable and may just take your money on the way, leaving you stranded." Michael knew the man was speaking with some accuracy.

How about buses? Trains? The tourist official rambled on, running his finger up and down grimy, complicated schedules, and Michael started thinking, C'mon, Tillman. For chrissake, what are you doing? You're here in a panic to find Jellie Braden, and you're standing around haggling over a few bucks. For a moment, the spurious masculine pride in cutting the sharp deal, which seemed to lie throbbing in the hormones until called upon, had caused him to lose his way. As it usually did.

The official arranged a car and driver, telling Michael to wait by the tourist desk. Michael asked the man if he had a guide to Pondicherry, maps, anything at all. The man produced a torn little magazine from under the counter, which he claimed was his only copy (Michael believed him) and started looking through it. A lecture on Pondicherry followed concerning the famous ashram founded there by a mystic-philosopher-poet-patriot named Sri Aurobindo, about hotels and restaurants and the beauty of the seawall.

Was there a city map in the booklet? Yes, there was one, indeed, sir, a very nice map. Michael laid a five-dollar bill on the counter, keeping most of it covered with his hand, and said he'd very much like to take the Pondicherry guide with him. It was Michael's in less than a second, and his driver in a smudged white outfit came up to the counter, smiling.

Outside, the sun was a hammer. Other taxi drivers swung open their doors and said they would take

Michael to wherever he was going for half of what the fellow in the smudged white uniform was charging. Michael said thanks, but he'd already booked a car. After that they stopped smiling and were not his friends anymore.

As Michael's car pulled away from the airport, the driver began rubbing his thumb and forefinger together in the universal symbol for legal tender and pointed at his gas gauge, all the while saying, "Petrol." Indian taxi drivers were always running on empty, and he needed an advance. On Michael's last trip, two drivers had run out of gas while he was riding with them.

Impatient, Michael tapped his foot while the tank was being filled. He noticed a fruit stand nearby and bought three bananas and two oranges, which he stuffed into the side pockets of his knapsack. Back in the car he waited for the driver. A ragged man bent down and looked in the window, displaying the grisly stump of an arm severed just above the elbow. Michael gave him five rupees. The man touched his forehead and backed away.

Finally they were rolling through the noise and smoke and dust that was India and would always be India. Michael's nose was still adjusting to the thick odors—smoke from factories and open cooking fires, leaded gas, excrement from humans and animals, all of it mixed together and forming the dense and penetrating smell defining India. He never completely lost that smell. Michael noticed when he watched a travelogue on India back in Cedar Bend, his brain immediately pulled up those old India smells from wherever the memories of smells are stored. No other country had drilled its odors into him in the way India had.

The women. He'd temporarily forgotten how beautiful were the Indian women, even the poorest ones. It was easy to fall in transient love every few seconds in India. A superb gene pool, male and female alike, maybe the best gene pool in the world when it came to physical appearance. Orange saris and green saris, red ones and blue ones, and gold upon their bodies, bracelets on their arms and combs in their hair. The women were lithe and walked just above the earth, so it seemed. Some with gold or silver chains running from nose to ear.

He watched them as the driver constantly honked at goats and cattle and people, weaving through traffic, waved on by cops standing on small pedestals at the busier intersections. Into the countryside on a two-lane, severely bruised blacktop. Ashok and Tata trucks with workmen riding on top, their headwraps blowing in the wind. Buses careening around the curves, bullock carts in front of them, an old woman pedaling a wheelchair contraption in the other lane, people walking, herds of goats crossing.

The driver turned up his radio, giving him and Michael the sound of a flute and drummers playing complex rhythms on tablas beneath it. He pounded the horn and made the occult Indian hand signals telling other drivers what his intentions were. India: moving . . . moving . . . tablas and flutes and dust, the road in front looking like a ragtag caravan put together with all the travelers and vehicles from the last five hundred years.

Michael held a banana over the front seat. The driver took it and gave Michael a flash of perfect white teeth, leaned on his horn, and peeled the banana, hot air roaring in through the open windows. They entered a town, and Michael unfolded his map of India. Must be Chengalpattu. They'd be going slightly southwest to Madurantakam and then would make a southeast turn at Tindivanam, where a small blue line ran over to Pondicherry on the Bay of Bengal.

Michael thumbed the five-dollar Pondicherry guide, looking at confusing street maps, reading the town's history. It was a union territory, a city-state much like Washington, D.C. The state of Tamil Nadu on its west, the bay on its east. Settled by French traders in the seventeenth century, returned to India in 1954. Jellie, are you there along the streets of Pondicherry? On the off chance she had ridden with this same driver to Pondicherry, if she had gone to Pondicherry at all, Michael took out her picture and handed it to the driver.

The driver looked at it, turned his head, and grinned, shouting over the wind and flute music, "Pretty lady. You go see her in Pondy?"

Michael worked back down into pidgin English. "Lady ride this car?" He pointed at Jellie in the photo, then at the driver and the interior of the car. Michael said it again: "Pretty lady ride this car?"

It took the driver a second, but he got the meaning and shook his head. "No, no see lady." Michael nodded and put the photo back in his bush jacket.

The guide said Pondicherry had a population of 150,000, but Michael knew that was probably a best guess, far under the true count. Where to start? Like all Indian cities, he figured it would be a maze of little streets and complex buildings tied in with one another via walkways and alleys. Even if she was in Pondy, it was not going to be easy. The ashram attracted people from all over the world who came to study the teachings of Sri Aurobindo and his consort, a French woman known only as "the Mother." Both of them were dead. But, according to the guide, the ashram flourished. A visionary settlement called Auroville, also known as the City of Dawn, supposedly fashioned around the teachings of Aurobindo and the Mother, had been developing for over a decade just outside of Pondicherry. The guide quoted Mother: "Auroville will be a site of material and spiritual researches for a living embodiment of an actual Human Unity."

That sounded like Jellie. Anthropologists, many of them, at least, had a strong inclination toward matters of the spirit, something to do with their trade. If Jellie was running and seeking spiritual guidance, the ashram and Auroville might be a good place to start.

He'd need a place to stay and looked at advertisements in the guide as the driver swerved and honked and signaled.

Ajantha Guest House—An Oasis of Luxury
Hotel Aristo—A Touch of Class, Truly an Aristocratic Experience
Hotel Ram International—It's a Whole New World

To the Western eye and ear, Indians had a penchant for overstatement, not to mention hyperbole, and Michael discounted heavily what he read. Not that he was fussy. He'd stayed many nights in small Indian hotels where a hole in the floor worked as a toilet and the shower was cold, if there was a shower at all. After a few nights, however, he'd forget there was any other way than cold showers and a hole in the floor, and it all worked just fine. A hot shower, in traditional south Indian terms, would justify the claim "Truly an Aristocratic Experience."

He concentrated on Jellie, thinking hard about her ways and what he knew of her preferences. Where would she stay? The Park Guest House was part of the ashram and had a Spartan attitude toward smoking, liquor, and human weaknesses in general. Jellie had come to think things over, according to her cable, and the guest house with its gardens, vegetarian restaurant, and meditative overtones spoke to that way of life.

Initially Michael thought that finding Jellie, if she was in Pondicherry, would not be all that difficult. White skin stood out in most of India. But it was a much larger town than he'd anticipated, and the guide stated many Westerners came to bathe in the rarefied spirit of Sri Aurobindo and the Mother. And, as Michael had already considered, it was easy to get lost in India if that's what you wanted. India could present a silent, impenetrable face when it chose, leaving you on the outside with no view to the interiors. Jellie was an old India hand, apparently with good connections, and would know how to conceal herself if she made up her mind to do that.

If you were in a hurry, India could be infuriating.

The driver decided lunch was in order at Madurantakam. He pulled over and went up to an outdoor food stand. Michael wasn't hungry but drank a cup of tea and ate one of the Snickers he'd bought in Heathrow. People gathered around him at a respectful distance and stared; routine curiosity, nothing more.

The sun was high and hard at noon. He clumped the old cotton hat on his head, fending off the kids who were less circumspect than their elders and wanted something, anything, from him. He bought some more oranges and handed them around, though the kids would have preferred something more wondrous, such as a cheap ballpoint pen from America. Sweat soaked through his shirt, ran down his chest and back. Michael was wiping his face and neck with a red bandanna when the driver signaled it was time to leave.

Forty-five minutes later they made the turn at Tindivanam and headed southeast toward Pondicherry, running along a rough surface in worse shape than the road they'd just left. This was semiarid land, palm trees arching over the road. People were spreading stalks of grain on the pavement, drying the grain, and letting vehicle wheels act as kind of a primitive threshing machine.

Outskirts of Pondicherry. The map fastened in the back of the city guide indicated they were coming in on Jawaharlal Nehru Street, apparently one of the main thoroughfares. Michael decided against staying at the ashram's guest house, mostly because he wasn't sure how Jellie might feel if he suddenly showed up. If she saw him before he saw her, she might retreat with whatever secrets she carried and become impossible to find once she knew he was here looking for her.

The Grand Hotel d'Europe at Number 12 Rue Suffren was in the same general area as most of the ashram's workshops and not far from the guest house. It was run by an old Frenchman, a Monsieur Maigrit, according to the guide. Michael suspected the food would be continental, which suited him fine, since he tended to burn down pretty fast on a straight Indian diet.

Michael motioned for the driver to pull over and showed him the map. The driver had trouble reading it, started talking rapidly, pointing ahead. Michael let him go on, and they halted at a busy street corner where two hundred bicycles waited for a green light. The driver got out with the map and talked to several men standing in front of a tea shop. Arms waved, heads shook, hands pointed. All of this went on for a minute or two before the driver returned. He said something Michael didn't understand, zigzagging his hand, which Michael took to mean they should work their way through the city and then turn right.

That seemed to fit, based on the map. They plowed up the busy main drag of Pondy and eventually hit a dead end at Rue St. Louis. The driver got out, went through the arms–head–hand language again, and came back to the car. A right turn, then skirting a large park on whose benches sat both Indians and aging French Legionnaires by the looks of their caps. A few blocks farther on another right, then a left. Painted on a building were the words *Rue Suffren*. Number 12 came up a half block later.

Michael knocked on the high wooden gate. An old Indian man in tan shorts and a white headwrap peeked out. Michael said, "Room?"

The gatekeeper glanced at the car and driver, then back at the tall American with wrinkled clothes and no luggage except a knapsack. Almost reluctantly he swung the gate open and indicated Michael should come into the courtyard. It was an old building, covered with vines and bougainvillea. Maigrit, Michael assumed it was him, came out of a doorway. Michael bowed slightly. "Do you have a room for a tired traveler?"

Maigrit looked at him, said nothing. Michael had arrived without prior reservations, which was probably considered a serious breach of decorum. Michael didn't speak much French, having forgotten most of what he'd learned as part of his Ph.D. language requirement. But he smiled the good midwestern smile that seemed to get him by in most of the world and gave it a try: "*Je voudrais une chambre?*"

Maigrit smiled back, recognizing incompetence but approving of the effort. Yes, a room was available for 150 rupees, about 9 dollars a night. Michael figured with advance reservations and a little haggling he could have knocked it down about a third or maybe half, but he was tired, and the location suited him.

Maigrit informed him the daily afternoon water shutoff was in progress, so a bath was not possible, but the *boy*, who was about seventy-five, would bring a small bucket of water if Monsieur Tillman wanted to wash up. Michael thanked him and said that would be appreciated. And was laundry service available? Shirts could be washed, ironed, and returned in four hours for double the normal price. The regular price was six cents a shirt.

The boy delivered water, took the shirts, and Michael washed his face, then lay down on the bed and thought. Home was forty-six hours behind, though his internal abacus lied and said it was longer, years maybe. A week ago he'd been sitting in his apartment waiting for Jellie to return from Syracuse. Ten days ago she lay naked on his kitchen table while he rubbed red wine over her breasts. "Jellie, are you somewhere on the other side of these walls, close by, living out what you never want me to know?"

Ten

ichael awakened a little before six when the old man rapped on his door. He'd slept for nearly four hours and got up feeling hot and stiff and road weary. He opened the door, took the shirts, and gave the man a tip. The old man bowed and left, looking back at Michael over his shoulder.

Michael checked the faucets. The water had come back on, and he was a little surprised when the left tap gave him a warm stream. He ran a small tub, shaved, and got himself presentable with a clean body, clean shirt, and fresh pair of Levi's.

The proprietor was on the veranda, reading a French newspaper. What Michael needed first was flexible transportation, a motorcycle. He'd seen a number of smaller bikes when the driver brought him through town. Yes, a small motorcycle could be

rented at a location on Mahatma Gandhi Road. Maigrit had the gatekeeper call a bicycle rickshaw for
Michael and spoke in Tamil to the rickshaw man,
giving him the address. Maigrit said the ride would
cost a quarter, and a dime tip would be about right.

Michael watched the bulging leg muscles of the
man pedaling him through the streets of Pondicherry.
Unlike some Westerners who had never traveled in
these places and frowned on the use of rickshaws as
something next to slavery, Michael didn't see it that
way. If you asked the rickshaw man how he felt about
it, he wouldn't understand the question. It was how
he made his living, and he was quite happy to deliver
you somewhere for a fee. It was called participating
in the local economy. As Michael once told a col-
league who disdained such colonialist behavior, "Pay
the rickshaw man New York cab fare, maybe it will
make you feel more politically correct." Taxi or rickshaw, it was all a matter of muscle power with differ-
ences in the degree of it used.

India was, in many ways, an evening country.
The heat and dust settled down late in the day, and
the streets were crowded. Merchants stayed open late.
Time then for long, leisurely dinners and laughter in
the cafes, commencing around nightfall. The rickshaw man turned left on Sastry Street, pedaling a
straight line toward MG Road. Michael sat there feeling exposed, not wanting Jellie to see him coasting
along through the streets of Pondicherry.

Christ, he thought, how strange this is. Here I
am looking for a woman with whom I've made love,
a woman who rolls in pleasure beneath my touch and
says over and over again how much she loves me.

Yet I'm worried about her seeing me. It's a curious world, Michael Tillman. That's what he said to himself as the rickshaw bumped along through the south India twilight.

The motorcycle rental outfit was located in a little garage next to the Cool Cat Coffee Bar with grease everywhere and parts scattered about. Michael felt at home. Two machines leaned against the door, two more were torn down inside. Michael could have either of the two by the door. He looked them over. They were rough as the roads they traveled and pretty well banged up. The old Kawasaki looked like it might run, and after a few kicks he had it going. The proprietor stood watching him, hands on hips, not smiling. Michael pointed to tools on the workbench.

Ten minutes later he had the chain tightened and the carburetor adjusted. The garage man was grinning. Technical competence always brought respect. Michael paid a fifty-dollar deposit and recalibrated his mind to driving on the left-hand side of the road, then took the Kawasaki out into evening traffic, running easy until he got the feel of driving in what always seemed the wrong way.

He took the same route back to the hotel as he'd come, picking up two plastic containers of bottled water on the way, and parked the bike in the courtyard. Tonight he'd walk. When the search needed to be expanded or he had to get somewhere in a hurry, the bike would take him there.

Maigrit greeted him and said what a handsome machine Michael had found. Michael took out the picture of Jellie and said he was looking for her.

Maigrit looked at it, then at Michael, and asked,

"*Amour?*" Michael smiled and nodded. Maigrit was sorry, but he'd never seen her. "There are many Western women who come here to participate in the ashram. They look for comfort and inner peace, perhaps a new way of life."

The Frenchman no longer operated a restaurant in his hotel, but if Michael wanted continental food, the Alliance Française was not far, just opposite the Park Guest House. It was a club, though membership rules were not tightly enforced. Simply walk through the gate, cross the courtyard, and go up the steps.

Michael thought twice about going there. He wasn't too worried about running into Jellie, because he figured she wanted to sink back into Indian ways and would take her meals at Indian restaurants or, more likely, cook for herself. But word moved fast in these Indian towns, and he had a feeling the Western community would pass the news about a newcomer who wore jeans and sandals and seemed to be looking for someone.

But he was hungry and wasn't ready for Indian cuisine yet, so he walked through quiet streets in the direction the Frenchman had directed him. A few people sat on steps in this section of the city, but most of the houses were behind high walls. Two white men with shaved heads and wearing saffron-colored wraps, bare legs poking out from thigh level down, went by in the opposite direction, paying no attention to Michael.

He turned left on Rue Bazare St. Laurent, missed his right turn on Rue Dumas, and came to Cours Chabrol—Beach Road—running along the seawall. The night breeze was kind, and Michael stood in the shadows at the end of Rue Bazare St. Laurent without crossing over to the seawall. The walkways were crowded with evening strollers. Off to his right, just up the road, was the gated entrance to the Park Guest House, the ashram's hotel.

When two Western women in Indian dress came along the sidewalk, he turned around, heading back up the street he had just come down, feeling odd, as if he were involved in an international espionage operation. Jellie, what have you done to me? I was content, if not supremely happy, before we met, and here I am walking the back streets of India looking for you, and in some small part of me not wanting to find you, fearful of what you might say, of what you might tell me you are going to do with the rest of your life.

A guard stood at the Alliance Française's gate. Michael pointed at his own chest, then pointed inside and said, "Restaurant?"

The guard nodded and motioned him through the gate. There were trees and flowers in the courtyard. Off to one side was a cement platform where an Indian woman was dancing to the rhythm of a drummer sitting cross-legged in the shadows behind her.

No one else was in the courtyard, but he could hear an accordion playing a French song in the building ahead of him. Michael watched the dancer for a moment. She was oblivious of him, stopping after a moment and speaking to the drummer, who then started off again in a slightly different rhythm.

The first floor of the place had a unisex bathroom and a black-and-white photography exhibition hanging on its gray walls. Music and laughter came from the floor above, and he went up the stairs into the restaurant. Half of it was covered, the rest was open to the night. Waiters were moving rapidly around in white uniforms, and a young Indian in dark slacks and purple shirt came toward Michael, speaking in French. Michael smiled and said, "Dinner, please?"

"Just one, monsieur?" His English was very good.

Michael nodded.

"Do you prefer indoors or outside?"

"Outside, please."

The maître d' seated Michael at a small table off in a corner. Michael's entrance caused a few curious heads to turn, but the laughter and eating and drinking quickly resumed. He ordered beer and a chicken brochette from the open-flame barbecue built into the wall across the room from where he was seated. Stars were out, the scent of jasmine came on the night wind, and he sat there alone, staring at his hands.

The food was excellent, served with rice and French bread. And chocolate cake with good strong coffee afterward. He was starting to feel somewhat whole again. On his way out, an older man had taken over the maître d' role. When Michael walked over to him, the man smiled warmly.

"Did you enjoy your dinner?"

Michael told him it was very good, then showed him the picture of Jellie. The maître d' looked at it, then at Michael, repeated those two moves, and stopped smiling.

"Have you seen her?" Michael asked.

The maître d' stared at him and didn't answer.

"I'm looking for her; it's very important I find her."

The man lit a cigarette, looked at the picture again, then handed it back to Michael. "Long time ago, maybe."

"How long? A week? How long?"

"Long time. Ten, fifteen years. It's hard to say; the woman I'm thinking of was much younger. Excuse me, I have work to do."

Michael took a deep breath and wondered. The man had looked at him and the photo, friendliness turning to curt dismissal afterward, almost as if the maître d' recognized Jellie's picture and wanted to be done with Michael as soon as possible. Michael walked back to his hotel through dark, quiet streets, still wondering.

For two days he wandered Pondicherry with no organized search strategy. On the third day he took the bike out to Auroville, but it was spread out over miles, little settlements and houses scattered about. If she was there, he'd never find her. In early evenings he sat on the seawall near the ashram guest house and watched traffic coming for the evening meal. He tried talking with the austere woman guarding the front desk of the guest house, but that was useless. People came there to get away and be left alone. When Michael showed her the photo of Jellie, the woman shook her head and went back to her ledgers.

He was getting nowhere and asked Maigrit for directions to the college he'd read about in the guide. Maigrit ran his finger along the street map, showing

Michael the location and how to get there. Michael wheeled the Kawasaki out of the hotel courtyard, kicked the starter, and rolled north through the city.

The college was in a shabby section of Pondicherry. Cruising around the small campus, Michael saw a weathered sign reading "Department of Management." Time to flash the credentials. He introduced himself to a secretary, telling her who he was and where he was from. This was a situation where titles would help. Indians loved credentials and respected professors only a little less than credentials. She went down a hallway into an office, coming back in less than a minute, followed by a short, round, Indian man in his fifties. He wore glasses and a necktie reaching about halfway down his chest.

Friendly smile. "Ah, Dr. Tillman, how good of you to call on us."

He wanted to know all about Michael's academic life. Michael ran the list of degrees and experience, impatient to get on with the reason he'd come. But India observed its courtesies with a fair amount of pomp, and he was bound to reciprocate. Before long they were joined by two economists, with tea served by the secretary shortly after. One of the professors excused himself, saying he would return momentarily. When he did, a copy of *The Atlantic* was in his hand. It was opened to Michael's article on tax incentives. He pointed to the article, then at Michael. "And did you write this, Dr. Tillman?" Michael nodded. The professor smiled then, big smile. "Quite a brilliant piece of work. Very nice indeed."

Credibility had been established, Michael was on his home ground, and these were bright, decent people he was dealing with. He told them about searching for Jellie, leaving out the background details, saying only it was extremely important he locate her. They didn't recognize her photo, but when Michael mentioned Jellie's interest in anthropology, the department head called to his secretary and spoke to her out in the hall.

"I have requested my secretary summon one of the anthropology professors to talk with you. There are many projects in anthropology going on in Pondicherry. The French especially have strong interests in those areas, having established an institute some years ago with which our college cooperates."

In ten minutes a woman appeared in the office doorway. She was fortyish and wore a pink sari. The department head stood, introducing her as Dr. Dhavale, professor of anthropology. The photo of Jellie, which was becoming a little shopworn after being held by a hundred hands in the last few days, was lying on the desk. Immediately the anthropology professor picked it up, glanced at it, then looked at Michael.

His heartbeat went up twenty points. "Is there any chance you know the woman in the picture?"

The professor's face was cautious. "You say your name is Tillman? Michael Tillman?"

"Yes."

"From a place called Cedar Bend?"

His pulse jumped another ten points. "Yes."

"May Dr. Tillman and I have words in private, please?" She was addressing the department head.

"Oh, yes, of course, Dr. Dhavale. Dr. Tillman, could we impose upon you to give a lecture or two while you are in town? I know our students and faculty would very much appreciate it."

They'd been helpful. Saying no was a problem, a matter of both courtesy and gratitude. "Dr. Ramani, I will be happy to do that sometime. First, however, I must not delay in finding Mrs. Braden. When I have done that, may I contact you and set up the lectures if I am going to be in Pondicherry?"

"Yes, yes, certainly. We understand, though we are disappointed you must hurry off. Please let us know when you can lecture for us, and we will set up a very nice afternoon with a reception afterwards."

Michael said he'd do that and followed Dr. Dhavale out of the building across a courtyard into another building, where her tiny office was located. For the first time in seventy-two hours he did not feel tired.

She sat across her desk from him, black eyes bold and cool, sizing him up. "Jellie Markham and I became friends years ago, during the time she was here for her thesis work." She used Jellie's maiden name and the French pronunciation with the soft j— JahLAY—for her first name. "We have corresponded with each other through the years and have remained close."

Michael said nothing but began to understand how dumb he'd been for the last three days, using Jellie's married name and the American pronunciation of her Christian name. Even if someone had known her, they wouldn't have recognized the names he was giving them if she'd assumed the French version when she lived in Pondicherry. And that would make sense, given the heavy French atmosphere permeating the city.

"Dr. Dhavale, I'm forty-three. It took a lot of years for me to be able to feel about someone the way I feel about Jellie. I care for her, I need to find her, I need your help to do it."

The anthropologist studied him as if she were deciding on a final course grade. "I do not wish to violate her confidence, so I'm not sure of how much to say, Dr. Tillman. But I know Jellie has strong feelings for you. She has lived a complicated life, more complicated than you can imagine. But those details are for her to tell you when she chooses. She sent a letter to you, giving you my name and address in case you wanted to contact her. But I don't think she anticipated you would show up on my doorstep. Did you receive her letter?"

"No. I must have left before it arrived in Cedar Bend. I found you quite by accident."

"This is very difficult for me, Dr. Tillman, please understand that. I want to help you, but I do not wish to upset Jellie and ruin our friendship by saying what I shouldn't. I know she felt bad about not saying a proper good-bye to you." Chitra Dhavale looked out the only window in her office, dusty window, then turned back to Michael. "She left several days ago for Thekkady. Do you know of it?"

"No."

"It is a village quite near a beautiful place called Lake Periyar. Jellie told me you spent time in south India, so I thought you might have heard of it. She is staying with people named Sudhana who live in the countryside near Thekkady."

"May I ask what she is doing there? Do you know?"

"Yes, I know, but that is part of what is not my place to tell you, and I am afraid I have already violated her confidence by saying what I have said."

"What is the best way to Thekkady? The best route?"

"You could go back to Madras and fly to Cochin or Madurai, taking a car after that. Perhaps a better, though more tiring way is to take the early afternoon train out of Pondicherry. It is a meter-gauge railway, so you ride it just down to Villupuram Junction, which is approximately forty kilometers from here. From there you take the *Trivandrum Mail* southward and get off in Madurai. After that you can either take a bus or hire a car and driver to take you on to Thekkady. It is an arduous trip, Dr. Tillman, but it is probably the quickest route. Your other alternative, flying out of Madras, may be frustrating. You might arrive there and not be able to find a seat on a flight for several days."

She looked at her watch. "It's a little before twelve. If you hurry, Dr. Tillman, you can catch the one o'clock train to Villupuram. I have a feeling you are anxious to be on your way, am I not correct?" She gave him a warm, Indian-woman smile. "If you find Jellie Markham, please tell her of my distress over this and ask her to forgive me if I have done wrong by telling you where she is."

"I will. Thank you, Dr. Dhavale."

As he went out her office door, Chitra Dhavale said, "Dr. Tillman?" He turned, paused.

"Jellie may be using the name Velayudum instead of Braden or Markham. Don't ask me why. Just accept what I have told you. And I should add this: If you find her, things may seem somewhat strange and perhaps quite disappointing, or at least unsettling to you. As I said before, Jellie has lived a complicated life."

So it was the *Trivandrum Mail* south to Madurai and a car westward after that.

Eleven

Thekkady lies on the border between the states of Tamil Nadu and Kerala, in the high country of southwest India. On the edge of town is a gate across the road, a red bar that reminded Michael of the old Checkpoint Charlie in Berlin. The driver halted and went into a small office near the road. Any moment Michael expected to hear Richard Burton's voice speaking the words from a John Le Carré novel, something about a man coming in from the East tonight.

All hell broke loose in the office. The driver showed his papers, but apparently crossing from one state to another in this area was pretty much the same as going from one country to the next. From what Michael could make out, the Kerala authorities refused to honor the much trumpeted, all-India driver's license.

Michael got out, leaned against the car. More words that turned into shouting and what sounded like threats. He pointed to the bar, lifted his knapsack, and asked with sign language if he could cross. It was more complicated than he'd thought, requiring a twenty-dollar bill in the hand of the border official to get him through after paying off the driver. Baksheesh, it's called, and it was everywhere and always had been.

Cool mountain air and thin yellow sunlight, quiet village in midafternoon, dusty road. Michael walked down it, his boots leaving deep footprints. "Hey, boss, you go lake?" The young Indian man was standing by a jeep.

Michael looked at a name scribbled in his pocket notebook, then walked over to the jeep man and said, "Maybe. Find people called Sudhana, first."

"No, boss, we go lake only." He whacked the side of the jeep. "Two hundred rupees for ride. Pretty place there."

It might be pretty, but that wasn't where Michael was going. He held up three one-hundred-rupee bank notes. "Find house of Sudhana, first. Then two hundred more if I want to go to the lake." It turned out maybe the jeep didn't have to go to the lake after all.

The young man was in no hurry and started talking to several others hanging around. They looked at Michael and laughed. The young bastards were always brave in groups. They knew he had cash, big cash to them. Stuck in his belt, under his wrinkled bush jacket, was a short-bladed hunting knife he carried in these parts of the world. He could feel the handle pressing into his back.

A few years ago he'd held the knife against the throat of a taxi driver late one night in Mysore, north of here, when things were getting rough and a crowd of young smart-asses was encouraging the driver to dump him and a female companion out of the cab. When the Mysore driver felt the blade against his skin he let out the clutch as if he were having a muscle spasm, knocking two of the smart boys on their rears.

An older man came out of a store, shouting. From what Michael could tell, the man owned the jeep and was ordering a general shaping up and getting on with business. There was chatter in multiple dialects, the name *Sudhana* mentioned several times. The older man sketched on a piece of cardboard and handed it to the younger one, who had called Michael "boss." He walked over to the jeep, grinning, patting the jump seat, and motioning with his head for Michael to climb in. The young one and another bundle of insolence about the same age got in the front seats.

They bounced off down the dirt road and turned south onto a different road running high above the eastern side of a fast mountain stream. More turns, winding around a low mountain, then left up a smaller road. The driver slammed to a stop in front of a house with tin patches on the sides and roof. "Sudhana, there—" He pointed. "Cigarettes?"

Michael gave them each an American cigarette, which was something of a luxury in these parts. Both lit up immediately, and Michael walked on unsteady legs toward the house. The old doubts? Was this the place? Was he doing the right thing? Jellie, don't turn me away, don't do that. Whatever is going on, let me be part of it.

The forehead and eyes of a crone appeared over a windowsill, then disappeared immediately when she saw the good-size white man walking toward her. "Sudhana?" Michael called out. Nothing. "Jellie? Jellie, it's Michael." Still nothing. Then slowly the door opened a crack, and the old woman looked out. She spoke rapidly in words he didn't understand. "Jellie . . . JahLAY. Jellie . . . JahLAY." He said her name over and over again, then added the surname he had been told she might be using, and the words were strange on his tongue. "Jellie *Velayudum*. JahLAY *Velayudum*."

The woman shook her head, spoke rapidly in a croaking voice, and pointed in a direction that looked as if it were inside the house. Christ, had something happened or what? Was Jellie lying in there?

The driver swaggered over to where Michael was trying to climb the wall between cultures. "Cigarette, boss? I know what old woman is saying." More baksheesh. You get a little tired of it after a while. It's not the money or the smokes, it's the bloody damned arrogance, the use of leverage.

Michael gave him half a pack of Merits. "She say woman called JahLAY Velayudum is at old hunting lodge in the middle of the lake, place called Lake Palace Hotel. You want go there?"

Michael nodded, and the driver flipped his head toward the jeep. They went down around the mountain and got on the road along the river again. Seven minutes later the jeep came over a rise, and Lake Periyar looked blue and calm in the distance.

The jeep driver dropped Michael off at the Aranya Nivas Hotel, a hundred yards from the lakeshore. He asked for more cigarettes, and Michael told him to stuff it. Michael Tillman was tired of smart young bastards, whatever country they come from, and said as much. He'd been too passive, too intent on finding Jellie, putting up with too much nonsense. The driver retreated in the face of Michael's anger, shrugged his shoulders, and backed his jeep out of the hotel driveway.

Michael went inside, grubby and tired. The woman at the desk was perfectly done, turquoise sari and a face that would launch a thousand Porsches back in the States. She was polite and efficient, and he was ready for some of that. He asked about the Lake Palace Hotel. She told him it was an old maharajah's hunting lodge with only six guest rooms and that reservations were handled here at the Aranya Nivas. While she flipped through a reservations book, Michael stared at a photograph on the wall behind her. It was slightly faded, but still a beautiful shot of a tiger coming out of tall grass on a foggy morning and carried the signature *Robert Kincaid*.

The clerk said there were rooms available for the next four nights. After that it was completely booked for a week. Three continental meals each day were included in the price.

The big question. He asked it: "I'm supposed to meet a woman at the Lake Palace. I wonder if she has checked in yet. Her first name is Jellie . . . JahLAY. I believe she is registered under the name Velayudum, though she might be using Markham or Braden." It all sounded rather suspicious, vaguely clandestine, but he had decided to cover all the bases.

"Three of the rooms are currently occupied out

there." She looked up at him. "And you say you are to meet someone?"

"Yes. My arrival date, however, was uncertain."

"I have a Velayudum listed here. There are two people registered under that name."

Michael staggered inside himself. All the months, all the miles, the dreams. Forty-three, and he was standing there looking stupid while Jellie was registered under an Indian name and sharing the room with someone, most likely a man named Velayudum from somewhere back in her India days. Jellie—all the things I don't know about you.

Michael would always remember how alone he felt at that moment, incredibly alone and lonely and discarded. It must have shown, because the woman asked, "Sir, would you still like a room at the Lake Palace?"

He could go back to Madurai, fly to Madras, and change his homeward flight. Then he thought, This is foolish male vanity you're suffering, Tillman. You're not thinking clearly, afraid of what you might find in the middle of the lake. You're not going anywhere except out to that hotel and hit the end of this at full speed, if that's what it comes to.

"Put me down for one night, please. The hotel is on an island, is that correct?"

"Yes, we call it an island. There is a narrow strip of swamp connecting it to the mainland. It's approximately a twenty-minute boat ride from the jetty."

"What boat, what jetty?"

"Go out the front door, turn right, and walk down the path. You'll see a small building with a sign reading 'Periyar Wildlife Sanctuary.' Purchase your boat ticket there. The ticket agent will direct you to the proper boat. The island is in one of India's largest tiger preserves, and since you will be staying there you must also purchase an entrance permit to the preserve. If you want to take a safari into the jungle, you can make arrangements for a guide at the same time you purchase your boat ticket. Without a guide, you will not be allowed to leave the hotel grounds, since there are large animals about and it is much too dangerous."

As Michael turned to leave he asked, "Was the photograph behind you taken here?"

"Yes, on the island where the Lake Palace is located. I'm told the photographer who took it came here often some years ago and always stayed at the Lake Palace."

Down the path to the sanctuary office. Hundreds of Indian tourists milling around on the jetty below and several old excursion boats rocking in the water. Michael handed the room voucher to a wildlife officer at the office. He issued a boat ticket, saying Michael should show his hotel voucher to the pilot of the *Miss Lake Periyar*. The pilot would then drop him off at the hotel.

It was a mess. Travel was never easy in India, and this was something altogether different. There were three excursion boats, two of them in the process of loading, one already packed with Indian tourists. Two hundred future boat passengers, porters, and assorted hangers-on were packed on the jetty. The loaded boat had *Miss Lake Periyar* painted on its starboard side.

He fought his way through the crowd, got on the boat, and showed one of the hands the hotel voucher. The man seemed disinterested but nodded and indicated with a toss of his head that Michael should find a seat. The dominant feeling permeating all travel in India was one of ambiguity, and Michael had serious doubts as to whether the pilot would be notified he was to be dropped at the hotel.

The boat was constructed with two levels, a glassed-in first level and an open upper deck. There were no seats left, but there was shouting and laughter and calls to those left on the jetty, the sum of which was pandemonium. Children ran up and down the steps between the first and second levels, people got off the boat to talk to those left behind, then got back on again.

The boathand Michael had talked to was making a reasonable attempt at crowd control but was failing miserably, overwhelmed by the crush. How, Michael wondered, could any animals be spotted along the shore, if that indeed was the main thrust of the boat tour. The boat would sound like pharaoh's army coming over the water toward them.

The boathand got tough when the engine turned over. He ordered people to sit down and stay seated. Michael checked again, but every seat on the boat was filled, so he hunkered down on the steps leading to the upper deck with a young boy sitting on the step just below his feet. The boy twisted his neck and looked at him while Michael stared out over the water.

The boat moved away from the jetty and chugged slowly down the huge, narrow lake, a reservoir stretching for miles behind the Periyar Dam, constructed by the British in 1895. A narration came from small loudspeakers mounted at various places on the boat, sometimes in English, sometimes in one of the Indian languages, telling the passengers they might see various animals ranging from leopards to tigers to elephants to wild pigs. Michael figured if they saw any animals at all, they'd be flopped down in laughter at the strange mammals packed onto an old green contraption that should've sunk twenty years ago.

Late afternoon now, sun dropping. Michael's boat and the two eventually following were the last sight-seeing runs of the day. Heavy jungle along the shore except for fifty feet or so of bare dirt running down to the water in some places. Michael stood up for a moment and could see a high hill with trees, looking as though it sat hard and straight in the boat's course.

Ten minutes later the boathand shook Michael's knee and said, "Lake Palace." Michael was tight, so tight his breath was coming in short little intakes and exhales, as if he were finishing a long sprint, which he was. Across the sunlit water of India on a December afternoon Michael Tillman went, fearful, terribly so, of what he was going to find ahead of him.

A wooden jetty stuck out fifteen feet from the island's shore, and he could see wide stone steps behind the jetty leading up into heavy forest. A long red tile roof was visible through breaks in the foliage. On the jetty was an Indian boy of about fifteen. The desk clerk at the Aranya Nivas had radioed the lodge to say a guest was on the *Miss Lake Periyar*.

The pilot expertly swung the boat broadside to the jetty's end, and Michael jumped off. The boy pointed at the knapsack on Michael's shoulder, and Michael gave it to him. They began the long climb up the stone steps to the lodge, which sat a hundred and fifty feet above them. Halfway up Michael touched the boy's shoulder, signaling he wanted to stop for a moment.

He sat on a wooden bench beside the steps, put his head in his hands, and thought, imagining what he might see at the top of the steps and thinking about how he would handle whatever was there. The boy stood patiently, looking off into the jungle.

After a minute or two, Michael got up and they continued. At the top of the stairs he followed the boy over a red dirt area where the jungle had been cut back around the entire circumference of the lodge. Off to Michael's right an Indian couple sat on the veranda in front of their room. They were drinking tea but paused to watch the new arrival come across the dirt and onto the veranda south of them. The manager appeared with a room key, looked Michael over, and said dinner would be served at seven, adding informal dress was appropriate. He asked if he could get Michael something to drink. Michael ordered two Kingfisher beers and followed the boy along the veranda.

The room was spacious with a double bed and a bath area in a separate room to the rear, furniture of slightly battered white wicker. Two large windows with heavy wooden shutters that were closed faced the veranda, and an overhead fan turned slowly. A smaller window in the bath area also had the same heavy shutters. The boy put Michael's knapsack on one of the beds and scurried around, turning on lights. Michael tipped him, and he was gone, closing the door behind him.

Michael looked at his watch. Three hours before dinner. He showered and dressed in a clean khaki shirt and jeans, traded his boots for sandals, drinking Kingfisher and preparing himself for what was to come. He was ready, if there was any real way to be ready for what he was sure he'd discover. No excuse to lounge around in the room, so he walked outside on the cement veranda, which was empty of people along the entire run of the lodge.

A trench, about five feet deep and three feet wide, circled the lodge out beyond the open dirt area where the jungle began. Michael was pretty sure the trench was designed to hold at bay unreliable things snarling along on short legs or crawling on scaled bellies, tongues flickering.

The Indian couple he'd seen earlier were standing near their room at the far end of the lodge. They were on the crest of a hill dropping off to the lake and were looking through binoculars at something across the water on the opposite shore. They called the boy over and asked him a question. "Wild pigs," he said.

Purple-blue flowers curled from the roof. Far down the lake Michael heard a sound. It took him a moment to recognize it: elephant. In the distance he could hear the low beating of an excursion boat's engine. He sat there on the south end of a veranda in south India, lit a cigarette, and started on his second beer, feeling like a warrior about to enter battle.

Behind him and north along the veranda he heard a door open and the sound of voices, one of them Jellie's, he thought. Adrenaline hit Michael Tillman's arteries in a surge faster and stronger than anything he'd experienced in his basketball days or, for that matter, ever before in any circumstance. The warrior had come to fight for his woman, his body was preparing itself.

Now was the moment. *Now*—do it, Tillman. Do it and get it over with, settle your affairs, here in the jungle. Where else have men ever settled their affairs? He turned and saw a young Indian woman, fifteen or sixteen years, come out of an open doorway. Her black shining hair was in a long braid, and she had on a sari of a deep orange color, bracelets on her arms and around one ankle, silver toe rings, and straw-colored sandals.

Jellie Markham/Braden/Velayudum, or whoever she was on that day, came out of the same doorway and looked across the stretch of open dirt toward the jungle. "It's a beautiful evening, Jaya," Michael heard her say.

The young woman answered her, "Yes, it is. This is the loveliest place I've ever seen. The mountain air is so clean and cool after the lowland heat. I've always looked forward to our time here."

Jellie looked down the veranda, gray eyes taking in the scenery, casually glancing at a man sitting by himself at a table. The young woman started to speak but saw Jellie's face and followed her eyes. They both stared for a moment, then the young woman looked again at Jellie's face, but Jellie never took her eyes off Michael Tillman. He waited for a man named Velayudum to come out of the doorway and put his arm around Jellie, but no one came.

Jellie was frozen where she stood. Michael looked back at her. She wore the traditional Indian woman's outfit called a *salwar kameese*—long tunic and loose, flowing bottoms gathering themselves just above her white sandals, all of it done in the palest of lavenders. She had a red scarf draped around her neck with the ends of it hanging over her shoulders and down her back. And, like the young woman, she wore an ankle bracelet and toe rings. Her hair shone in the half-light on the veranda, and hung straight and long, parted off to one side, just as she wore it back in Cedar Bend, sometimes tucking it up under a tweed cap.

Cedar Bend? Where in the hell was that? Did it exist anymore, or had it ever existed? Maybe . . . maybe somewhere in another time, somewhere back down along the crinkled chain of living and loving and working, it had once existed. Back in the same, forgotten, and ancient world as Custer, South Dakota, where a boy worked late in the night shooting baskets and repairing an old English motorcycle that would take him over the roads of his life, eventually with a woman named Jellie riding behind him.

Jellie took the girl's hand and came toward him. He stood up, saying nothing, watching her eyes, which never left his. She let go of the girl's hand, put her arms around his waist, and laid her head against his chest. He touched her hair. She lifted her face and kissed him.

She turned to the girl. "Jaya, this is Michael Tillman, the man I've been telling you about." Her eyes on Michael's face again, steady eyes. "Michael, this is my daughter, Jaya Velayudum."

Twelve

Dhiren Velayudum: revolutionary, member of a radical separatist group that fought everyone and everything connected with the central Indian government. And Jellie Markham, young and idealistic back in the middle sixties, young and idealistic and off to India to write her thesis. Movie stuff: Tamil warrior-poet meets young American woman with her own dreams of how things ought to be. At bottom, Dhiren Velayudum was a terrorist, and Jellie became his lover and confidante. Though it didn't seem like terrorism in their nights of loving and days filled with quixotic visions of a great revolutionary flow that could not be halted. She married Dhiren in a traditional Indian ceremony. The shrieking death-dance of her parents when they found out could be heard all the way from Syracuse.

Things went bad for the radicals, and there were

wild months of running with Dhiren, hiding in villages and cities. Then came an afternoon road winding high into the Western Ghats, the same road Michael would travel one day years later. The car in which Dhiren and Jellie were riding moved slowly around hairpin curves.

Suddenly Dhiren was pushing Jellie, shouting for her to get out of the car and hide. She got out, carrying Jaya, and crouched behind a jumble of deadfall. Dhiren pitched from the other side of the car and ran for the trees on the opposite side of the road, nine-millimeter, Russian-made pistol in his hand. The sound of automatic weapons. Bullets spitting into the dust like an animal with a hundred claws tracking him and closing fast, then crawling up and across his body. Dhiren spinning, stumbling into the forest.

That night at the Lake Palace Hotel, Jellie and Michael sat on the veranda for two hours after Jaya went to bed. She told the story, all of it, leaving out nothing. How she felt about Dhiren, her memories of him. How she carried her baby along the night roads of south India after Dhiren had been shot, walking all night into Thekkady, where there were sympathizers with the radicals' cause. How the India government punished her by refusing to issue an exit visa for Jaya so Jellie could take her to the States.

She told him how Leonard Markham had come for her, all the way to Delhi, and the words he'd said: "Let's go home, Jellie. We'll find a way to get your baby to America." She looked off into the night. "It's amazing what parents can forgive."

Jellie told him how she fought for years to get Jaya a visa and failed, her father helping her and pounding on authorities from Washington, D.C., to New Delhi. But India put on its silent, impenetrable face, and nothing happened.

Jellie sat with her knees pulled up, her arms wrapped around them while she talked. "Chitra kept track of things on the Indian side and wrote to say it was still not possible to get the necessary papers for Jaya. I tried to come back, but the Indian government denied me an entrance visa.

"Can you imagine the agony, Michael? Three years it went on that way. I kept applying for a visa, and then for no reason I've ever been able to figure out, they issued me one. I simply became unimportant to them after a while, I guess.

"I could have given up my U.S. citizenship and perhaps become an Indian citizen, but I wasn't ready to do that, and I'm not sure India would have accepted me. I still believed I could get Jaya out of the country. I even thought about smuggling her out, but everyone I talked to said it was too risky, that I could end up in an Indian prison for years and leave Jaya without any mother at all."

Michael nodded, his face serious. When something important was being said, when attention was called for, Michael Tillman was a world-class listener. And he was listening now to what Jellie Braden was saying. He narrowed his eyes, then rubbed them with his palms, trying to settle himself as he started to understand things he hadn't anticipated. It began to sink in, hard: he'd underestimated Jellie. She wasn't simply a bright, good-looking woman married to one of his colleagues. Instead, she had lived another life alien to anything he could have imagined. She was

far more an adult than he had realized, far more sophisticated in a worldly fashion than he would ever
be. She was talking about a different Jellie, who had
lived before, one he would not be able to comprehend
or experience, no matter how much she told him,
how much he thought about it. Jesus, automatic
weapons and mountain roads, a man who had given
her a child in a swirl of flight and idealistic revolutionary doctrine. She had laughed and cried with' this
man, and loved him wildly and freely and carried her
baby as she ran with him. He felt a strange combination of sadness for her and envy for Dhiren Velayudum, who had touched places in her that he, Michael
Tillman, could never touch. What a goddamned stupid joke, he thought, his wrong and undue assump-
tions about himself and Jellie and how he presumed
Jellie saw him—for the last year he had been measuring Michael Tillman against Jimmy Braden, not
against a man with the power and spirit of Dhiren
Velayudum, a man who had lived for just the right
amount of time and died at just the right moment to
create a larger-than-life image in the far back memories of Jellie Braden. It was an image that would never
have any equal, for it had never been lessened by the
slog of ordinary, daily existence. Michael let out a
long breath, while Jellie caught hers and continued.

"All of this time Jaya was becoming a young
Indian girl. I finally decided maybe it was best she be
raised in Indian ways. I didn't seem to have any other
choice. The decision was made: Jaya would continue
to live with the Sudhanas until she was old enough
for boarding school, and I would visit her as often as
I could.

"I sent money to the Sudhanas, tormenting myself all these years that I was not here to see my little girl growing up. Yet I don't know if it could have worked out any better. Jaya is a fine young woman. But I did visit every year, and we always came out here to the Lake Palace for a while. So at least she got to know her real mother pretty well, though we have become more like sisters than mother and daughter. I've always saved most of my salary from whatever job I've had over the years, and that money went to India, to the Sudhanas and to Jaya. She entered boarding school when she was six and has been there since.

"When I met Jimmy Braden and married him, all I said was I'd been involved with an Indian man who had died and I still had a lot of friends over here who needed financial help. The lie rested in what I didn't say. I told him I would be coming alone to visit every year. Jimmy, I think, would have agreed to anything, just to get me to marry him—I know that sounds terrible, but it's true—so he said it was not a problem. He's never complained once about my visits to India, and he's never asked any questions about what it is I do when I'm over here. As I've said before, Jimmy has his good qualities."

Michael got up and walked behind her, put his arms around her, and kissed her hair. Jellie Braden looked off into the night. Something large and moving fast crashed through the jungle fifty yards back of the lodge.

Jellie stood and looked up at him, put her hands on his face. "Michael, Dhiren was a lot like you, in some ways, but I don't want you to think you're some kind of latter-day surrogate for him. That's not true at all, and you must believe me when I say it."

He smiled and said, "I believe you, Jellie," though he wasn't quite as sure about it as he sounded.

"I came to India this time because I needed to think and to talk with Jaya about us. I wanted to make sure of how I felt and for her to understand. When you found me this evening I was already turning for home, Michael. I was turning for home, toward you."

In his room he laid her down and kissed her in all the places she liked to be kissed. Later there was heavy scratching at the door and the sense of great bulk moving around outside. Michael sat up. "What the hell is that? Sounds like a bear."

"I think that's what it is. I heard it last night."

"There used to be a lot of them in the Black Hills. They go on like that. I have some fruit in my knapsack, and the bear can probably smell it. He'll go away after a bit."

The bear left and was replaced by the tickety-tick of fast little feet running over roof tiles. Michael and Jellie lay in the darkness together. "Sounds like India on the move again," he whispered to her.

Jellie went back to her room an hour before dawn. Michael lay awake, thinking about all they had talked about. Twenty minutes in front of first light he dressed and went outside into heavy, dripping fog wrapped around the lodge and turning open spaces into closed ones, turning the jungle into vague, threatening shapes in gray camouflage. Across the lake,

which was only about a hundred yards wide where
the island divided it, a monkey called, sounding far
and lonesome. The classic jungle sound from old Tar-
zan movies. Elephants again, closer now. The monkey let go once more and was joined by a few others,
along with intermittent calls from awakening birds.

His small flashlight took him through the fog
and down the stone steps to the water. Why he was
doing this he wasn't certain. Something to do with
loving Jellie and knowing where he stood with her, a
little early morning celebration of his own, some time
to rearrange how he saw her in light of what she'd
told him about her early years in India. He sat on a
jetty post where he could look out to the opposite
side of the lake and down the shoreline to his right.
He sat there and waited, listening for sounds beyond
the lapping of small waves. First light came up, trans-
lucent through the fog.

He was staring off into space, thinking about
Jellie and Jaya asleep in the lodge above him, not
looking at anything in particular. The fog swayed in
an early breeze and began turning into a yellowish
mist as the sun poked its way through a gap in the
eastern hills.

The tiger saw Michael before Michael saw him.
The cat was thirty yards down the shore, drops of
water coming off its muzzle as it lifted its head after
drinking. It didn't move, just kept that big head pointing in Michael's direction, its body still perpendicular
to the water. Long red tongue came out and flicked
away the droplets on its white chin.

The plan? What plan? Stupid, Tillman, real
dumb, Michael was thinking. The lodge was a forty-

second sprint up a flight of steep, rough steps, or longer via a jungle route, and a Bengal in full stride could cover a hundred yards in four seconds. If the tiger wanted him, Michael could do nothing. Running would be pointless. And pathetic.

Somehow, though, Michael wasn't worried. He never quite understood why when he thought back on it. He just wasn't. In fact, all the time he was thinking how serious wildlife watchers would give up their butterfly nets for life if they could have this experience. Talk about a *Saw-It!* merit badge, talk about counting coup. A lot of folks were out there practicing a kind of visual banditry and grunted sourly when the stagecoach didn't stop. It had stopped here, in the fog, at dawn.

Michael began to take pleasure in just staring back at the tiger, in the simple purity of contemplating its existence, in knowing not everything wild and strong had been snuffed out by condos and shopping malls. There was something good and exhilarating about that, about knowing that creatures who crawled toward trenches or went bump against your shutters in the darkness or stared at you from a misty shoreline in south India were out there, and they cared nothing for your passing joys and sorrows, and they were free to return to the jungle when they chose.

The tiger lowered its head, lapped at the water, looked at Michael again, then shambled down the shore in the opposite direction. At fifty yards it turned to look at Michael once more, looked at him for a long time. At a hundred yards the big cat angled off into the jungle. The sun ran up its flag hard and bright, and the fog lifted.

"Good morning, Michael."

It was Jellie, and Jaya, carrying cups of hot tea for themselves and a big cup of coffee for the tiger expert who was busy sewing a merit badge on his sleeve: *Saw It!* Michael said nothing about the tiger, thinking they might feel sorry about having missed it and thereby spoiling a first-class sunrise for them. When he told them later they were both sorry and glad—sorry they'd missed it, glad they weren't there.

"Michael"—her gray eyes were full of good, loving signals as they looked at him—"we didn't talk about travel plans. Jaya and I are booked here for another three nights, can you stay?"

Stay? He'd have slugged it out with the Bengal for the privilege. "Jellie, I'm free until mid-January. My return flight is January twelfth. What's your program, as they say in India?" Jaya smiled.

"Well . . ." Jellie was a little hesitant. He sensed it was money.

"Let me suggest something. You're looking at a guy who lives in a cheap apartment, drives a thirty-year-old motorcycle and a fifteen-year-old Dodge Dart, and makes a passable salary. If the two of you feel like it, let's travel, go where we want to go. Take the canal boats through the Kerala estuaries, lay around up on the Goa coast for a while, ride the steamer up to Bombay and stay in the Taj Hotel. My treat and no holds barred."

"That will cost a lot of money." She bent over and kissed him good morning.

He whispered, "We can work it out on the kitchen table back in Cedar Bend."

She rolled her eyes. "My new profession now

becomes clear." Then Jellie laughed, and Jaya laughed, too, though she seemed a little unsure of why she was laughing. But Michael thought he knew—she was laughing because her mother was laughing, because her mother was happy and loved a man and wasn't afraid to let her see it. She'd figure it out after a while.

And they did that, traveled. Stayed on at the Lake Palace for three more nights, then went off to Kerala to see the famous Chinese fishing nets and stayed in the Malabar Hotel, where they swam in the pool and had late suppers served on white linen by the bay. They hit Goa and lounged on the beach, took the steamer to Bombay and checked into the Taj Hotel for five days. Flew up to Jaipur to see the Pink City and took a camel safari into the Rajasthani desert.

On January 5 they put Jaya on a plane for Cochin and school, which left Jellie and Michael a week to themselves. They spent it in Pondicherry, staying with Innkeeper Maigrit ("Ah, monsieur, you found her, I see. May I politely say she was worth the search") and taking their evening meals in the small restaurants of Pondicherry. They went far up the beach one afternoon and made love in the sand, then swam naked in the warm Bay of Bengal and made love again in the water. And Michael lectured at the college, paying his debt to Dr. Ramani.

Jellie was moved by the fact Michael had booked his return flight for the twelfth of January, that he'd been prepared to spend over seven weeks looking for her. He said, and meant it, "If I hadn't found you by the sixth, I was going to call home and tell them to find a substitute for the spring semester. I was—Jellie,

I truly mean this—fully prepared to go on with my knapsack until I found you, no matter how long it might have taken."

On January 12 they rode British Airways toward Heathrow, reading, laughing, holding hands. Then serious at times, preparing themselves for laying all of this in front of Jimmy.

Between London and Chicago, somewhere over the Greenland ice pack, Jellie leaned her head against Michael's shoulder. He looked at the gray eyes, noticed something pensive in them.

"What is it, Jellie?"

"I was just thinking. People once called Dhiren 'the Tiger of Morning.' "

She went to sleep then, resting against him. He gently fished a notebook out of his pocket and wrote, "The Tiger of Morning lives forever."

Thirteen

James Lee Braden III was a middle-grade rationalist. What could not be explained in terms of empirical evidence did not exist. Except for God, who received immunity from rational inspection and was dealt with on Sundays at the First Presbyterian Church. Turn of the key, click of a door lock, and Jimmy looked up from the autobiography of John Maynard Keynes he was reading. His wife walked in with Michael Tillman behind her.

This time Jimmy didn't cry. And he wasn't all that surprised. Parallel events—Jellie gone, Michael pulling out a few days later. Teeter-totters in the park, a faculty wife who had seen Jellie and Michael leaving the Ramada together, speculation in the offices. Matters passed over originally but recalled later on when the time was right—data, incomplete and soft, but data nonetheless. Induction and tentative conclusion:

Maybe Jellie Braden and Michael Tillman were more than friends.

January evening 1982, conclusion no longer tentative. Jimmy said he understood how Jellie and Michael would be attracted to each other. His primary concern was, in his words, "how we all carry on from here." He seemed almost relieved, more worried about style than substance.

Jellie was less rational and quite a lot less stylish than her husband at that moment. She'd been married to Jimmy Braden for eleven years, that counted for something. She got herself worked up pretty good, telling Jimmy how sorry she was, how it was not right to behave as she had. Jimmy eventually said, "Our decision to marry was probably a good one at the time, but people change. There's no point living with choices made by people who were different eleven years ago than they are now."

Jellie gathered herself and her things and moved in with Michael. They painted his old apartment and gradually converted it into something both of them could tolerate. The Shadow stayed in the living room. That was not open for debate or compromise. Jellie did suggest a dropcloth to protect the nice oak flooring from greasy tools. Michael smiled and said it was a large concession but agreed.

He rolled back into teaching, dog-paddling his way through the wash of sideways looks and gossip that ultimately became a minor part of the university saga. Jellie retrieved her maiden name, finished her M.A., and was accepted in the anthropology Ph.D. program. And Jimmy? He went away. Arthur Wilcox found him an associate deanship at a private school in the Northeast, near Jimmy's parents. All were pleased.

Well, not everyone. Eleanor Markham was appalled and forever would view Michael as a social misfit and home wrecker. She was especially appalled at his travel habits and happened to be looking out the window of her Syracuse home one afternoon when the Black Shadow rolled up her driveway. The Shadow was no longer an amusing abstraction sitting in some lunatic professor's living room. It was real now, and her forty-four-year-old daughter was riding behind the lunatic. Probably it was Jellie's leather jacket, boots, and mirrored sunglasses that got her. It'd been a long life, and she'd hoped for something better.

Michael and Jellie's father escaped to the trout streams. Leonard Markham never said harsh words about anybody, and he mentioned Jimmy only once in Michael's presence. He was laying out a Royal Coachman fly after several elegant backcasts. The Coachman landed soft as you please below a big rock where the water eddied. He puffed on his pipe, twitched the fly, and said, "Jim Braden was afraid of water. Can you imagine that, Michael?" Michael didn't say anything. Leonard twitched the fly again. A brookie rolled beside it but thought better of the enterprise and left the fly alone, in the way Leonard Markham left the subject of Jimmy Braden and never came back to it.

Jellie and Michael traveled to India once a year. In 1984 they brought Jaya back to meet her grandparents. Afterward the three of them visited Michael's

mother, who was confined to a nursing home in
Rapid City. She was old and pretty wobbly, but sen-
tient most of the time. Ruth Tillman took Jaya's hand
and held it for a long time, smiling. It was the best
Michael could do in the way of a grandchild, and in
some strange way Ruth Tillman found it enough.

So it went. Not undiluted peace and tranquillity,
but workable part of the time, most of the time. Michael Tillman was a loner, something of a recluse,
always had been, always would be. He would go
away from Jellie, sometimes on the Shadow, sometimes only in his mind. And she resented that.

"People aren't motorcycles, Michael. You can't
just take the chain off and hang it over a chair until
you get around to it."

He grinned at her. "You're right. You're always
right about that stuff. Women know things men don't
when it comes to the gender interface. . . . Jesus,
how's that for psychobabble . . . gender interface.
Next thing you know I'll become a 'gender reconciliation facilitator.' Saw that in a magazine the other day.
There are hot new job opportunities out there I never
dreamed of."

She rolled her eyes, crossed her arms. "I don't
think you're the least bit interested in facilitating gender reconciliation, here or anywhere else."

"You're right again, mostly, wrong about here.
I'm a good ol' boy from the bad ol' days in certain
respects. Nadia Koslowski made some inroads in
taming the Y chromosome, but she left before the
work was finished. You've continued where Nadia
left off and already discovered I'm only marginally
educable in that area. I'm interested in peaceful coexis-

tence, but I'm also interested in my work and fishing and riding around on shadows, two-wheeled ones and otherwise. My attention shifts, I wobble like Mercury's orbit. I'll try to do better, really I will. But I probably won't improve a whole lot. And I'm not altogether sure you really want me to change all that much. You might end up with a limp, obsequious piece of crap you don't care for."

"Michael, sometimes I think I should pour plastic over you and preserve you just the way you are in these moments. We could prop you up in the Smithsonian and hang a sign around your neck that says *Homo past-hopeus*, let future and more enlightened generations stare at you. Carolyn was right when she said you're incorrigible."

He held up his hands in a position of surrender. "Hell, I'm guilty as charged. I've discovered it's easier to plead guilty to everything. Less argument that way. And even though I don't share your faith in the wisdom of future generations, I kind of like the Smithsonian idea. But make sure I'm sitting on the Shadow with a fly rod in my hand. And make sure you remember Dhiren and how happy you were with him, and how unhappy you were with Jimmy Braden. You once told me Jimmy was so conciliatory and ambivalent it damn near drove you crazy. You're a strong woman in a lot of ways, Jellie Markham, but you like your men a little wild and untamed. I will, however—and being completely aware of my failings and general unworthiness—extend my offer of marriage once again, as I do almost weekly."

She scuffed her tennis shoe on the floor and looked down it. In some ways he was right. She'd never quite sorted it out, the tradeoffs. The men she truly cared for made her happy in some ways, unhappy in others. Still looking at her shoe, she said, "As I've mentioned before, being married twice is enough. Three times seems a bit much somehow." She cooled down and smiled at him. "Thanks for the proposal, however. I always appreciate it when you ask. Maybe sometime I'll surprise you and say 'yes.' "

"The offer remains open. How about two fingers' worth of Jack Daniel's, a bath, and then the kind of reconciliation we seem to do best. Cut and paste, make peace and make love."

"We need groceries. You always get hungry afterwards."

He pulled on his leather jacket, grinning. "So do you. In atonement for my many sins I'll go to the store. Got a list?"

"No, do you?"

"No. I'll buy beer, potatoes, and whatever else I think of on the way."

An hour later they were sitting in the small tub together, hot water deep and soapy. She put her feet on his shoulders, he ran his hands along her thighs and told her for the thousandth time she had the greatest breasts in the universe. She looked at him over the rim of her glass and started laughing.

"What's the matter? Your breasts are serious business."

"Nothing. I was just thinking about plastic and the Smithsonian again. Think I'll do it when you're gone and defenseless."

"Okay by me. You can prop Arthur Wilcox up

beside me, label him *Homo go-squatis, Driven Bonkers by Homo past-hopeus*. Put some blueprints in his hand." He leaned back in the tub. "Let me change the subject. Remember that nice area in the Black Hills called White Bear Canyon I showed you once?"

"Yes."

"After you finish your degree, let's move out there. I'll quit teaching, get my retirement annuity under way, and do a little writing. There's a small college called Spearfish State nearby. Maybe you could get a teaching job there if it suits you."

"It's a possible; I'll think about it later." She put her legs around him and slid up on his lap, arms around his neck. "Right now I'm getting a lot more interested in moving to the bedroom." She leaned her head back and shook it. "UUhhh, men! You're all nuttier'n hell."

Michael kissed her long and sweet, on her mouth, on both her breasts, and ran his tongue along her throat. "Not all of us are nutty . . . only the ones you like."

Jellie received her doctorate in 1987. Michael was allowed to attend the ceremony in full academic regalia, though his robe and soft, six-pointed cap, which had lain unused for years, needed two runs at the dry cleaners before they were presentable. When she walked across the stage and was handed her diploma, he damn near fainted with pride, knowing how much it meant to her. Michael threw a small party for her at the apartment and had a bottle of champagne all to himself, grinning while he sat on the Shadow and watched her gray eyes as people congratulated her. Jellie Markham had become whole, professionally, at least.

Later that evening when the guests had stumbled back to wherever guests go when they leave, she came out of the bathroom with her academic gown and mortarboard on. Michael was still sitting on the Shadow, barefoot in T-shirt and jeans, a bottle of champagne balanced on the gas tank. He said, "*Dr.* Markham, I presume."

She grinned that old salacious grin of hers, the one she put on when it was time for serious matters of the flesh, then parted the robe and showed him she was wearing nothing beneath it. "Dr. Markham is now ready for her graduation present, if Dr. Tillman is prepared." He was indeed, and the evening concluded in splendid fashion with Michael straddling the Shadow and Jellie straddling Michael, Miles on the tape deck. Jellie chewed on his ear and whispered "Vroom, vroom," while she moved slowly up and down with quiet, blissful intensity on the motorcycle man.

Michael's mother died in 1988. A realtor called eight months later and said he had a buyer for the little house in Custer. Classes started in a week, but Michael cranked up the Shadow and headed out.

It all went smoothly, and he brought the Shadow back toward Cedar Bend, starting with the Black Hills and staying on secondary highways for the entire distance. He ran into heavy rains a little east of the Missouri River, but he was short of time and pushing hard, his yellow slicker flapping in the wind. Night caught him at the Iowa border.

He looked down at his old friend, patting the gas tank. The engine was bolted directly to the frame, and he could feel the vibrations at the level of his cells. "Let's open things up a bit, big guy, see what you're made of here on your thirty-seventh birthday." The Shadow responded and ran like a black cat over the wet pavement, its headlights sweeping across woodlands on the curves.

It happened in the hills east of Sioux City. The semi slid around a blind curve, drifting into the other lane. Michael's visor was a little fogged, and his night vision wasn't what it used to be. He blinked, then squinted hard. The truck was moving fast in the hands of a sleepy driver hammering eighty thousand pounds of vehicle and its load of tractor parts toward Omaha. The driver came to full alert as the truck skidded, fought to control his rig, and saw the yellow slicker fluttering a hundred feet straight ahead of where his hood ornament pointed.

Michael was blinded by the lights, truck closing and no way to lay the Shadow down and slide. He thought of Jellie and tigers. For some reason he thought of Jellie and tigers in that instant, then took the Shadow off the road and into the trees at seventy miles an hour. A yellow blur rocketing 30 feet into the forest . . . 100 feet . . . 200 feet . . . steering and braking and running the maze in a wild flash of tigers and Jellie and the way she looked at him in those times, holding her breath, eyes wide and her breasts and belly coming up to meet the tiger and him, Michael Tillman, and he smiled, and for a moment, just a wild and fleeting moment that became vanishingly small, he believed he was going to make it. Until the yellow blur became a butterfly gone.

* * *

In those stretches when he was conscious, Michael could hear the hum of life-support systems to which he was fastened. Sort of a faint and steady background noise. Sometimes a certain machine kicked in and the noise would get louder, which he didn't like but which he couldn't do anything about.

He was pretty well beat up. The doctors laid it out straight and hard: cracked pelvis, two broken arms, compound fracture of one leg, internal injuries. He thought he was dying, so did the doctors, and he tried to come to grips with that fact, hanging on until Jellie could get there, hanging on to see her again. He concentrated on Jellie's face, formed it up cool and clean in his mind, got her to smile for him, and he was still around in the morning.

Outside his room at the desk guarding the intensive care unit, he vaguely heard a panicked voice. "Where's Michael Tillman, please, I'm his wife." His wife—he'd never thought of Jellie that way.

She bent over him: "Oh, Michael . . . Michael. I came as fast as I could. Michael, get better, and I'll take care of you forever. Don't worry, it'll all be fine."

"Jellie, touch my face." His throat was wrapped around a tube, and he couldn't talk above a whisper, a hoarse one, but she heard him and stroked his cheek. He felt tears, big tears, coming out of both eyes, his eyes. It wasn't self-pity . . . well, maybe it was. He didn't know, didn't matter. He was feeling the touch of her hand on his face, thinking about how much he loved her and that they'd never make their old, sweet laughing love again, and that he'd never take her out to Heron Lake on the back of the Shadow again, and that they'd never sit on the veranda of the Lake Palace Hotel again, looking for tigers he knew were out there because he saw one once on a foggy morning when the world was beginning to turn his way.

Jellie was crying but trying to hide it from him. He floated in and out of consciousness for days, but finally the old body decided to give him another chance. He blinked open his eyes on a rainy Tuesday. She was sitting near his bed and looked up at him, smiling. "Welcome back, Michael."

In a few weeks Michael was on his feet, with Jellie's help, looking like a clumsy snowman, in his casts. He was not a patient patient; his mind called for action while his body wanted rest. After the casts were off, Jellie would come home from the university, where she was working as a temporary instructor, and find him attempting push-ups or sitting bent over his desk chair, trying to make the muscles in his arms learn to type again.

"For God's sake, Michael, I'm doing all I can do to get you better, and you're not helping. I have classes and shopping and you, and that's a full load. You have to cooperate a little, take things slow as the doctor said. And don't look at me in that little boy cranky way of yours; I'm too busy for nonsense."

"I feel inadequate, that's all. Sloppy, too, lying around here drawing disability pay."

"Think of it as if you were practicing the jumpshot, Michael. Invest now, get the benefits later."

"Too logical, nurse Jellie, too logical."

"You're the logician, Michael, except when it comes to yourself."

"That puts me in the great mainstream, right? Only time I've ever been there, and I don't like the feel of it."

"Well, you can like it or not like it. I'm going to the library. I have six hours of preparation to do for the survey course."

She put on her coat and stomped out. Two hours later she called him from a pay phone in the library. "You okay?"

"Yep. The little boy is no longer cranky and will attempt to remain as such. Sorry for the hassle. Christ, I did this to myself, and now I'm externalizing the results of my own stupidity on to you."

"Michael, I love you, really I do. But it's not easy sometimes. You understand that, don't you?"

"Yep again. Do you really have six hours of class preparation?"

"No. I was just escaping from the Walnut Street rehab ward for a while. I think I'll come home and fix us something to eat."

"Wrong. I'll rustle up some soup or its equivalent, have it bubbling when you get here."

Eventually, Michael's ability to type came back, ideas started to form, and the computer screen glowed blue in the evenings. After three months he could walk outside by himself and started jogging slowly a few weeks afterward. There was laughter again, and there was loving.

But living with Michael's intensity was not easy. Jellie had known it before the accident, and that intensity came back even stronger as he recovered. It was constant, unrelenting, a never-ending push toward frontiers of the mind and spirit, frontiers he redefined as he approached them, causing them to recede so the chase could go on. Michael chased frontiers and Jellie helped him chase the things he lost because his mind was always somewhere else, never paying attention to where he put car keys or checks or his latest draft of an article.

"Michael, you don't 'look' well. You riffle around through a stack of something or shove things here and there on top of the refrigerator and think you've really searched. After that, you yell, 'Jellie, have you seen . . . ?' "

"I use the lost horse method for finding things." He was eating an apple and had just finished complaining that he couldn't find last month's paycheck, which he was taking to the bank as soon as he located his car keys and found his gloves.

"What's the lost horse method?"

He was holding the apple between his teeth and scrounging around on top of the refrigerator, talking through the apple at the same time. He sounded as if he had a severe speech defect. "If you lose a horse, go where you saw him last and start there."

"What if you took the horse somewhere, to start with, and forgot where he was before you took him somewhere else? Your system wouldn't work, would it?"

"All my methods are flawed." He grinned, flipping the half-eaten apple over his shoulder from behind his back and catching it with his other hand. "Help me find the goddamn check, Jellie, so I can then look for my goddamned keys after which I'll search for my goddamned gloves. Please, Jellie. You're looking at a disabled searcher. All men have the disability; it's another one of those many flaws in the Y chromosome."

Jellie continued working as a temporary instructor at the university and enjoyed the teaching. Michael became more and more unhappy with the constraints of an academic bureaucracy that operated, as he saw it, for its own benefit, for its own survival and nothing else. Jellie could ignore that, and took delight instead in her students and her own research. This was new territory for her; Michael was more than two decades into it.

In 1990, after talking it over, they moved to White Bear Canyon. Jellie had misgivings about the move, about surrendering her own professional life to follow the drift of Michael's ways. But he had been unhappy at the university, and there was the possibility of a teaching position for her at Spearfish State. Life in the canyon was quiet and pleasant, but Jellie was restless. Though Michael worked alone and enjoyed it, Jellie needed an organization, a place where she could teach and do conventional research in her field.

A year later Jellie went to India alone. The birth of Jaya's second child was a complicated delivery, and she needed help afterward. Jellie stayed on longer than she'd intended. Two months, three months. India starting pulling on her again, Elsa Markham's genes turning her in directions that pointed a long way from White Bear Canyon and the problems of living close with a difficult man. A French architect from Auroville invited her out to dinner. He was handsome, worldly. She went with him once to the Alliance Française but declined the next time he asked. It didn't seem fair to Michael. The architect continued to call her. He sent flowers, left notes tacked to her door.

Michael knew nothing about the Frenchman, but he was worried. He called and asked, "When are you coming back?" His voice was pensive.

"I don't know," she said in a flat, noncommittal way.

"There's a job for you at Spearfish State beginning next fall. They called two days ago."

"I don't know right now. That's all I can say."

Spearfish State versus the excitement of a cosmopolitan life in Pondicherry. Dinners at the Alliance Française, a handsome Frenchman who was smooth and attentive, who seemed to understand and appreciate the feelings of women. She went out with him again. He wanted to take her to Paris and show her around. It was simple, uncomplicated, living this way. No problems. And she was near Jaya and the grandchildren, which enabled her to do penance for the mother she never had been. The university in Pondicherry offered her a part-time job, and she almost went to bed with the Frenchman on a night when the sweet smell of jasmine rode on slow winds from the Bay of Bengal, but she pulled back at the last minute. She was falling into something different, another life that seemed far off now. The next time she wouldn't pull back.

Michael called again. His voice was cooler than she remembered. He'd lived alone before, he could do it again, she knew that. He'd come to India after her once; he wouldn't do it a second time. When they said good-bye, his voice changed, got a little soft and sad.

"I miss you, Jellie/JahLAY."

And she cried then for reasons she didn't understand.

In the white sun of an India morning, the seawall at Pondicherry curved into the distance and looked like something from Mediterranean lands. Come evening, the locals strolled there while the streets and buildings of the city breathed out the heat of the day just past. After talking with Michael, Jellie walked to the seawall and sat there for a long time. A slice of yellow moon hung thirty degrees up, off in the general direction of Burma.

Back home she went to a mirror and looked at herself. Fifty-one. The Frenchman said she looked no more than forty. Men still turned to watch her when she passed, and that was good, she supposed. She brushed her long black hair, straightened her scarf, and returned to the mirror. She whispered, "Jellie Markham . . . Jellie . . . the song is almost finished. Just what the hell are you doing here when the only man you truly care for is half a world away?"

Two days later she walked slowly along a winding road in the high country near Thekkady. Dhiren seemed far back. Twenty-five years had passed since that day of blood and fear in the dust now covering her feet. The afternoon breeze lifted her hair while she sat quietly on a log and remembered her warrior-poet, remembered him and the way he touched her, remembered him running for the trees. That evening she visited an old woman named Sudhana. They ate simple food and talked of other times.

Chitra Dhavale rode with Jellie to the airport in Madras. "I'll miss you, Jellie, but I am glad you are going back. It's the right thing."

"What a strange, messy life it's been, Chitra. Irresponsible, too." Jellie had tears in her eyes. They were standing near the gate to Jellie's plane.

Chitra put her arms around her and said, "Yes . . . strange and messy . . . and irresponsible in some ways, I suppose. All of that . . . and quite wonderful also when you think about it, depending on who's doing the measuring and by what standards. But you at least know what it's like to come into high plumage and catch the southern winds. Most of us don't and never will. It's a lucky person who can have a single great love in her life. You've had two. One when you were a girl, and the other when you became a woman."

Jellie smiled then. "And one was a warrior-poet and the other is a motorcycle man. God help us all." They laughed together while she dried her tears, and forty minutes later Air India lifted off. Chitra Dhavale watched morning light flash from the 747's wings as it turned toward South Dakota.

Jellie had not told Michael she was returning and rode the airport limo by herself from Rapid City through the Black Hills. On the front porch of the cabin in White Bear Canyon was a disassembled motorcycle, the Shadow II. Michael had found it six months before at a convention of motorcycle enthusiasts and was rebuilding it. It would never take the place of the old Shadow destroyed in the accident, he knew that. The original was a symbol of his youth, and when it was gone, some boyish part of him went with it. He mourned both the losses.

The cabin was empty. But she could smell traces of pipe smoke. Her father's suitcase was in the spare bedroom. Michael had said Leonard Markham was planning on visiting him to fish the trout. Packages of fly line lay on the kitchen table along with lures, a bottle of Jack Daniel's, and Michael's beat-up cap with its *Real Men Don't Bond* logo. She'd given the cap to him as a birthday present just after his accident. When she'd handed him the sack containing the cap, she'd said, "This is in no way capitulation to the good ol' boy in you. Understand that. I just thought you'd like it."

She stood quietly, looking around. It felt a little strange, but also familiar in good ways. Casserole lay on Michael's desk, old but doing fine apparently. Jellie walked over and petted her. The cat stretched and yawned. Out back, Malachi was barking at something.

Michael's first novel, *Traveling with Pythagoras*, lay on the desk. He'd written it from the viewpoint of Pythagoras' mother, who, legend had it, accompanied her mystic son on his journeys through Egypt and Babylonia. It had done pretty well for a first novel, thirty thousand copies. She picked it up and read the inscription on the title page: "For Leonard Markham, who gave me a woman to love." Beside it lay Michael's second book, a nonfiction work dealing with philosophical issues in applied mathematics, *The Algebras of Illusion*.

Underneath the books was a manuscript. She

stared at the cover page—*The Tiger of Morning*—then laid the books on top of it again. She knew Michael carried a low, burning, and unspoken sense that he could never replace Dhiren. Maybe this was his way of getting it out of his system. Jellie figured he'd tell her about the manuscript when he was ready.

She opened the back screen door and looked out through the trees toward the trout stream fifty yards away. Her father was bent down along the shore, fussing with his tackle. Michael, wearing sunglasses, and the sleeves of his blue denim shirt rolled to the elbow, was wading deep water that surged around him, cigar clenched in his teeth, favoring the leg he'd injured in the motorcycle accident. He was fifty-three, and the leg was going to give him trouble the rest of his life. She held her breath for an instant when he stumbled and nearly fell, but he caught himself on a boulder in midstream.

He straightened up and began his backcasts. Jellie Markham leaned against the door frame and watched him, remembering what Chitra had said about high plumage and southern winds, about warrior-poets and motorcycle men. And she smiled, shook her head, and began laughing softly to herself. "God help us all." She changed out of her India clothing and walked down toward the stream in an old sweater, jeans, and hiking boots. Malachi saw her and came running, bouncing and barking. Leonard Markham heard the dog and looked up, put his hand high above his head, and waved to her. Behind him, water sprayed jewellike off Michael Tillman's fly line as he reached back in the last sunlight of a blue, mountain evening.

Acknowledgments

Thanks to the usual suspects—Georgia Ann, Rachael, Carol, Shirley, Gary and Kathe, Susan, J.R., Linda, Mike, Bill, and Pam—who are kind enough to read various drafts of what I write and offer comment. And thanks also to Maureen Egen and the rest of the folks at Warner Books for their patience with a wandering man. The standard disclaimer is in effect: my work is better because of these people, the weaknesses are mine. And, of course, thanks to the Aaron Priest Literary Agency and all the readers out there who make this curious, reclusive life of words and imagination possible.

RJW
Cedar Falls, Iowa
January 28, 1993

THE BRIDGES
OF MADISON
COUNTY

For the peregrines

The Beginning

There are songs that come free from the blue-eyed grass, from the dust of a thousand country roads. This is one of them. In late afternoon, in the autumn of 1989, I'm at my desk, looking at a blinking cursor on the computer screen before me, and the telephone rings.

On the other end of the wire is a former Iowan named Michael Johnson. He lives in Florida now. A friend from Iowa has sent him one of my books. Michael Johnson has read it; his sister, Carolyn, has read it; and they have a story in which they think I might be interested. He is circumspect, refusing to say anything about the story, except

The Beginning

that he and Carolyn are willing to travel to Iowa to talk with me about it.

That they are prepared to make such an effort intrigues me, in spite of my skepticism about such offers. So I agree to meet with them in Des Moines the following week. At a Holiday Inn near the airport, the introductions are made, awkwardness gradually declines, and the two of them sit across from me, evening coming down outside, light snow falling.

They extract a promise: If I decide not to write the story, I must agree never to disclose what transpired in Madison County, Iowa, in 1965 or other related events that followed over the next twenty-four years. All right, that's reasonable. After all, it's their story, not mine.

So I listen. I listen hard, and I ask hard questions. And they talk. On and on they talk. Carolyn cries openly at times, Michael struggles not to. They show me documents and magazine clippings and a set of journals written by their mother, Francesca.

Room service comes and goes. Extra coffee is ordered. As they talk, I begin to see the images. First you must have the images, then come the words. And I begin to hear the words, begin to see them on pages of writing. Sometime just after midnight, I agree to write the story—or at least attempt it.

Their decision to make this information public

The Beginning

was a difficult one for them. The circumstances are delicate, involving their mother and, more tangentially, their father. Michael and Carolyn recognized that coming forth with the story might result in tawdry gossip and unkind debasement of whatever memories people have of Richard and Francesca Johnson.

Yet in a world where personal commitment in all of its forms seems to be shattering and love has become a matter of convenience, they both felt this remarkable tale was worth the telling. I believed then, and I believe even more strongly now, they were correct in their assessment.

In the course of my research and writing, I asked to meet with Michael and Carolyn three more times. On each occasion, and without complaint, they traveled to Iowa. Such was their eagerness to make sure the story was told accurately. Sometimes we merely talked; sometimes we slowly drove the roads of Madison County while they pointed out places having a significant role in the story.

In addition to the help provided by Michael and Carolyn, the story as I tell it here is based on information contained in the journals of Francesca Johnson; research conducted in the northwestern United States, particularly Seattle and Bellingham, Washington; research carried out quietly in Madison County, Iowa; information gleaned from the

The Beginning

photographic essays of Robert Kincaid, assistance provided by magazine editors, detail supplied by manufacturers of photographic films and equipment, and long discussions with several wonderful elderly people in the county home at Barnesville, Ohio, who remembered Kincaid from his boyhood days.

In spite of the investigative effort, gaps remain. I have added a little of my own imagination in those instances, but only when I could make reasoned judgments flowing from the intimate familiarity with Francesca Johnson and Robert Kincaid I gained through my research. I am confident that I have come very close to what actually happened.

One major gap involves the exact details of a trip made across the northern United States by Kincaid. We knew he made this journey, based on a number of photographs that subsequently were published, a brief mention of it by Francesca Johnson in her journals, and handwritten notes he left with a magazine editor. Using these sources as my guide, I retraced what I believe was the path he took from Bellingham to Madison County in August of 1965. Driving toward Madison County at the end of my travels, I felt I had, in many ways, become Robert Kincaid.

Still, attempting to capture the essence of Kincaid was the most challenging part of my research and writing. He is an elusive figure. At times he seems rather ordinary. At other times ethereal, perhaps even spectral. In his work he was a consummate professional. Yet he saw himself as a peculiar kind of male animal becoming obsolete in a world given over to increasing amounts of organization. He once talked about the "merciless wail" of time in his head, and Francesca Johnson characterized him as living "in strange, haunted places, far back along the stems of Darwin's logic."

Two other intriguing questions are still unanswered. First, we have been unable to determine what became of Kincaid's photographic files. Given the nature of his work, there must have been thousands, probably hundreds of thousands, of photographs. These never have been recovered. Our best guess—and this would be consistent with the way he saw himself and his place in the world —is that he destroyed them prior to his death.

The second question deals with his life from 1975 to 1982. Very little information is available. We know he earned a sparse living as a portrait photographer in Seattle for several years and continued to photograph the Puget Sound area. Other than that, we have nothing. One interesting note is that all letters mailed to him by the Social Security Administration and Veterans Administration were marked "Return to Sender" in his handwriting and sent back.

Preparing and writing this book has altered my

world view, transformed the way I think, and, most of all, reduced my level of cynicism about what is possible in the arena of human relationships. Coming to know Francesca Johnson and Robert Kincaid as I have through my research, I find the boundaries of such relationships can be extended farther than I previously thought. Perhaps you will have the same experience in reading this story.

That will not be easy. In an increasingly callous world, we all exist with our own carapaces of scabbed-over sensibilities. Where great passion leaves off and mawkishness begins, I'm not sure. But our tendency to scoff at the possibility of the former and to label genuine and profound feelings as maudlin makes it difficult to enter the realm of gentleness required to understand the story of Francesca Johnson and Robert Kincaid. I know I had to overcome that tendency initially before I could begin writing.

If, however, you approach what follows with a willing suspension of disbelief, as Coleridge put it, I am confident you will experience what I have experienced. In the indifferent spaces of your heart, you may even find, as Francesca Johnson did, room to dance again.

Summer 1991

The Bridges of
Madison County

Robert Kincaid

On the morning of August 8, 1965, Robert Kincaid locked the door to his small two-room apartment on the third floor of a rambling house in Bellingham, Washington. He carried a knapsack full of photography equipment and a suitcase down wooden stairs and through a hallway to the back, where his old Chevrolet pickup truck was parked in a space reserved for residents of the building.

Another knapsack, a medium-size ice chest, two tripods, cartons of Camel cigarettes, a Thermos, and a bag of fruit were already inside. In the truck box was a guitar case. Kincaid arranged the knapsacks on the seat and put the cooler and tripods on the floor. He climbed into the truck box and wedged the guitar case and suitcase into a corner of the box, bracing them with a spare tire lying on its side and securing both cases to the tire with a length of clothesline rope. Under the worn spare he shoved a black tarpaulin.

He stepped in behind the wheel, lit a Camel, and went through his mental checklist: two hundred rolls of assorted film, mostly slow-speed Kodachrome; tripods; cooler; three cameras and five lenses; jeans and khaki slacks; shirts; wearing photo vest. Okay. Anything else he could buy on the road if he had forgotten it.

Kincaid wore faded Levi's, well-used Red Wing field boots, a khaki shirt, and orange suspenders. On his wide leather belt was fastened a Swiss Army knife in its own case.

He looked at his watch: eight-seventeen. The truck started on the second try, and he backed out, shifted gears, and moved slowly down the alley under hazy sun. Through the streets of Bellingham he went, heading south on Washington 11, running along the coast of Puget Sound for a few miles, then following the highway as it swung east a little before meeting U.S. Route 20.

Turning into the sun, he began the long, winding drive through the Cascades. He liked this country and felt unpressed, stopping now and then to make notes about interesting possibilities for future expeditions or to shoot what he called "memory snapshots." The purpose of these cursory photographs was to remind him of places he might want to visit again and approach more seriously. In late afternoon he turned north at Spokane, picking up U.S. Route 2, which would take him halfway across the northern United States to Duluth, Minnesota.

He wished for the thousandth time in his life that he had a dog, a golden retriever, maybe, for travels like this and to keep him company at home. But he was frequently away, overseas much of the time, and it would not be fair to the animal. Still, he thought about it anyway. In a few years he would be getting too old for the hard fieldwork. "I might get a dog then," he said to the coniferous green rolling by his truck window.

Drives like this always put him into a taking-stock mood. The dog was part of it. Robert Kincaid was as alone as it's possible to be—an only child, parents both dead, distant relatives who had lost track of him and he of them, no close friends.

He knew the names of the man who owned the corner market in Bellingham and the proprietor of the photographic store where he bought his supplies. He also had formal, professional relationships with several magazine editors. Other than that, he knew scarcely anyone well, nor they him. Gypsies make difficult friends for ordinary people, and he was something of a gypsy.

He thought about Marian. She had left him nine years ago after five years of marriage. He was fifty-two now; that would make her just under forty. Marian had dreams of becoming a musician, a folksinger. She knew all of the Weavers' songs and sang them pretty well in the coffeehouses of Seattle. When he was home in the old days, he drove her to gigs and sat in the audience while she sang.

His long absences—two or three months sometimes—were hard on the marriage. He knew that. She was aware of what he did when they decided to get married, and each of them had a vague sense that it could all be handled somehow. It couldn't. When he came home from photographing a story in Iceland, she was gone. The note read: "Robert, it didn't work out. I left you the Harmony guitar. Stay in touch."

He didn't stay in touch. Neither did she. He signed the divorce papers when they arrived a year later and caught a plane for Australia the next day. She had asked for nothing except her freedom.

At Kalispell, Montana, he stopped for the night, late. The Cozy Inn looked inexpensive, and was. He carried his gear into a room containing two table lamps, one of which had a burned-out bulb. Lying in bed, reading _The Green Hills of Africa_ and drinking a beer, he could smell the paper mills of Kalispell. In the morning he jogged for forty minutes, did fifty push-ups, and used his cameras as small hand weights to complete the routine.

Across the top of Montana he drove, into North Dakota and the spare, flat country he found as fascinating as the mountains or the sea. There was a kind of austere beauty to this place, and he stopped several times, set up a tripod, and shot some black-and-whites of old farm buildings. This landscape appealed to his minimalist leanings. The Indian reservations were depressing, for all of the reasons everybody knows and ignores. Those kinds of settlements were no better in northwestern Washington, though, or anywhere else he had seen them.

On the morning of August 14, two hours out of Duluth, he sliced northeast and took a back road up to Hibbing and the iron mines. Red dust floated in the air, and there were big machines and trains specially designed to haul the ore to freighters at Two Harbors on Lake Superior. He spent an afternoon looking around Hibbing and found it not to his liking, even if Bob Zimmerman-Dylan was from there originally.

The only song of Dylan's he had ever really cared for was "Girl from the North Country." He could play and sing that one, and he hummed the words to himself as he left behind the place with giant red holes in the earth. Marian had shown him some chords and how to handle basic arpeggios to accompany himself. "She left me with more than I left her," he said once to a boozy riverboat pilot in a place called McElroy's Bar, somewhere in the Amazon basin. And it was true.

The Superior National Forest was nice, real nice. Voyageur country. When he was young, he'd wished the old voyageur days were not over so he could become one. He drove by meadows, saw three moose, a red fox, and lots of deer. At a pond he stopped and shot some reflections on the water made by an odd-shaped tree branch. When he finished he sat on the running board of his truck, drinking coffee, smoking a Camel, and listening to the wind in the birch trees.

"It would be good to have someone, a woman," he thought, watching the smoke from his cigarette blow out over the pond. "Getting older puts you in that frame of mind." But with him gone so much, it would be tough on the one left at home. He'd already learned that.

When he was home in Bellingham, he occasionally dated the creative director for a Seattle advertising agency. He had met her while doing a corporate job. She was forty-two, bright, and a nice person, but he didn't love her, would never love her.

Sometimes they both got a little lonely, though, and would spend an evening together, going to a movie, having a few beers, and making pretty decent love later on. She'd been around—two marriages, worked as a waitress in several bars while attending college. Invariably, after they'd completed their lovemaking and were lying together, she'd tell him, "You're the best, Robert, no competition, nobody even close."

He supposed that was a good thing for a man to hear, but he was not all that experienced and had no way of knowing whether or not she was telling the truth anyway. But she did say something one time that haunted him: "Robert, there's a creature inside of you that I'm not good enough to bring out, not strong enough to reach. I sometimes have the feeling you've been here a long time, more than one lifetime, and that you've dwelt in private places none of the rest of us has even dreamed about. You frighten me, even though you're gentle with me. If I didn't fight to control myself with you, I feel like I might lose my center and never get back."

He knew in an obscure way what she was talking about. But he couldn't get his hands on it himself. He'd had these drifting kinds of thoughts, a wistful sense of the tragic combined with intense physical and intellectual power, even as a young boy growing up in a small Ohio town. When other kids were singing "Row, Row, Row Your Boat," he was learning the melody and English words to a French cabaret song.

He liked words and images. "Blue" was one of his favorite words. He liked the feeling it made on his lips and tongue when he said it. Words have physical feeling, not just meaning, he remembered thinking when he was young. He liked other words, such as "distant," "woodsmoke," "highway," "ancient," "passage," "voyageur," and "India" for how they sounded, how they tasted, and what they conjured up in his mind. He kept lists of words he liked posted in his room.

Then he joined the words into phrases and posted those as well:

Too close to the fire.

I came from the East with a small band of travelers.

The Bridges of Madison County

The constant chirping of those who would
save me and those who would sell me.

Talisman, Talisman, show me your secrets.
Helmsman, Helmsman, turn me for home.

Lying naked where blue whales swim.

She wished him steaming trains that left from
winter stations.

Before I became a man, I was an arrow—
long time ago.

Then there were the places whose names he liked: the Somali Current, the Big Hatchet Mountains, the Malacca Strait, and a long list of others. The sheets of paper with words and phrases and places eventually covered the walls of his room.

Even his mother noticed something different about him. He never spoke a word until he was three, then began talking in complete sentences, and he could read extremely well by five. In school he was an indifferent student, frustrating the teachers.

They looked at his IQ scores and talked to him about achievement, about doing what he was capable of doing, that he could become anything he wanted to become. One of his high school teachers wrote the following in an evaluation of him: "He believes that 'IQ tests are a poor way to judge people's abilities, failing as they do to account for magic, which has its own importance, both by itself and as a complement to logic.' I suggest a conference with his parents."

His mother met with several teachers. When the teachers talked about Robert's quietly recalcitrant behavior in light of his abilities, she said, "Robert lives in a world of his own making. I know he's my son, but I sometimes have the feeling that he came not from my husband and me, but from another place to which he's trying to return. I appreciate your interest in him, and I'll try once more to encourage him to do better in school."

But he had been content to read all the adventure and travel books in the local library and kept to himself otherwise, spending days along the river that ran through the edge of town, ignoring proms and football games and other things that bored him. He fished and swam and walked and lay in long grass listening to distant voices he fancied only he could hear. "There are wizards out there," he used to say to himself. "If you're quiet and open enough to hear them, they're out there." And he wished he had a dog to share these moments.

There was no money for college. And no desire for it, either. His father worked hard and was good to his mother and him, but the job in a valve factory didn't leave much for other things, including the care of a dog. He was eighteen when his father died, so with the Great Depression bearing down hard, he enlisted in the army as a way of supporting his mother and himself. He stayed there four years, but those four years changed his life.

In the mysterious way that military minds work, he was assigned to a job as photographer's assistant, though he had no idea of even how to load a camera. But in that work, he discovered his profession. The technical details were easy for him. Within a month he was not only doing the darkroom work for two of the staff photographers, but also was allowed to shoot simple projects himself.

One of the photographers, Jim Peterson, liked him and spent extra time showing him the subtleties of photography. Robert Kincaid checked out photo books and art books from the Fort Monmouth town library and studied them. Early on, he particularly liked the French impressionists and Rembrandt's use of light.

Eventually he began to see that light was what he photographed, not objects. The objects merely were the vehicles for reflecting the light. If the light was good, you could always find something to photograph. The 35-millimeter camera was beginning to emerge then, and he purchased a used

Leica at a local camera store. He took it down to Cape May, New Jersey, and spent a week of his leave there photographing life along the shore.

Another time he rode a bus to Maine and hitch-hiked up the coast, caught the dawn mail boat out of Isle au Haut from Stonington, and camped, then took a ferry across the Bay of Fundy to Nova Scotia. He began keeping notes of his camera settings and places he wanted to visit again. When he came out of the army at twenty-two, he was a pretty decent shooter and found work in New York assisting a well-known fashion photographer.

The female models were beautiful; he dated a few and fell partially in love with one before she moved to Paris and they drifted apart. She had said to him: "Robert, I don't know who or what you are for sure, but please come visit me in Paris." He told her he would, meant it when he said it, but never got there. Years later when he was doing a story on the beaches of Normandy, he found her name in the Paris book, called, and they had coffee at an outdoor cafe. She was married to a cinema director and had three children.

He couldn't get very keen on the idea of fashion. People threw away perfectly good clothes or hastily had them made over according to the instructions of European fashion dictators. It seemed dumb to him, and he felt lessened doing the photography. "You are what you produce," he said as he left this work.

His mother died during his second year in New York. He went back to Ohio, buried her, and sat before a lawyer, listening to the reading of the will. There wasn't much. He didn't expect there would be anything. But he was surprised to find his parents had accumulated a little equity in the tiny house on Franklin Street where they had lived all their married lives. He sold the house and bought first-class equipment with the money. As he paid the camera salesman, he thought of the years his father had worked for those dollars and the plain life his parents had led.

Some of his work began to appear in small magazines. Then *National Geographic* called. They had seen a calendar shot he had taken out on Cape May. He talked with them, got a minor assignment, executed it professionally, and was on his way.

The military asked him back in 1943. He went with the marines and slogged his way up South Pacific beaches, cameras swinging from his shoulders, lying on his back, photographing the men coming off amphibious landing craft. He saw the terror on their faces, felt it himself. Saw them cut in two by machine-gun fire, saw them plead to

God and their mothers for help. He got it all, survived, and never became hooked on the so-called glory and romance of war photography.

Coming out of the service in 1945, he called *National Geographic*. They were ready for him, anytime. He bought a motorcycle in San Francisco, ran it south to Big Sur, made love on a beach with a cellist from Carmel, and turned north to explore Washington. He liked it there and decided to make it his base.

Now, at fifty-two, he was still watching the light. He had been to most of the places posted on his boyhood walls and marveled he actually was there when he visited them, sitting in the Raffles Bar, riding up the Amazon on a chugging riverboat, and rocking on a camel through the Rajasthani desert.

The Lake Superior shore was as nice as he'd heard it was. He marked down several locations for future reference, took some shots to jog his memory later on, and headed south along the Mississippi River toward Iowa. He'd never been to Iowa but was taken with the hills of the northeast part along the big river. Stopping in the little town of Clayton, he stayed at a fisherman's motel and spent two mornings shooting the towboats and an afternoon on a tug at the invitation of a pilot he met in a local bar.

Cutting over to U.S. Route 65, he went through

Des Moines early on a Monday morning, August 16, 1965, swung west at Iowa 92, and headed for Madison County and the covered bridges that were supposed to be there, according to _National Geographic_. They were there all right; the man in the Texaco station said so and gave him directions, just fairish directions, to all seven.

The first six were easy to find as he mapped out his strategy for photographing them. The seventh, a place called Roseman Bridge, eluded him. It was hot, he was hot, Harry—his truck—was hot, and he was wandering around on gravel roads that seemed to lead nowhere except to the next gravel road.

In foreign countries, his rule of thumb was, "Ask three times." He had discovered that three responses, even if they all were wrong, gradually vectored you in to where you wanted to go. Maybe twice would be enough here.

A mailbox was coming up, sitting at the end of a lane about one hundred yards long. The name on the box read "Richard Johnson, RR 2." He slowed down and turned up the lane, looking for guidance.

When he pulled into the yard, a woman was sitting on the front porch. It looked cool there, and she was drinking something that looked even cooler. She came off the porch toward him. He stepped from the truck and looked at her, looked closer, and then closer still. She was lovely, or had been at one time, or could be again. And immediately he began to feel the old clumsiness he always suffered around women to whom he was even faintly attracted.

Francesca

Deep autumn was birthday time for Francesca, and cold rain swept against her frame house in the south Iowa countryside. She watched the rain, looked through it toward the hills along Middle River, thinking of Richard. He had died on a day like this, eight years ago, from something with a name she would rather not remember. But Francesca thought of him now and his sturdy kindness, his steady ways, and the even life he had given her.

The children had called. Neither of them could make it home again this year for her birthday, though it was her sixty-seventh. She understood, as she always did. Always had. Always would. They were both in midcareer, running hard, managing a hospital, teaching students, Michael getting into his second marriage, Carolyn struggling with her first. Secretly she was glad they never seemed to arrange a visit on her birthday; she had her own ceremonies reserved for that day.

This morning her friends from Winterset had stopped by with a birthday cake. Francesca made coffee, while the talk ran to grandchildren and the town, to Thanksgiving and what to get for Christmas for whom. The quiet laughter and the rise and fall of conversation from the living room were comforting in their familiarity and reminded Francesca of one small reason why she had stayed here after Richard's death.

Michael had touted Florida, Carolyn New England. But she had remained in the hills of south Iowa, on the land, keeping her old address for a special reason, and she was glad she had done that.

Francesca had watched them leave at lunchtime. They drove their Buicks and Fords down the lane, turned onto the paved county road, and headed toward Winterset, wiper blades pushing aside the rain. They were good friends, though they would never understand what lay inside of her, would not understand even if she told them.

Her husband had said she would find good friends, when he brought her here after the war, from Naples. He said, "Iowans have their faults, but one of them is not lack of caring." And that was true, is true.

She had been twenty-five when they met—out of the university for three years, teaching at a private school for girls, wondering about her life. Most of the young Italian men were dead or injured or in POW camps or broken by the fighting. Her affair with Niccolo, a professor of art at the university, who painted all day and took her on wild, reckless tours of the underside of Naples at night, had been over for a year, done in finally by the unceasing disapproval of her traditional parents.

She wore ribbons in her black hair and clung to her dreams. But no handsome sailors disembarked looking for her, no voices came up to her window from the streets below. The hard press of reality brought her to the recognition that her choices were constrained. Richard offered a reasonable alternative: kindness and the sweet promise of America.

She had studied him in his soldier's uniform as

they sat in a cafe in the Mediterranean sunlight, saw him looking earnestly at her in his midwestern way, and came to Iowa with him. Came to have his children, to watch Michael play football on cold October nights, to take Carolyn to Des Moines for her prom dresses. She exchanged letters with her sister in Naples several times each year and had returned there twice, when each of her parents had died. But Madison County was home now, and she had no longing to go back again.

The rain stopped in midafternoon, then resumed its ways just before evening. In the twilight, Francesca poured a small glass of brandy and opened the bottom drawer of Richard's rolltop desk, the walnut piece that had passed down through three generations of his family. She took out a manila envelope and brushed her hand across it slowly, as she did each year on this day.

The postmark read "Seattle, WA, Sep 12 '65." She always looked at the postmark first. That was part of the ritual. Then to the address written in longhand: "Francesca Johnson, RR 2, Winterset, Iowa." Next the return address, carelessly scrabbled in the upper left: "Box 642, Bellingham, Washington." She sat in a chair by the window, looked at the addresses, and concentrated, for contained in them was the movement of his hands, and she wanted to bring back the feel of those hands on her twenty-two years ago.

When she could feel his hands touching her, she opened the envelope, carefully removed three letters, a short manuscript, two photographs, and a complete issue of *National Geographic* along with clippings from other issues of the magazine. There, in gray light fading, she sipped her brandy, looking over the rim of her glass to the handwritten note clipped on the typed manuscript pages. The letter was on his stationery, simple stationery that said only "Robert Kincaid, Writer-Photographer" at the top in discreet lettering.

September 10, 1965

Dear Francesca,

Enclosed are two photographs. One is the shot I took of you in the pasture at sunrise. I hope you like it as much as I do. The other is of Roseman Bridge before I removed your note tacked to it.

I sit here trolling the gray areas of my mind for every detail, every moment, of our time together. I ask myself over and over, "What happened to me in Madison County, Iowa?" And

I struggle to bring it together. That's why I wrote the little piece, "Falling from Dimension Z," I have enclosed, as a way of trying to sift through my confusion.

I look down the barrel of a lens, and you're at the end of it. I begin work on an article, and I'm writing about you. I'm not even sure how I got back here from Iowa. Somehow the old truck brought me home, yet I barely remember the miles going by.

A few weeks ago, I felt self-contained, reasonably content. Maybe not profoundly happy, maybe a little lonely, but at least content. All of that has changed.

It's clear to me now that I have been moving toward you and you toward me for a long time. Though neither of us was aware of the other before we met, there was a kind of mindless certainty humming blithely along beneath our ignorance that ensured we would come together. Like two solitary birds flying the great prairies by celestial reckoning, all of these years and lifetimes we have been moving toward one another.

The road is a strange place. Shuffling along, I looked up and you were there walking across the grass toward my truck on an August day. In retrospect, it seems inevitable—it could not have been any other way—a case of what I call the high probability of the improbable.

So here I am walking around with another person inside of me. Though I think I put it better the day we parted when I said there is a third person we have created from the two of us. And I am stalked now by that other entity.

Somehow, we must see each other again. Any place, anytime.

Call me if you ever need anything or simply want to see me. I'll be there, pronto. Let me know if you can come out here sometime—anytime. I can arrange plane fare, if that's a problem. I'm off to southeast India next week, but I'll be back in late October.

I Love You,
Robert

P. S., The photo project in Madison County turned out fine. Look for it in NG next year. Or tell me if you want me to send a copy of the issue when it's published.

Francesca Johnson set her brandy glass on the wide oak windowsill and stared at an eight-by-ten black-and-white photograph of herself. Sometimes it was hard for her to remember how she had looked then, twenty-two years ago. In tight faded jeans, sandals, and a white T-shirt, her hair blowing in the morning wind as she leaned against a fence post.

Through the rain, from her place by the window, she could see the post where the old fence still circumscribed the pasture. When she rented out the land, after Richard died, she stipulated the pasture must be kept intact, left untouched, even though it was empty now and had turned to meadow grass.

The first serious lines were just beginning to show on her face in the photograph. His camera had found them. Still, she was pleased with what she saw. Her hair was black, and her body was full and warm, filling out the jeans just about right. Yet it was her face at which she stared. It was the face of a woman desperately in love with the man taking the picture.

She could see him clearly also, down the flow of her memory. Each year she ran all of the images through her mind, meticulously, remembering everything, forgetting nothing, imprinting all of it, forever, like tribesmen passing down an oral history through the generations. He was tall and thin and hard, and he moved like the grass itself, without effort, gracefully. His silver-gray hair hung well below his ears and nearly always looked disheveled, as if he had just come in from a long sea voyage through a stiff wind and had tried to brush it into place with his hands.

His narrow face, high cheekbones, and hair falling over his forehead set off light blue eyes that seemed never to stop looking for the next photograph. He had smiled at her, saying how fine and warm she looked in early light, asked her to lean against the post, and then moved around her in a wide arc, shooting from knee level, then standing, then lying on his back with the camera pointed up at her.

She had been slightly embarrassed at the amount of film he used but pleased by the amount of attention he paid to her. She hoped none of the neighbors were out early on their tractors. Though on that particular morning she hadn't cared too much about neighbors and what they thought.

He shot, loaded film, changed lenses, changed cameras, shot some more, and talked quietly to her as he worked, always telling her how good she looked to him and how much he loved her. "Francesca, you're incredibly beautiful." Sometimes he stopped and just stared at her, through her, around her, inside of her.

Her nipples were clearly outlined where they pressed against the cotton T-shirt. She had been strangely unconcerned about that, about being naked under the shirt. More, she was glad of it and was warmed knowing that he could see her breasts so clearly down his lenses. Never would she have dressed this way around Richard. He would not have approved. Indeed, before meeting Robert Kincaid, she would not have dressed this way any-time.

Robert had asked her to arch her back ever so slightly, and he had whispered then, "Yes, yes, that's it, stay there." That was when he had taken the photograph at which she now stared. The light was perfect, that's what he had said—"cloudy bright" was his name for it—and the shutter clicked steadily as he moved around her.

He was lithe; that was the word she had thought of while watching him. At fifty-two his body was all lean muscle, muscle that moved with the kind of intensity and power that comes only to men who work hard and take care of themselves. He told her he had been a combat photographer in the Pacific, and Francesca could imagine him coming up smoke-drenched beaches with the marines, cameras banging against him, one to his eye, the shutter almost on fire with the speed of his picture taking.

She looked at the picture again, studied it. I did look good, she thought, smiling to herself at the mild self-admiration. "I never looked that good

The Bridges of Madison County

before or after. It was him." And she took another sip of brandy while the rain climbed up and rode hard on the back of November wind.

Robert Kincaid was a magician of sorts, who lived within himself in strange, almost threatening places. Francesca had sensed as much immediately on a hot, dry Monday in August 1965, when he stepped out of his truck onto her driveway. Richard and the children were at the Illinois State Fair, exhibiting the prize steer that received more attention than she did, and she had the week to herself.

She had been sitting on the front porch swing, drinking iced tea, casually watching the dust spiral up from under a pickup coming down the county road. The truck was moving slowly, as if the driver were looking for something, stopped just short of her lane, then turned up it toward the house. Oh, God, she had thought. Who's this?

She was barefoot, wearing jeans and a faded blue workshirt with the sleeves rolled up, shirttail out. Her long black hair was fastened up by a tortoiseshell comb her father had given her when she left the old country. The truck rolled up the lane and stopped near the gate to the wire fence surrounding the house.

Francesca stepped off the porch and walked unhurriedly through the grass toward the gate.

And out of the pickup came Robert Kincaid, looking like some vision from a never-written book called *An Illustrated History of Shamans*.

His tan military-style shirt was tacked down to his back with perspiration; there were wide, dark circles of it under his arms. The top three buttons were undone, and she could see tight chest muscles just below the plain silver chain around his neck. Over his shoulders were wide orange suspenders, the kind worn by people who spent a lot of time in wilderness areas.

He smiled. "I'm sorry to bother you, but I'm looking for a covered bridge out this way, and I can't find it. I think I'm temporarily lost." He wiped his forehead with a blue bandanna and smiled again.

His eyes looked directly at her, and she felt something jump inside. The eyes, the voice, the face, the silver hair, the easy way he moved his body, old ways, disturbing ways, ways that draw you in. Ways that whisper to you in the final moment before sleep comes, when the barriers have fallen. Ways that rearrange the molecular space between male and female, regardless of species.

The generations must roll, and the ways whisper only of that single requirement, nothing more. The power is infinite, the design supremely elegant. The ways are unswerving, their goal is clear.

The Bridges of Madison County

The ways are simple; we have made them seem complicated. Francesca sensed this without knowing she was sensing it, sensed it at the level of her cells. And there began the thing that would change her forever.

A car went past on the road, trailing dust behind it, and honked. Francesca waved back at Floyd Clark's brown arm sticking out of his Chevy and turned back to the stranger. "You're pretty close. The bridge is only about two miles from here." Then, after twenty years of living the close life, a life of circumscribed behavior and hidden feelings demanded by a rural culture, Francesca Johnson surprised herself by saying, "I'll be glad to show it to you, if you want."

Why she did that, she never had been sure. A young girl's feelings rising like a bubble through water and bursting out, maybe, after all these years. She was not shy, but not forward, either. The only thing she could ever conclude was that Robert Kincaid had drawn her in somehow, after only a few seconds of looking at him.

He was obviously taken aback, slightly, by her offer. But he recovered quickly and with a serious look on his face said he'd appreciate that. From the back steps she picked up the cowboy boots she wore for farm chores and walked out to his truck, following him around to the passenger side.

"Just take me a minute to make room for you;

lots of gear 'n' stuff in here." He mumbled mostly to himself as he worked, and she could tell he was a little flustered, and a little shy about the whole affair.

He was rearranging canvas bags and tripods, a Thermos bottle and paper sacks. In the back of the pickup were an old tan Samsonite suitcase and a guitar case, both dusty and battered, both tied to a spare tire with a piece of clothesline rope.

The door of the truck swung shut, banging him in the rear as he mumbled and sorted and stuffed paper coffee cups and banana peels into a brown grocery bag that he tossed into the truck box when he was finished. Finally he removed a blue-and-white ice chest and put that in the back as well. In faded red paint on the green truck door was printed "Kincaid Photography, Bellingham, Washington."

"Okay, I think you can squeeze in there now." He held the door, closed it behind her, then went around to the driver's side and with a peculiar, animal-like grace stepped in behind the wheel. He looked at her, just a quick glance, smiled slightly, and said, "Which way?"

"Right." She motioned with her hand. He turned the key, and the out-of-tune engine ground to a start. Along the lane toward the road, bouncing, his long legs working the pedals automatically, old Levi's running down over leather-laced, brown field boots that had seen lots of foot miles go by.

He leaned over and reached into the glove compartment, his forearm accidentally brushing across her lower thigh. Looking half out the windshield and half into the compartment, he took out a business card and handed it to her. "Robert Kincaid, Writer-Photographer." His address was printed there, along with a phone number.

"I'm out here on assignment for *National Geographic*," he said. "You familiar with the magazine?"

"Yes." Francesca nodded, thinking, Isn't everybody?

"They're doing a piece on covered bridges, and Madison County, Iowa, apparently has some interesting ones. I've located six of them, but I guess there's at least one more, and it's supposed to be out in this direction."

"It's called Roseman Bridge," said Francesca over the noise of the wind and tires and engine. Her voice sounded strange, as if it belonged to someone else, to a teenage girl leaning out of a window in Naples, looking far down city streets toward the trains or out at the harbor and thinking of distant lovers yet to come. As she spoke, she watched the muscles in his forearm flex when he shifted gears.

Two knapsacks were beside her. The flap of one

was closed, but the other was folded back, and she could see the silver-colored top and black back of a camera sticking out. The end of a film box, "Kodachrome II, 25. 36 Exposures," was taped to the camera back. Stuffed behind the packs was a tan vest with many pockets. Out of one pocket dangled a thin cord with a plunger on the end.

Behind her feet were two tripods. They were badly scratched, but she could read part of the worn label on one: "Gitzo." When he had opened the glove box, she noticed it was crammed with notebooks, maps, pens, empty film canisters, loose change, and a carton of Camel cigarettes.

"Turn right at the next corner," she said. That gave her an excuse to glance at the profile of Robert Kincaid. His skin was tanned and smooth and shiny with sweat. He had nice lips, for some reason she had noticed that right away. And his nose was like that she had seen on Indian men during a vacation the family had taken out west when the children were young.

He wasn't handsome, not in any conventional sense. Nor was he homely. Those words didn't seem to apply to him. But there was something, something about him. Something very old, something slightly battered by the years, not in his appearance, but in his eyes.

On his left wrist was a complicated-looking watch with a brown, sweat-stained leather band.

A silver bracelet with some intricate scrollwork clung to his right wrist. It needed a good rubbing with silver polish, she thought, then chastised herself for being caught up in the trivia of small-town life she had silently rebelled against through the years.

Robert Kincaid pulled a pack of cigarettes from his shirt pocket, shook one halfway out, and offered it to her. For the second time in five minutes, she surprised herself and took the cigarette. What am I doing? she thought. She had smoked years ago but gave it up under the steady thump of criticism from Richard. He shook out another one, put it between his lips, and flicked a gold Zippo lighter into flame, holding it toward her while he kept his eyes on the road.

She cupped her hands around the lighter to hold the wind in abeyance and touched his hand to steady it against the bouncing of the truck. It took only an instant for her to light the cigarette, but that was long enough to feel the warmth of his hand and the tiny hairs along the back of it. She leaned back and he swung the lighter toward his own cigarette, expertly forming his wind cup, taking his hands off the steering wheel for no more than a second.

Francesca Johnson, farmer's wife, rested against the dusty truck seat, smoked the cigarette, and pointed. "There it is, just around the curve." The old bridge, peeling red in color, tilting slightly from all the years, sat across a small stream.

Robert Kincaid had smiled then. He quickly looked at her and said, "It's great. A sunrise shot." He stopped a hundred feet from the bridge and got out, taking the open knapsack with him. "I'm going to do a little reconnaissance for a few minutes, do you mind?" She shook her head and smiled back.

Francesca watched him walk up the country road, taking a camera from the knapsack and then slinging the bag over his left shoulder. He had done that thousands of times, that exact movement. She could tell by the fluidity of it. As he walked, his head never stopped moving, looking from side to side, then at the bridge, then at the trees behind the bridge. Once he turned and looked back at her, his face serious.

In contrast with the local folks, who fed on gravy and potatoes and red meat, three times a day for some of them, Robert Kincaid looked as if he ate nothing but fruit and nuts and vegetables. Hard, she thought. He looks hard, physically. She noticed how small his rear was in his tight jeans —she could see the outlines of his billfold in the left pocket and the bandanna in the right one— and how he seemed to move over the ground with unwasted motion.

It was quiet. A redwing blackbird sat on fence

wire and looked in at her. A meadowlark called from the roadside grass. Nothing else moved in the white sun of August.

Just short of the bridge, Robert Kincaid stopped. He stood there for a moment, then squatted down, looking through the camera. He walked to the other side of the road and did the same thing. Then he moved into the cover of the bridge and studied the beams and floor planks, looked at the stream below through a hole in the side.

Francesca snuffed out her cigarette in the ashtray, swung open the door, and put her boots on the gravel. She glanced around to make sure none of her neighbors' cars were coming and walked toward the bridge. The sun was a hammer in late afternoon, and it looked cooler inside the bridge. She could see his silhouette at the other end until he disappeared down the incline toward the stream.

Inside, she could hear pigeons burbling softly in their nests under the eves and put the palm of her hand on the side planking, feeling the warmth. Graffiti was scrawled on some of the planks: "Jimbo—Denison, Iowa." "Sherry + Dubby." "Go Hawks!" The pigeons kept on burbling softly.

Francesca peeked through a crack between two of the side planks, down toward the stream where Robert Kincaid had gone. He was standing on a rock in the middle of the little river, looking toward the bridge, and she was startled to see him wave. He jumped back to the bank and moved easily up the steep grade. She kept watching the water until she sensed his boots on the bridge flooring.

"It's real nice, real pretty here," he said, his voice reverberating inside the covered bridge.

Francesca nodded. "Yes, it is. We take these old bridges for granted around here and don't think much about them."

He walked to her and held out a small bouquet of wildflowers, black-eyed Susans. "Thanks for the guided tour." He smiled softly. "I'll come back at dawn one of these days and get my shots." She felt something inside of her again. Flowers. Nobody gave her flowers, even on special occasions.

"I don't know your name," he said. She realized then that she had not told him and felt dumb about that. When she did, he nodded and said, "I caught the smallest trace of an accent. Italian?"

"Yes. A long time ago."

The green truck again. Along the gravel roads with the sun lowering itself. Twice they met cars, but it was nobody Francesca knew. In the four minutes it took to reach the farm, she drifted, feeling unraveled and strange. More of Robert Kincaid, writer-photographer, that's what she wanted. She wanted to know more and clutched the flowers on her lap, held them straight up, like a schoolgirl coming back from an outing.

The blood was in her face. She could feel it. She hadn't done anything or said anything, but she felt as if she had. The truck radio, indistinguishable almost in the roar of road and wind, carried a steel guitar song, followed by the five o'clock news.

He turned the truck up the lane. "Richard is your husband?" He had seen the mailbox.

"Yes," said Francesca, slightly short of breath. Once her words started, they kept on coming. "It's pretty hot. Would you like an ice tea?"

He looked over at her. "If it's all right, I sure would."

"It's all right," she said.

She directed him—casually, she hoped—to park the pickup around behind the house. What she didn't need was for Richard to come home and have one of the neighbor men say, "Hey, Dick, havin' some work done at the place? Saw a green pickup there last week. Knew Frannie was home so I did'n bother to check on it."

Up broken cement steps to the back porch door. He held the door for her, carrying his camera knapsacks. "Awful hot to leave the equipment in the truck," he had said when he pulled them out.

A little cooler in the kitchen, but still hot. The

collie snuffled around Kincaid's boots, then went out on the back porch and flopped down while Francesca removed ice from metal trays and poured sun tea from a half-gallon glass jug. She knew he was watching her as he sat at the kitchen table, long legs stretched in front of him, brushing his hair with both hands.

"Lemon?"

"Yes, please."

"Sugar?"

"No, thanks."

The lemon juice dribbled slowly down the side of a glass, and he saw that, too. Robert Kincaid missed little.

Francesca set the glass before him. Put her own on the other side of the Formica-topped table and her bouquet in water, in an old jelly glass with renderings of Donald Duck on it. Leaning against the counter, she balanced on one leg, bent over, and took off a boot. Stood on her bare foot and reversed the process for the other boot.

He took a small drink of tea and watched her. She was about five feet six, fortyish or a little older, pretty face, and a fine, warm body. But there were pretty women everywhere he traveled. Such physical matters were nice, yet, to him, intelligence and passion born of living, the ability to move and be moved by subtleties of the mind and spirit, were what really counted. That's why he found most young women unattractive, regardless of their exterior beauty. They had not lived long enough or hard enough to possess those qualities that interested him.

But there was something in Francesca Johnson that did interest him. There was intelligence; he could sense that. And there was passion, though he couldn't quite grasp what that passion was directed toward or if it was directed at all.

Later, he would tell her that in ways undefinable, watching her take off her boots that day was one of the most sensual moments he could remember. Why was not important. That was not the way he approached his life. "Analysis destroys wholes. Some things, magic things, are meant to stay whole. If you look at their pieces, they go away." That's what he had said.

She sat at the table, one leg curled under her, and pulled back strands of hair that had fallen over her face, refastening them with the tortoiseshell comb. Then, remembering, she rose and went to the end cupboard, took down an ashtray, and set it on the table where he could reach it.

With that tacit permission, he pulled out a pack of Camels and held it toward her. She took one and noticed it was slightly wet from his heavy perspiring. Same routine. He held the gold Zippo,

Robert James Waller

she touched his hand to steady it, felt his skin with her fingertips, and sat back. The cigarette tasted wonderful, and she smiled.

"What is it you do, exactly—I mean with the photography?"

He looked at his cigarette and spoke quietly. "I'm a contract shooter—uh, photographer—for *National Geographic*, part of the time. I get ideas, sell them to the magazine, and do the shoot. Or they have something they want done and contact me. Not a lot of room for artistic expression, it's a pretty conservative publication. But the pay is decent. Not great, but decent, and steady. The rest of the time I write and photograph on my own hook and send pieces to other magazines. If things get tough, I do corporate work, though I find that awfully confining.

"Sometimes I write poetry, just for myself. Now and then I try to write a little fiction, but I don't seem to have a feeling for it. I live north of Seattle and work around that area quite a bit. I like shooting the fishing boats and Indian settlements and landscapes.

"The *Geographic* work often keeps me at a location for a couple of months, particularly for a major piece on something like part of the Amazon or the North African desert. Ordinarily I fly to an assignment like this and rent a car. But I felt like driving through some places and scouting them out for future reference. I came down along Lake Superior; I'll go back through the Black Hills. How about you?"

Francesca hadn't expected him to ask. She stammered for a moment. "Oh, gosh, nothing like you do. I got my degree in comparative literature. Winterset was having trouble finding teachers when I arrived here in 1946, and the fact that I was married to a local man who was a veteran made me acceptable. So I picked up a teaching certificate and taught high school English for a few years. But Richard didn't like the idea of me working. He said he could support us, and there was no need for it, particularly when our two children were growing. So I stopped and became a farm wife full-time. That's it."

She noticed his iced tea was almost gone and poured him some more from the jug.

"Thanks. How do you like it here in Iowa?"

There was a moment of truth in this. She knew it. The standard reply was, "Just fine. It's quiet. The people are real nice."

She didn't answer immediately. "Could I have another cigarette?" Again the pack of Camels, again the lighter, again touching his hand, lightly. Sunlight walked across the back porch floor and onto the dog, who got up and moved out of sight. Francesca, for the first time, looked into the eyes of Robert Kincaid.

Robert James Waller

"I'm supposed to say, 'Just fine. It's quiet. The people are real nice.' All of that's true, mostly. It is quiet. And the people *are* nice, in certain ways. We all help each other out. If someone gets sick or hurt, the neighbors pitch in and pick corn or harvest oats or do whatever needs to be done. In town, you can leave your car unlocked and let your children run without worrying about them. There are a lot of good things about the people here, and I respect them for those qualities.

"But"—she hesitated, smoked, looked across the table at Robert Kincaid—"it's not what I dreamed about as a girl." The confession, at last. The words had been there for years, and she had never said them. She had said them now to a man with a green pickup truck from Bellingham, Washington.

He said nothing for a moment. Then: "I scribbled something in my notebook the other day for future use, just had the idea while driving along; that happens a lot. It goes like this: 'The old dreams were good dreams; they didn't work out, but I'm glad I had them.' I'm not sure what that means, but I'll use it somewhere. So I think I kind of know how you feel."

Francesca smiled at him then. For the first time, she smiled warm and deep. And the gambler's instincts took over. "Would you like to stay for supper? My family's away, so I don't have too much on hand, but I can figure out something."

"Well, I get pretty tired of grocery stores and restaurants. That's for sure. So if it's not too much bother, I'd like that."

"You like pork chops? I could fix that with some vegetables from the garden."

"Just the vegetables would be fine for me. I don't eat meat. Haven't for years. No big deal, I just feel better that way."

Francesca smiled again. "Around here that point of view would not be popular. Richard and his friends would say you're trying to destroy their livelihood. I don't eat much meat myself, I'm not sure why, I just don't care for it. But every time I try a meatless supper on the family, there are howls of rebellion. So I've pretty much given up trying. It'll be fun figuring out something different for a change."

"Okay, but don't go to a lot of trouble on my account. Listen, I've got a bunch of film in my cooler. I need to dump out the melted ice water and organize things a bit. It'll take me a little while." He stood up and drank the last of his tea.

She watched him go through the kitchen doorway, across the porch, and into the yard. He didn't let the screen door bang like everyone else did but instead shut it gently. Just before he went out, he squatted down to pet the collie, who acknowledged the attention with several sloppy licks along his arms.

Upstairs, Francesca ran a quick bath and, while drying off, peered over the top of the cafe curtain toward the farmyard. His suitcase was open, and he was washing himself, using the old hand pump. She should have told him he could shower in the house if he wanted. She had meant to, balked for a moment at the level of familiarity that implied to her, and then, floating around in her own confusion, forgot to say anything.

But Robert Kincaid had washed up under worse conditions. Out of buckets of rancid water in tiger country, out of his canteen in the desert. In her farmyard, he had stripped to the waist and was using his dirty shirt as a combination washcloth and towel. "A towel," she scolded herself. "At least a towel, I could have done that for him."

His razor caught the sunlight, where it lay on cement beside the pump, and she watched him soap his face and shave. He was—there's the word again, she thought—hard. He wasn't big-bodied, a little over six feet, a little toward thin. But he had large shoulder muscles for his size, and his belly was flat as a knife blade. He didn't look however old he was, and he didn't look like the local men with too much gravy over biscuits in the morning.

During the last shopping trip to Des Moines, she had bought new perfume—Wind Song—and she used it now, sparingly. What to put on? It didn't seem right for her to dress up too much, since he was still in his working clothes. Long-sleeved white shirt, sleeves rolled to just below the elbows, a clean pair of jeans, sandals. The gold hoop earrings Richard said made her look like a hussy and a gold bracelet. Hair pulled back with a clip, hanging down her back. That felt right.

When she came into the kitchen, he was sitting there with his knapsacks and cooler, wearing a clean khaki shirt, with the orange suspenders running over it. On the table were three cameras and five lenses, and a fresh package of Camels. The cameras all said "Nikon" on them. So did the black lenses, short ones and middling ones and a longer one. The equipment was scratched, dented in places. But he handled it carefully, yet casually, wiping and brushing and blowing.

He looked up at her, serious face again, shy face. "I have some beer in the cooler. Like one?"

"Yes, that would be nice."

He took out two bottles of Budweiser. When he lifted the lid, she could see clear plastic boxes with film stacked like cordwood in them. There were four more bottles of beer besides the two he removed.

Francesca slid open a drawer to look for an opener. But he said, "I've got it." He took the Swiss Army knife from its case on his belt and flicked out the bottle opener on it, using it expertly.

He handed her a bottle and raised his in a half salute: "To covered bridges in the late afternoon or, better yet, on warm, red mornings." He grinned.

Francesca said nothing but smiled softly and raised her bottle a little, hesitantly, awkwardly. A strange stranger, flowers, perfume, beer, and a toast on a hot Monday in late summer. It was almost more than she could deal with.

"There was somebody a long time ago who was thirsty on an August afternoon. Whoever it was studied their thirst, rigged up some stuff, and invented beer. That's where it came from, and a problem was solved." He was working on a camera, almost talking to it as he tightened a screw on its top with a jeweler's screwdriver.

"I'm going out to the garden for a minute. I'll be right back."

He looked up. "Need help?"

She shook her head and walked past him, feeling his eyes on her hips, wondering if he watched her all the way across the porch, guessing that he did.

She was right. He watched her. Shook his head and looked again. Watched her body, thought of the intelligence he knew she possessed, wondered about the other things he sensed in her. He was drawn to her, fighting it back.

The Bridges of Madison County

The garden was in shade now. Francesca moved through it with a dishpan done in cracked white enamel. She gathered carrots and parsley, some parsnips and onions and turnips.

When she entered the kitchen, Robert Kincaid was repacking the knapsacks, neatly and precisely, she noticed. Everything obviously had its place and always was placed in its place. He had finished his beer and opened two more, even though she was not quite done with hers. She tilted back her head and finished the first one, handing him the empty bottle.

"Can I do something?" he asked.

"You can bring in the watermelon from the porch and a few potatoes from the bucket out there."

He moved so easily that she was amazed at how quickly he went to the porch and returned, melon under his arm, four potatoes in his hands. "Enough?"

She nodded, thinking how ghostlike he seemed. He set them on the counter beside the sink where she was cleaning the garden vegetables and returned to his chair, lighting a Camel as he sat down.

"How long will you be here?" she asked, looking down at the vegetables she was working on.

"I'm not sure. This is a slow time for me, and

my deadline for the bridge pictures is still three weeks away. As long as it takes to get it right, I guess. Probably about a week."

"Where are you staying? In town?"

"Yes. A little place with cabins. Something-or-other Motor Court. I just checked in this morning. Haven't even unloaded my gear yet."

"That's the only place to stay, except for Mrs. Carlson's; she takes in roomers. The restaurants will be a disappointment, though, particularly for someone with your eating habits."

"I know. It's an old story. But I've learned to make do. This time of year it's not so bad; I can find fresh produce in the stores and at stands along the road. Bread and a few other things, and I make it work, approximately. It's nice to be invited out like this, though. I appreciate it."

She reached along the counter and flipped on a small radio, one with only two dials and tan cloth covering the speakers. "With time in my pocket, and the weather on my side . . ." a voice sang, guitars chunking along underneath. She kept the volume low.

"I'm pretty good at chopping vegetables," he offered.

"Okay, there's the cutting board, a knife's in the drawer right below it. I'm going to fix a stew, so kind of cube the vegetables."

He stood two feet from her, looking down,

cutting and chopping the carrots and turnips, parsnips and onions. Francesca peeled potatoes into
the sink, aware of being so close to a strange man.
She had never thought of peeling potatoes as having little slanting feelings connected with it.

"You play the guitar? I saw the case in your
truck."

"A little bit. It keeps me company, not too much
more than that. My wife was an early folkie, way
before the music became popular, and she got me
going on it."

Francesca had stiffened slightly at the word *wife*.
Why, she didn't know. He had a right to be married, but somehow it didn't fit him. She didn't want
him to be married.

"She couldn't stand the long shoots when I'd be
gone for months. I don't blame her. She pulled
out nine years ago. Divorced me a year later. We
never had children, so it wasn't complicated. Took
one guitar, left the el cheapo with me."

"You hear from her?"

"No, never."

That was all he said. Francesca didn't push it.
But she felt better, selfishly, and wondered again
why she should care one way or the other.

"I've been to Italy, twice," he said. "Where you
from, originally?"

"Naples."

"Never made it there. I was in the north once,

doing some shooting along the River Po. Then again for a piece on Sicily."

Francesca peeled potatoes, thinking of Italy for a moment, conscious of Robert Kincaid beside her.

Clouds had moved up in the west, splitting the sun into rays that splayed in several directions. He looked out the window above the sink and said, "God light. Calendar companies love it. So do religious magazines."

"Your work sounds interesting," Francesca said. She felt a need to keep neutral conversation going.

"It is. I like it a lot. I like the road, and I like making pictures."

She noticed he'd said "making" pictures. "You make pictures, not take them?"

"Yes. At least that's how I think of it. That's the difference between Sunday snapshooters and someone who does it for a living. When I'm finished with that bridge we saw today, it won't look quite like you expect. I'll have made it into something of my own, by lens choice, or camera angle, or general composition, and most likely by some combination of all of those.

"I don't just take things as given; I try to make them into something that reflects my personal consciousness, my spirit. I try to find the poetry in the image. The magazine has its own style and demands, and I don't always agree with the editors' taste; in fact, most of the time I don't. And that bothers them, even though they decide what goes in and what gets left out. I guess they know their readership, but I wish they'd take a few more chances now and then. I tell them that, and it bothers them.

"That's the problem in earning a living through an art form. You're always dealing with markets, and markets—mass markets—are designed to suit average tastes. That's where the numbers are. That's the reality, I guess. But, as I said, it can become pretty confining. They let me keep the shots they don't use, so at least I have my own private files of stuff I like.

"And, once in a while, another magazine will take one or two, or I can write an article on a place I've been and illustrate it with something a little more daring than *National Geographic* prefers.

"Sometime I'm going to do an essay called 'The Virtues of Amateurism' for all of those people who wish they earned their living in the arts. The market kills more artistic passion than anything else. It's a world of safety out there, for most people. They want safety, the magazines and manufacturers give them safety, give them homogeneity, give them the familiar and comfortable, don't challenge them.

"Profit and subscriptions and the rest of that stuff dominate art. We're all getting lashed to the great wheel of uniformity.

"The marketing people are always talking about something called 'consumers.' I have this image of a fat little man in baggy Bermuda shorts, a Hawaiian shirt, and a straw hat with beer-can openers dangling from it, clutching fistfuls of dollars."

Francesca laughed quietly, thinking about safety and comfort.

"But I'm not complaining too much. Like I said, the traveling is good, and I like fooling with cameras and being out of doors. The reality is not exactly what the song started out to be, but it's not a bad song."

Francesca supposed that, for Robert Kincaid, this was everyday talk. For her, it was the stuff of literature. People in Madison County didn't talk this way, about these things. The talk was about weather and farm prices and new babies and funerals and government programs and athletic teams. Not about art and dreams. Not about realities that kept the music silent, the dreams in a box.

He finished chopping vegetables. "Anything else I can do?"

She shook her head. "No, it's about under control."

He sat at the table again, smoking, taking a drink of beer now and then. She cooked, sipping on her beer between tasks. She could feel the alcohol, even this small amount of it. On New

The Bridges of Madison County

Year's Eve, at the Legion Hall, she and Richard would have some drinks. Other than that, not much, and there seldom was liquor in the house, except for a bottle of brandy she had bought once in some vague spasm of hope for romance in their country lives. The bottle was still unopened.

Vegetable oil, one and one-half cups of vegetables. Cook until light brown. Add flour and mix well. Add water, a pint of it. Add remaining vegetables and seasonings. Cook slowly, about forty minutes.

With the cooking under way, Francesca sat across from him once again. Modest intimacy descended upon the kitchen. It came, somehow, from the cooking. Fixing supper for a stranger, with him chopping turnips and, therefore, distance, beside you, removed some of the strangeness. And with the loss of strangeness, there was space for intimacy.

He pushed the cigarettes toward her, the lighter on top of the package. She shook one out, fumbled with the lighter, felt clumsy. It wouldn't catch. He smiled a little, carefully took the lighter from her hand, and flipped the flint wheel twice before it caught. He held it, she lit her cigarette. Around men she usually felt graceful in comparison to them. Not around Robert Kincaid, though.

A white sun had turned big red and lay just over the corn fields. Through the kitchen window she could see a hawk riding the early evening updrafts. The seven o'clock news and market summary were on the radio. And Francesca looked across the yellow Formica toward Robert Kincaid, who had come a long way to her kitchen. A long way, across more than miles.

"It already smells good," he said, pointing toward the stove. "It smells . . . quiet." He looked at her.

"Quiet? Could something smell quiet?" She was thinking about the phrase, asking herself. He was right. After the pork chops and steaks and roasts she cooked for the family, this was quiet cooking. No violence involved anywhere down the food chain, except maybe for pulling up the vegetables. The stew cooked quietly and smelled quiet. It was quiet here in the kitchen.

"If you don't mind, tell me a little about your life in Italy." He was stretched out on the chair, his right leg crossed over his left at the ankles.

Silence bothered her around him, so she talked. Told him about her growing years, the private school, the nuns, her parents—housewife, bank manager. About standing along the sea wall as a teenager and watching ships from all over the world. About the American soldiers that came later. About meeting Richard in a cafe where she and some girlfriends were drinking coffee. The war had disrupted lives, and they wondered if they would ever get married. She was silent about Niccolo.

He listened, saying nothing, nodding in understanding occasionally. When she finally paused, he said, "And you have children, did you say?"

"Yes. Michael is seventeen. Carolyn is sixteen. They both go to school in Winterset. They're in 4-H; that's why they're at the Illinois State Fair. Showing Carolyn's steer.

"Something I've never been able to adapt to, to understand, is how they can lavish such love and care on the animals and then see them sold for slaughter. I don't dare say anything about it, though. Richard and his friends would be down on me in a flash. But there's some kind of cold, unfeeling contradiction in that business."

She felt guilty mentioning Richard's name. She hadn't done anything, anything at all. Yet she could feel guilt, a guilt born of distant possibilities. And she wondered how to manage the end of the evening and if she had gotten herself into something she couldn't handle. Maybe Robert Kincaid would just leave. He seemed pretty quiet, nice enough, even a little bashful.

As they talked on, the evening turned blue, light fog brushing the meadow grass. He opened two more beers for them while Francesca's stew cooked, quietly. She rose and dropped dumplings into boiling water, turned, and leaned against the sink, feeling warm toward Robert Kincaid from Bellingham, Washington. Hoping he wouldn't leave too early.

He ate two helpings of the stew with quiet good manners and told her twice how fine it was. The watermelon was perfect. The beer was cold. The evening was blue. Francesca Johnson was forty-five years old, and Hank Snow sang a train song on KMA, Shenandoah, Iowa.

Ancient Evenings, Distant Music

Now what? thought Francesca. Supper over, sitting there.

He took care of it. "How about a walk out in the meadow? It's cooling down a little." When she said yes, he reached into a knapsack and pulled out a camera, draping the strap over his shoulder.

Kincaid pushed open the back porch door and held it for her, followed her out, then shut it gently. They went down the cracked sidewalk, across the graveled farmyard, and onto the grass east of the machine shed. The shed smelled like warm grease.

When they came to the fence, she held down the barbed wire with one hand and stepped over it, feeling the dew on her feet around the thin sandal straps. He executed the same maneuver, easily swinging his boots over the wire.

"Do you call this a meadow or a pasture?" he asked.

"Pasture, I guess. The cattle keep the grass short. Watch out for their leavings." A moon nearly full was coming up the eastern sky, which had turned azure with the sun just under the horizon. On the road below, a car rocketed past, loud muffler. The Clark boy. Quarterback on the Winterset team. Dated Judy Leverenson.

It had been a long time since she had taken a walk like this. After supper, which was always at five, there was the television news, then the evening programs, watched by Richard and sometimes by the children when they had finished their homework. Francesca usually read in the kitchen —books from the Winterset library and the book club she belonged to, history and poetry and fiction—or sat on the front porch in good weather. The television bored her.

When Richard would call, "Frannie, you've got to see this!" she'd go in and sit with him for a while. Elvis always generated such a summons. So did the Beatles when they first appeared on *The Ed Sullivan Show*. Richard looked at their hair and kept shaking his head in disbelief and disapproval.

For a short time, red streaks cut across part of the sky. "I call that 'bounce,' " Robert Kincaid said, pointing upward. "Most people put their cameras away too soon. After the sun goes down, there's often a period of really nice light and color in the sky, just for a few minutes, when the sun is below the horizon but bounces its light off the sky."

Francesca said nothing, wondering about a man to whom the difference between a pasture and a meadow seemed important, who got excited about sky color, who wrote a little poetry but not much fiction. Who played the guitar, who earned his living by images and carried his tools in knapsacks. Who seemed like the wind. And moved like it. Came from it, perhaps.

He looked upward, hands in his Levi's pockets, camera hanging against his left hip. "The silver apples of the moon/The golden apples of the sun." His midrange baritone said the words like that of a professional actor.

She looked over at him. "W. B. Yeats, 'The Song of Wandering Ængus.' "

"Right. Good stuff, Yeats. Realism, economy, sensuousness, beauty, magic. Appeals to my Irish heritage."

Robert James Waller

He had said it all, right there in five words. Francesca had labored to explain Yeats to the Winterset students but never got through to most of them. She had picked Yeats partly because of what Kincaid had just said, thinking all of those qualities would appeal to teenagers whose glands were pounding like the high school marching band at football halftimes. But the bias against poetry they had picked up, the view of it as a product of unsteady masculinity, was too much even for Yeats to overcome.

She remembered Matthew Clark looking at the boy beside him and then forming his hands as if to cup them over a woman's breasts when she read, "The golden apples of the sun." They had snickered, and the girls in the back row with them blushed.

They would live with those attitudes all their lives. That's what had discouraged her, knowing that, and she felt compromised and alone, in spite of the outward friendliness of the community. Poets were not welcome here. The people of Madison County liked to say, compensating for their own self-imposed sense of cultural inferiority, "This is a good place to raise kids." And she always felt like responding, "But is it a good place to raise adults?"

Without any conscious plan, they had walked slowly into the pasture a few hundred yards, made a loop, and were headed back toward the house. Darkness came about them as they crossed the fence, with him pushing down the wire for her this time.

She remembered the brandy. "I have some brandy. Or would you like some coffee?"

"Is the possibility of both open?" His words came out of the darkness. She knew he was smiling.

As they came into the circle inscribed on grass and gravel by the yard light, she answered, "Of course," hearing the sound of something in her voice that worried her. It was the sound of easy laughter in the cafes of Naples.

It was difficult finding two cups without some kind of chip on them. Though she was sure that chipped cups were part of his life, she wanted perfect ones this time. The brandy glasses, two of them back in the cupboard, turned upside down, had never been used, like the brandy. She had to stretch on her tiptoes to reach them and was aware of her wet sandals and the jeans stretched tight across her bottom.

He sat on the same chair he had used before and watched her. The old ways. The old ways coming into him again. He wondered how her hair would feel to his touch, how the curve of her back would fit his hand, how she would feel underneath him.

The old ways struggling against all that is learned, struggling against the propriety drummed in by centuries of culture, the hard rules of civilized man. He tried to think of something else, photography or the road or covered bridges. Anything but how she looked just now.

But he failed and wondered again how it would feel to touch her skin, to put his belly against hers. The questions eternal, and always the same. The goddamned old ways, fighting toward the surface. He pounded them back, pushed them down, lit a Camel, and breathed deeply.

She could feel his eyes on her constantly, though his watching was circumspect, never obvious, never intrusive. She knew that he knew brandy had never been poured into those glasses. And with his Irishman's sense of the tragic, she also knew he felt something about such emptiness. Not pity. That was not what he was about. Sadness, maybe. She could almost hear his mind forming the words:

> the bottle unopened,
> and glasses empty,
> she reached to find them,
> somewhere north of Middle River,
> in Iowa.
> I watched her with eyes

> *that had seen a Jivaro's Amazon*
> *and the Silk Road*
> *with caravan dust*
> *climbing behind me,*
> *reaching into unused*
> *spaces of Asian sky.*

As Francesca stripped the Iowa liquor seal from the top of the brandy bottle, she looked at her fingernails and wished they were longer and better cared for. Farm life did not permit long fingernails. Until now it hadn't mattered.

Brandy, two glasses, on the table. While she arranged the coffee, he opened the bottle and poured just the right amount into each glass. Robert Kincaid had dealt with after-dinner brandy before.

She wondered in how many kitchens, how many good restaurants, how many living rooms with subdued light he had practiced that small trade. How many sets of long fingernails had he watched delicately pointing toward him from the stems of brandy glasses, how many pairs of blue-round and brown-oval eyes had looked at him through foreign evenings, while anchored sailboats rocked offshore and water slapped against the quays of ancient ports?

The overhead kitchen light was too bright for coffee and brandy. Francesca Johnson, Richard

Johnson's wife, would leave it on. Francesca Johnson, a woman walking through after-supper grass and leafing through girlhood dreams, would turn it off. A candle was in order, but that would be too much. He might get the wrong idea. She put on the small light over the kitchen sink and turned off the overhead. It was still not perfect, but it was better.

He raised his glass to shoulder level and moved it toward her. "To ancient evenings and distant music." For some reason those words made her take a short, quick breath. But she touched her glass to his, and even though she wanted to say, "To ancient evenings and distant music," she only smiled a little.

They both smoked, saying nothing, drinking brandy, drinking coffee. A pheasant called from the fields. Jack, the collie, barked twice out in the yard. Mosquitoes tested the window screen near the table, and a single moth, circuitous of thought yet sure of instinct, was goaded by the sink light's possibilities.

It was still hot, no breeze, some humidity now. Robert Kincaid was perspiring mildly, his top two shirt buttons undone. He was not looking at her directly, though she sensed his peripheral vision could find her, even as he seemed to stare out the window. In the way he was turned, she could see the top of his chest through the open buttons of his shirt and small beads of moisture lying there upon his skin.

Francesca was feeling good feelings, old feelings, poetry and music feelings. Still, it was time for him to go, she thought. Nine fifty-two on the clock above the refrigerator. Faron Young on the radio. Tune from a few years back: "The Shrine of St. Cecilia." Roman martyr of the third century A.D., Francesca remembered that. Patron saint of music and the blind.

His glass was empty. Just as he swung around from looking out the window, Francesca picked up the brandy bottle by the neck and gestured with it toward the empty glass. He shook his head. "Roseman Bridge at dawn. I'd better get going."

She was relieved. But she sank in disappointment. She turned around inside of herself. Yes, please leave. Have some more brandy. Stay. Go. Faron Young didn't care about her feelings. Neither did the moth above the sink. She didn't know for sure what Robert Kincaid thought.

He stood, swung one knapsack onto his left shoulder, put the other on top of his cooler. She came around the table. His hand moved toward her, and she took it. "Thanks for the evening, the supper, the walk. They were all nice. You're a good person, Francesca. Keep the brandy toward the front of the cupboard, maybe it'll work out after a while."

He had known, just as she thought. But she wasn't offended by his words. He was talking about romance, and he meant it in the best possible way. She could tell by the softness of his language, the way he said the words. What she didn't know was that he wanted to shout at the kitchen walls, bas-reliefing his words in the plaster: "For Christ's sake, Richard Johnson, are you as big a fool as I think you must be?"

She followed him out to his truck and stood by while he put his gear into it. The collie came across the yard, sniffing around the truck. "Jack, come here," she whispered sharply, and the dog moved to sit by her, panting.

"Good-bye. Take care," he said, stopping by the truck door to look at her for a moment, straight at her. Then, in one motion, he was behind the wheel and shutting the door after him. He turned the old engine over, stomped at the accelerator, and it rattled into a start. He leaned out the window, grinning, "Tune-up required, I think."

He clutched it, backed up, shifted again, and headed across the yard under the light. Just before he reached the darkness of the lane, his left hand came out of the window and waved back at her. She waved, too, even though she knew he couldn't see it.

As the truck moved down the lane, she jogged over and stood in shadow, watching the red lights rising and falling with the bumps. Robert Kincaid turned left on the main road toward Winterset, while heat lightning cut the summer sky and Jack slumbered toward the back porch.

After he left, Francesca stood before the bureau mirror, naked. Her hips flared only a little from the children, her breasts were still nice and firm, not too large, not too small, belly slightly rounded. She couldn't see her legs in the mirror, but she knew they were still good. She should shave more often, but there didn't seem much point to it.

Richard was interested in sex only occasionally, every couple of months, but it was over fast, rudimentary and unmoving, and he didn't seem to care much about perfume or shaving or any of that. It was easy to get a little sloppy.

She was more of a business partner to him than anything else. Some of her appreciated that. But rustling yet within her was another person who wanted to bathe and perfume herself . . . and be taken, carried away, and peeled back by a force she could sense, but never articulate, even dimly within her mind.

She dressed again and sat at the kitchen table writing on half a sheet of plain paper. Jack followed her out to the Ford pickup and jumped in when she opened the door. He went to the passenger side and stuck his head out the window as she backed the truck out of the shed, looking over at her, then out the window again as she drove down the lane and turned right onto the county road.

Roseman Bridge was dark. But Jack loped on ahead, checking things out while she carried a flashlight from the truck. She tacked the note on the left side of the entrance to the bridge and went home.

The Bridges of Tuesday

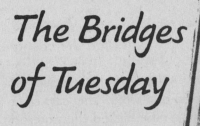

Robert Kincaid drove past Richard Johnson's mailbox an hour before dawn, alternately chewing on a Milky Way and taking bites from an apple, squeezing the coffee cup on the seat between his thighs to keep it from tipping over. He looked up at the white house standing in thin, late moonlight as he passed and shook his head at the stupidity of men, some men, most men. They could at least drink the brandy and not bang the screen door on their way out.

Francesca heard the out-of-tune pickup go by. She lay there in bed, having slept naked for the first time as far back as she could remember. She could imagine Kincaid, hair blowing in the wind curling through the truck window, one hand on the wheel, the other holding a Camel.

She listened as the sound of his wheels faded toward Roseman Bridge. And she began to roll words over in her mind from the Yeats poem: "I went out to the hazel wood, because a fire was in my head. . . ." Her rendering of it fell somewhere between that of teacher and supplicant.

He parked the truck well back from the bridge so it wouldn't interfere with his compositions. From the small space behind the seat, he took a knee-high pair of rubber boots, sitting on the running board to unlace his leather ones and pull on the others. One knapsack with straps over both shoulders, tripod slung over his left shoulder by its leather strap, the other knapsack in his right hand, he worked his way down the steep bank toward the stream.

The trick would be to put the bridge at an angle for some compositional tension, get a little of the stream at the same time, and miss the graffiti on the walls near the entrance. The telephone wires in the background were a problem, too, but that could be handled through careful framing.

He took out the Nikon loaded with Koda-chrome and screwed it onto the heavy tripod. The camera had the 24-millimeter lens on it, and he replaced that with his favorite 105-millimeter. Gray light in the east now, and he began to experiment with his composition. Move tripod two feet left, readjust legs sticking in muddy ground by the stream. He kept the camera strap wound over his left wrist, a practice he always followed when working around water. He'd seen too many cameras go into the water when tripods tipped over.

Red color coming up, sky brightening. Lower camera six inches, adjust tripod legs. Still not there. A foot more to the left. Adjust legs again. Level camera on tripod head. Set lens to f/8. Estimate depth of field, maximize it via hyperfocal technique. Screw in cable release on shutter button. Sun 40 percent above the horizon, old paint on the bridge turning a warm red, just what he wanted.

Light meter out of left breast pocket. Check it at f/8. One-second exposure, but the Kodachrome would hold well for that extreme. Look through the viewfinder. Fine-tune leveling of camera. He pushed the plunger of the shutter release and waited for a second to pass.

Just as he fired the shutter, something caught his eye. He looked through the viewfinder again. "What the hell is hanging by the entrance to the bridge?" he muttered. "A piece of paper. Wasn't there yesterday."

Tripod steady. Run up the bank with sun coming fast behind him. Paper neatly tacked to bridge. Pull it off, put tack and paper in vest pocket. Back toward the bank, down it, behind the camera. Sun 60 percent up.

Breathing hard from the sprint. Shoot again. Repeat twice for duplicates. No wind, grass still. Shoot three at two seconds and three at one-half second for insurance.

Click lens to f/16 setting. Repeat entire process. Carry tripod and camera to the middle of the stream. Get set up, silt from footsteps moving away behind. Shoot entire sequence again. New roll of Kodachrome. Switch lenses. Lock on the 24-millimeter, jam the 105 into a pocket. Move closer to the bridge, wading upstream. Adjust, level, light check, fire three, and bracket shots for insurance.

Flip the camera to vertical, recompose. Shoot again. Same sequence, methodical. There never was anything clumsy about his movements. All were practiced, all had a reason, the contingencies were covered, efficiently and professionally.

Up the bank, through the bridge, running with the equipment, racing the sun. Now the tough one. Grab second camera with faster film, sling both cameras around neck, climb tree behind bridge. Scrape arm on bark—"Dammit!"—keep climbing. High up now, looking down on the bridge at an angle with the stream catching sunlight.

Use spot meter to isolate bridge roof, then shady side of bridge. Take reading off water. Set camera for compromise. Shoot nine shots, bracketing, camera resting on vest wedged into tree crotch. Switch cameras. Faster film. Shoot a dozen more shots.

Down the tree. Down the bank. Set up tripod, reload Kodachrome, shoot composition similar to the first series only from the opposite side of the stream. Pull third camera out of bag. The old SP, rangefinder camera. Black-and-white work now. Light on bridge changing second by second.

After twenty intense minutes of the kind understood only by soldiers, surgeons, and photographers, Robert Kincaid swung his knapsacks into the truck and headed back down the road he had come along before. It was fifteen minutes to Hogback Bridge northwest of town, and he might just get some shots there if he hurried.

Dust flying, Camel lit, truck bouncing, past the white frame house facing north, past Richard Johnson's mailbox. No sign of her. What did you expect? She's married, doing okay. You're doing okay. Who needs those kinds of complications? Nice evening, nice supper, nice woman. Leave it at that. God, she's lovely, though, and there's something about her. Something. I have trouble taking my eyes away from her.

Francesca was in the barn doing chores when he barreled past her place. Noise from the livestock cloaked any sound from the road. And Robert Kincaid headed for Hogback Bridge, racing the years, chasing the light.

Things went well at the second bridge. It sat in a valley and still had mist rising around it when he arrived. The 300-millimeter lens gave him a big sun in the upper-left part of his frame, with the rest taking in the winding white rock road toward the bridge and the bridge itself.

Then into his viewfinder came a farmer driving a team of light brown Belgians pulling a wagon along the white road. One of the last of the old-style boys, Kincaid thought, grinning. He knew when the good ones came by and could already see what the final print would look like as he worked. On the vertical shots he left some light sky where a title could go.

When he folded up his tripod at eight thirty-five, he felt good. The morning's work had some keepers. Bucolic, conservative stuff, but nice and solid. The one with the farmer and horses might even be a cover shot; that's why he had left the space at the top of the frame, room for type, for a logo. Editors liked that kind of thoughtful craftsmanship. That's why Robert Kincaid got assignments.

He had shot all or part of seven rolls of film, emptied the three cameras, and reached into the lower-left pocket of his vest to get the other four. "Damn!" The thumbtack pricked his index finger. He had forgotten about dropping it in the pocket when he'd removed the piece of paper from Roseman Bridge. In fact, he had forgotten about the piece of paper. He fished it out, opened it, and read: "If you'd like supper again when 'white moths are on the wing,' come by tonight after you're finished. Anytime is fine."

He couldn't help smiling a little, imagining Francesca Johnson with her note and thumbtack driving through the darkness to the bridge. In five minutes he was back in town. While the Texaco man filled the tank and checked the oil ("Down half a quart"), Kincaid used the pay telephone at the station. The thin phone book was grimy from being thumbed by filling station hands. There were two listings under "R. Johnson," but one had a town address.

He dialed the rural number and waited. Francesca was feeding the dog on the back porch when the phone rang in the kitchen. She caught it at the front of the second ring: "Johnson's."

"Hi, this is Robert Kincaid."

Her insides jumped again, just as they had yesterday. A little stab of something that started in her chest and plunged to her stomach.

"Got your note. W. B. Yeats as a messenger and all that. I accept the invitation, but it might be late. The weather's pretty good, so I'm planning on shooting the—let's see, what's it called?—the Cedar Bridge . . . this evening. It could be after nine before I'm finished. Then I'll want to clean up a bit. So I might not be there until nine-thirty or ten. Is that all right?"

No, it wasn't all right. She didn't want to wait that long, but she only said, "Oh, sure. Get your work done, that's what's important. I'll fix something that'll be easy to warm up when you get here."

Then he added, "If you want to come along while I'm shooting, that's fine. It won't bother me. I could stop by for you about five-thirty."

Francesca's mind worked the problem. She wanted to go with him. But what if someone saw her? What could she say to Richard if he found out?

Cedar Bridge sat fifty yards upstream from and parallel to the new road and its concrete bridge. She wouldn't be too noticeable. Or would she? In less than two seconds, she decided. "Yes, I'd like that. But I'll drive my pickup and meet you there. What time?"

"About six. I'll see you then. Okay? 'Bye."

He spent the rest of the day at the local newspaper office looking through old editions. It was a pretty town, with a nice courthouse square, and he sat there on a bench in the shade at lunch with a small sack of fruit and some bread, along with a Coke from a cafe across the street.

When he had walked in the cafe and asked for a Coke to take out, it was a little after noon. Like an old Wild West saloon when the regional gunfighter appeared, the busy conversation had stopped for a moment while they all looked him over. He hated that, felt self-conscious, but it was the standard procedure in small towns. Someone new! Someone different! Who is he? What's he doing here?

"Somebody said he's a photographer. Said they saw him out by Hogback Bridge this morning with all sorts of cameras."

"Sign on his truck says he's from Washington, out west."

"Been over to the newspaper office all morning. Jim says he's looking through the papers for information on the covered bridges."

"Yeah, young Fischer at the Texaco said he stopped in yesterday and asked directions to all the covered bridges."

"What's he wanna know about them for, anyway?"

"And why in the world would anybody wanna take pictures of 'em? They're just all fallin' down in bad shape."

"Sure does have long hair. Looks like one of them Beatle fellows, or what is it they been callin' some of them other people? Hippies, ain't that it?" That brought laughter in the back booth and to the table next to it.

Kincaid got his Coke and left, the eyes still on him as he went out the door. Maybe he'd made a mistake in inviting Francesca, for her sake, not his. If someone saw her at Cedar Bridge, word would hit the cafe next morning at breakfast, relayed by young Fischer at the Texaco station after taking a handoff from the passerby. Probably quicker than that.

He'd learned never to underestimate the tele-communicative flash of trivial news in small towns. Two million children could be dying of hunger in the Sudan, and that wouldn't cause a bump in consciousness. But Richard Johnson's wife seen with a long-haired stranger—now that was news! News to be passed around, news to be chewed on, news that created a vague carnal lapping in the minds of those who heard it, the only such ripple they'd feel that year.

He finished his lunch and walked over to the

public phone on the parking of the courthouse. Dialed her number. She answered, slightly breathless, on the third ring. "Hi, it's Robert Kincaid again."

Her stomach tightened instantly as she thought, He can't come, he's called to say that.

"Let me be direct. If it's a problem for you to come out with me tonight, given the curiosity of small-town people, don't feel pressured to do it. Frankly, I could care less what they think of me around here, and one way or the other, I'll come by later. What I'm trying to say is that I might have made an error in inviting you, so don't feel compelled in any way to do it. Though I'd love to have you along."

She'd been thinking about just that since they'd talked earlier. But she had decided. "No, I'd like to see you do your work. I'm not worried about talk." She was worried, but something in her had taken hold, something to do with risk. Whatever the cost, she was going out to Cedar Bridge.

"Great. Just thought I'd check. See you later."

"Okay." He was sensitive, but she already knew that.

At four o'clock he stopped by his motel and did some laundry in the sink, put on a clean shirt, and tossed a second one in the truck, along with a pair of khaki slacks and brown sandals he'd picked up in India in 1962 while doing a story on the baby railroad up to Darjeeling. At a tavern he purchased two six-packs of Budweiser. Eight of the bottles, all that would fit, he arranged around his film in the cooler.

Hot, real hot again. The late afternoon sun in Iowa piled itself on top of its earlier damage, which had been absorbed by cement and brick and earth. It fairly blistered down out of the west.

The tavern had been dark and passably cool, with the front door open and big fans on the ceiling and one on a stand by the door whirring at about a hundred and five decibels. Somehow, though, the noise of the fans, the smell of stale beer and smoke, the blare of the jukebox, and the semihostile faces staring at him from along the bar made it seem hotter than it really was.

Out on the road the sunlight almost hurt, and he thought about the Cascades and fir trees and breezes along the Strait of San Juan de Fuca, near Kydaka Point.

Francesca Johnson looked cool, though. She was leaning against the fender of her Ford pickup where she had parked it behind some trees near the bridge. She had on the same jeans that fit her so well, sandals, and a white cotton T-shirt that did nice things for her body. He waved as he pulled up next to her truck.

"Hi. Nice to see you. Pretty hot," he said. Innocuous talk, around-the-edges-of-things talk.

That old uneasiness again, just being in the presence of a woman for whom he felt something. He never knew quite what to say, unless the talk was serious. Even though his sense of humor was well developed, if a little bizarre, he had a fundamentally serious mind and took things seriously. His mother had always said he was an adult at four years of age. That served him well as a professional. To his way of thinking, though, it did not serve him well around women such as Francesca Johnson.

"I wanted to watch you make your pictures. 'Shoot,' as you call it."

"Well, you're about to see it, and you'll find it pretty boring. At least other people generally do. It's not like listening to someone practice the piano, where you can be part of it. In photography, production and performance are separated by a long time span. Today I'm doing production. When the pictures appear somewhere, that's the performance. All you're going to see is a lot of fiddling around. But you're more than welcome. In fact, I'm glad you came."

She hung on those last four words. He needn't have said them. He could have stopped with "welcome," but he didn't. He was genuinely glad to see her; that was clear. She hoped the fact she was here implied something of the same to him.

"Can I help you in some way?" she asked as he pulled on his rubber boots.

"You can carry that blue knapsack. I'll take the tan one and the tripod."

So Francesca became a photographer's assistant. He had been wrong. There was much to see. There *was* a performance of sorts, though he was not aware of it. It was what she had noticed yesterday and part of what drew her toward him. His grace, his quick eyes, the muscles along his forearms working. Mostly the way he moved his body. The men she knew seemed cumbrous compared to him.

It wasn't that he hurried. In fact, he didn't hurry at all. There was a gazellelike quality about him, though she could tell he was strong in a supple way. Maybe he was more like a leopard than a gazelle. Yes. Leopard, that was it. He was not prey. Quite the reverse, she sensed.

"Francesca, give me the camera with the blue strap, please."

She opened the knapsack, feeling a little overcautious about the expensive equipment he handled so casually, and took out the camera. It said "Nikon" on the chrome plating of the viewfinder, with an "F" to the upper left of the name.

He was on his knees northeast of the bridge, with the tripod low. He held out his left hand without taking his eye from the viewfinder, and she gave him the camera, watching his hand close about the lens as he felt it touch him. He worked the plunger on the end of the cord she had seen hanging out of his vest yesterday. The shutter fired. He cocked the shutter and fired again.

He reached under the tripod head and un-screwed the camera on it, which was replaced by the one she had given him. While he fastened on the new one, he turned his head toward her and grinned. "Thanks, you're a first-class assistant." She flushed a little.

God, what was it about him! He was like some star creature who had drafted in on the tail of a comet and dropped off at the end of her lane. Why can't I just say "you're welcome"? she thought. I feel sort of slow around him, though it's nothing he does. It's me, not him. I'm just not used to being with people whose minds work as fast as his does.

He moved into the creek, then up the other bank. She went through the bridge with the blue knapsack and stood behind him, happy, strangely happy. There was energy here, a power of some kind in the way he worked. He didn't just wait for nature, he took it over in a gentle way, shaping it to his vision, making it fit what he saw in his mind.

He imposed his will on the scene, countering changes in light with different lenses, different films, a filter occasionally. He didn't just fight back, he dominated, using skill and intellect. Farmers also dominated the land with chemicals and bull-dozers. But Robert Kincaid's way of changing nature was elastic and always left things in their original form when he finished.

She looked at the jeans pulling themselves tight around his thigh muscles as he knelt down. At the faded denim shirt sticking to his back, gray hair over the collar of it. At how he sat back on his haunches to adjust a piece of equipment, and for the first time in ever so long, she grew wet between her legs just watching someone. When she felt it, she looked up at the evening sky and breathed deeply, listening to him quietly curse a jammed filter that wouldn't unscrew from a lens.

He crossed the creek again back toward the trucks, sloshing along in his rubber boots. Francesca went into the covered bridge, and when she came out the other end, he was crouched and pointing a camera toward her. He fired, cocked the shutter, and fired a second and third time as she walked toward him along the road. She felt herself grin in mild embarrassment.

"Don't worry." He smiled. "I won't use those anywhere without your permission. I'm finished here. Think I'll stop by the motel and rinse off a bit before coming out."

"Well, you can if you want. But I can spare a

towel or a shower or the pump or whatever," she said quietly, earnestly.

"Okay, you're on. Go ahead. I'll load the equipment in Harry—that's my truck—and be right there."

She backed Richard's new Ford out of the trees and took it up on the main road away from the bridge, turned right, and headed toward Winterset, where she cut southwest toward home. The dust was too thick for her to see if he was following, though once, coming around a curve, she thought she could see his lights a mile back, rattling along in the truck he called Harry.

It must have been him, for she heard his truck coming up the lane just after she arrived. Jack barked at first but settled down right away, muttering to himself, "Same guy as last night, okay, I guess." Kincaid stopped for a moment to talk with him.

Francesca stepped out of the back porch door. "Shower?"

"That'd be great. Show me the way."

She took him upstairs to the bathroom she had insisted Richard put in when the children were growing up. That was one of the few demands on which she had stood firm. She liked long hot baths in the evening, and she wasn't going to deal with teenagers tromping around in her private spaces.

Robert James Waller

Richard used the other bath, said he felt uncomfortable with all the feminine things in hers. "Too fussy," were his words.

The bath could be reached only through their bedroom. She opened the door to it and took out an assortment of towels and a washcloth from a cupboard under the sink. "Use anything you want." She smiled while biting her lower lip slightly.

"I might borrow some shampoo if you can spare it. Mine's at the motel."

"Sure. Take your pick." She set three different bottles on the counter, each partly used.

"Thanks." He tossed his fresh clothes on the bed, and Francesca noted the khakis, white shirt, and sandals. None of the local men wore sandals. A few of them from town had started wearing Bermuda shorts at the golf course, but not the farmers. And sandals . . . never.

She went downstairs and heard the shower come on. He's naked now, she thought, and felt funny in her lower belly.

Earlier in the day, after he called, she had driven the forty miles into Des Moines and went to the state liquor store. She was not experienced in this and asked a clerk about a good wine. He didn't know any more than she did, which was nothing. So she looked through the rows of bottles until she came across a label that read "Valpolicella." She remembered that from a long time ago. Dry,

The Bridges of Madison County

Italian red wine. She bought two bottles and another decanter of brandy, feeling sensual and worldly.

Next she looked for a new summer dress from a shop downtown. She found one, light pink with thin straps. It scooped down in back, did the same in front rather dramatically so the tops of her breasts were exposed, and gathered around her waist with a narrow sash. And new white sandals, expensive ones, flat-heeled, with delicate handiwork on the straps.

In the afternoon she fixed stuffed peppers, filling them with a mixture of tomato sauce, brown rice, cheese, and chopped parsley. Then came a simple spinach salad, corn bread, and an applesauce soufflé for dessert. All of it, except the soufflé, went into the refrigerator.

She hurried to shorten her dress to knee length. The Des Moines *Register* had carried an article earlier in the summer saying that was the preferred length this year. She always had thought fashion and all it implied pretty weird, people behaving sheeplike in the service of European designers. But the length suited her, so that's where the hem went.

The wine was a problem. People around here kept it in the refrigerator, though in Italy they never had done that. Yet it was too warm just to let it sit on the counter. Then she remembered the spring house. It was about sixty degrees in there in the summer, so she put the wine along the wall.

The shower shut off upstairs just as the phone rang. It was Richard, calling from Illinois.

"Everything okay?"

"Yes."

"Carolyn's steer'll be judged on Wednesday. Some other things we want to see next day. Be home Friday, late."

"All right, have a good time and drive carefully."

"Frannie, you sure you're okay? Sound a little strange."

"No, I'm fine. Just hot. I'll be better after my bath."

"Okay. Say hello to Jack for me."

"Yes, I'll do that." She glanced at Jack sprawled on the cement of the back porch floor.

Robert Kincaid came down the stairs and into the kitchen. White button-down—collar shirt, sleeves rolled up to just above the elbow, light khaki slacks, brown sandals, silver bracelet, top two buttons of his shirt open, silver chain. His hair was still damp and brushed neatly, with a part in the middle. And she marveled at the sandals.

"I'll just take my field duds out to the truck and bring in the gear for a little cleaning."

"Go ahead. I'm going to take a bath."

"Want a beer with your bath?"

The Bridges of Madison County

"If you have an extra one."

He brought in the cooler first, lifted out a beer for her, and opened it, while she found two tall glasses that would serve as mugs. When he went back to the truck for the cameras, she took her beer and went upstairs, noted that he had cleaned the tub, and then ran a high, warm bath for herself, settling in with her glass on the floor beside her while she shaved and soaped. He had been here just a few minutes before; she was lying where the water had run down his body, and she found that intensely erotic. Almost everything about Robert Kincaid had begun to seem erotic to her.

Something as simple as a cold glass of beer at bath time felt so elegant. Why didn't she and Richard live this way? Part of it, she knew, was the inertia of protracted custom. All marriages, all relationships, are susceptible to that. Custom brings predictability, and predictability carries its own comforts; she was aware of that, too.

And there was the farm. Like a demanding invalid, it needed constant attention, even though the steady substitution of equipment for human labor had made much of the work less onerous than it had been in the past.

But there was something more going on here. Predictability is one thing, fear of change is something else. And Richard was afraid of change, any kind of change, in their marriage. Didn't want to talk about it in general. Didn't want to talk about sex in particular. Eroticism was, in some way, dangerous business, unseemly to his way of thinking.

But he wasn't alone and really wasn't to blame. What was the barrier to freedom that had been erected out here? Not just on their farm, but in the rural culture. Maybe urban culture, for that matter. Why the walls and the fences preventing open, natural relationships between men and women? Why the lack of intimacy, the absence of eroticism?

The women's magazines talked about these matters. And women were starting to have expectations about their allotted place in the grander scheme of things, as well as what transpired in the bedrooms of their lives. Men such as Richard— most men, she guessed—were threatened by these expectations. In a way, women were asking for men to be poets and driving, passionate lovers at the same time.

Women saw no contradiction in that. Men did. The locker rooms and stag parties and pool halls and segregated gatherings of their lives defined a certain set of male characteristics in which poetry, or anything of subtlety, had no place. Hence, if eroticism was a matter of subtlety, an art form of its own, which Francesca knew it to be, it had no place in the fabric of their lives. So the distracting and conveniently clever dance that held them apart went on, while women sighed and turned their faces to the wall in the nights of Madison County.

There was something in the mind of Robert Kincaid that understood all of this, implicitly. She was sure of that.

Walking into the bedroom, toweling off, she noted it was a little after ten. Still hot, but the bath had cooled her. From the closet she took the new dress.

She pulled her long black hair behind her and fastened it with a silver clasp. Silver earrings, large hooped ones, and a loose-fitting silver bracelet she also had bought in Des Moines that morning.

The Wind Song perfume again. A little lipstick on the high-cheekboned, Latin face, the shade of pink even lighter than the dress. Her tan from working outdoors in shorts and midriff tops accented the whole outfit. Her slim legs came out from under the hem looking just fine.

She turned first one way, then the other, looking at herself in the bureau mirror. That's about as good as I can do, she thought. And then, pleased, said half out loud, "It's pretty good, though."

Robert Kincaid was working on his second beer and repacking the cameras when she came into the kitchen. He looked up at her.

"Jesus," he said softly. All of the feelings, all of the searching and reflecting, a lifetime of feeling and searching and reflecting, came together at that moment. And he fell in love with Francesca Johnson, farmer's wife, of Madison County, Iowa, long ago from Naples.

"I mean"—his voice was a little shaky, a little rough—"if you don't mind my boldness, you look stunning. Make-'em-run-around-the-block-howling-in-agony stunning. I'm serious. You're big-time elegant, Francesca, in the purest sense of that word."

His admiration was genuine, she could tell. She reveled in it, bathed in it, let it swirl over her and into the pores of her skin like soft oil from the hands of some deity somewhere who had deserted her years ago and had now returned.

And, in the catch of that moment, she fell in love with Robert Kincaid, photographer-writer, from Bellingham, Washington, who drove an old pickup truck named Harry.

Room to Dance Again

On that Tuesday evening in August of 1965, Robert Kincaid looked steadily at Francesca Johnson. She looked back in kind. From ten feet apart they were locked in to one another, solidly, intimately, and inextricably.

The telephone rang. Still looking at him, she did not move on the first ring, or the second. In the long silence after the second ring, and before the third, he took a deep breath and looked down at his camera bags.

With that she was able to move across the kitchen toward the phone hanging on the wall just behind his chair.

"Johnson's. . . . Hi, Marge. Yes, I'm fine. Thursday night?" She calculated: He said he'd be here a week, he came yesterday, this is only Tuesday. The decision to lie was an easy one.

She was standing by the door to the porch, phone in her left hand. He sat within touching distance, his back to her. She reached out with her right hand and rested it on his shoulder, in the casual way that some women have with men they care for. In only twenty-four hours she had come to care for Robert Kincaid.

"Oh, Marge, I'm tied up then. I'm going shopping in Des Moines. Good chance to get a lot of things done I've been putting off. You know, with Richard and the kids gone."

Her hand lay quietly upon him. She could feel the muscle running from his neck along his shoulder, just back of his collarbone. She was looking down on the thick gray hair, neatly parted. Saw how it drifted over his collar. Marge babbled on.

"Yes, Richard called a little while ago. . . . No, the judging's not till Wednesday, tomorrow. Richard said it'd be late Friday before they're home. Something they want to see on Thursday. It's a long drive, particularly in the stock truck. . . . No, football practice doesn't start for another week. Uh-huh, a week. At least that's what Michael said."

She was conscious of how warm his body felt through the shirt. The warmth came into her hand, moved up her arm, and from there spread through her to wherever it wanted to go, with no effort —indeed, with no control—from her. He was still, not wanting to make any noise that might cause Marge to wonder. Francesca understood this.

"Oh, yes, that was a man asking directions." As she guessed, Floyd Clark had gone right home and told his wife about the green pickup he had seen in the Johnsons' yard on his way by yesterday.

"A photographer? Gosh, I don't know. I didn't pay much attention. Could have been." The lies were coming easier now.

"He was looking for Roseman Bridge. . . . Is that right? Taking pictures of the old bridges, huh? Oh, well, that's harmless enough.

"Hippie?" Francesca giggled and watched Kincaid's head shake slowly back and forth. "Well, I'm not sure what a hippie looks like. This fellow was polite. He only stayed a minute or two and then was gone. . . . I don't know whether they have hippies in Italy, Marge. I haven't been there for eight years. Besides, like I said, I'm not sure I'd know a hippie if I saw one."

Marge was talking on about free love and communes and drugs she'd read about somewhere. "Marge, I was just getting ready to step into my bath when you called, so I'd better run before the water gets cold. . . . Okay, I'll call soon. 'Bye."

She disliked removing her hand from his shoulder, but there was no good excuse not to remove it. So she walked to the sink and turned on the radio. More country music. She adjusted the dial until the sound of a big band came on and left it there.

" 'Tangerine,' " he said.

"What?"

"The song. It's called 'Tangerine.' It's about an Argentinian woman." Talking around the edges of things again. Saying anything, anything. Fighting for time and the sense of it all, hearing somewhere back in his mind the faint click of a door shutting behind two people in an Iowa kitchen.

She smiled softly at him. "Are you hungry? I have supper ready whenever you want."

"It was a long, good day. I wouldn't mind another beer before I eat. Will you have one with me?" Stalling, looking for his center, losing it moment by moment.

She would. He opened two and set one on her side of the table.

Francesca was pleased with how she looked and

how she felt. Feminine. That's how she felt. Light and warm and feminine. She sat on the kitchen chair, crossed her legs, and the hem of her skirt rode up well above her right knee. Kincaid was leaning against the refrigerator, arms folded across his chest, Budweiser in his right hand. She was pleased that he noticed her legs, and he did.

He noticed all of her. He could have walked out on this earlier, could still walk. Rationality shrieked at him. "Let it go, Kincaid, get back on the road. Shoot the bridges, go to India. Stop in Bangkok on the way and look up the silk merchant's daughter who knows every ecstatic secret the old ways can teach. Swim naked with her at dawn in jungle pools and listen to her scream as you turn her inside out at twilight. Let go of this"—the voice was hissing now—"it's outrunning you."

But the slow street tango had begun. Somewhere it played, he could hear it, an old accordion. It was far back, or far ahead, he couldn't be sure. Yet it moved toward him steadily. And the sound of it blurred his criteria and funneled down his alternatives toward unity. Inexorably it did that, until there was nowhere left to go, except toward Francesca Johnson.

"We could dance, if you like. The music's pretty good for it," he said in that serious, shy way of his. Then he quickly tacked on his caveat: "I'm not much of a dancer, but if you'd like to, I can probably handle it in a kitchen."

Jack scratched at the porch door, wanting in. He could stay out.

Francesca blushed only a little. "Okay. But I don't dance much, either . . . anymore. I did as a young girl in Italy, but now it's just pretty much on New Year's Eve, and then only a little bit."

He smiled and put his beer on the counter. She rose, and they moved toward each other. "It's your Tuesday night dance party from WGN, Chicago," said the smooth baritone. "We'll be back after these messages."

They both laughed. Telephones and commercials. Something there was that kept inserting reality between them. They knew it without saying it.

But he had reached out and taken her right hand anyway, in his left. He leaned easily against the counter, legs crossed at the ankles, right one on top. She rested beside him, against the sink, and looked out the window near the table, feeling his slim fingers around her hand. There was no breeze, and the corn was growing.

"Oh, just a minute." She reluctantly removed her hand from his and opened the bottom right cupboard. From it she took two white candles she had bought in Des Moines that morning, along with a small brass holder for each candle. She put them on the table.

He walked over, tilted each one, and lit it, while she snapped off the overhead light. It was dark now, except for the small flames pointing straight upward, barely fluttering on a windless night. The plain kitchen had never looked this good.

The music started again. Fortunately for both of them, it was a slow rendition of "Autumn Leaves."

She felt awkward. So did he. But he took her hand, put an arm around her waist, she moved into him, and the awkwardness vanished. Somehow it worked in an easy kind of way. He moved his arm farther around her waist and pulled her closer.

She could smell him, clean and soaped and warm. A good, fundamental smell of a civilized man who seemed, in some part of himself, aboriginal.

"Nice perfume," he said, bringing their hands in to lie upon his chest, near his shoulder.

"Thank you."

They danced, slowly. Not moving very far in any direction. She could feel his legs against hers, their stomachs touching occasionally.

The song ended, but he held on to her, hummed the melody that had just played, and they stayed as they were until the next song began. He automatically led her into it, and the dance went on, while locusts complained about the coming of September.

She could feel the muscles of his shoulder through the light cotton shirt. He was real, more real than anything she'd ever known. He bent slightly to put his cheek against hers.

During the time they spent together, he once referred to himself as one of the last cowboys. They had been sitting on the grass by the pump out back. She didn't understand and asked him about it.

"There's a certain breed of man that's obsolete," he had said. "Or very nearly so. The world is getting organized, way too organized for me and some others. Everything in its place, a place for everything. Well, my camera equipment is pretty well organized, I admit, but I'm talking about something more than that. Rules and regulations and laws and social conventions. Hierarchies of authority, spans of control, long-range plans, and budgets. Corporate power; in 'Bud' we trust. A world of wrinkled suits and stick-on name tags.

"Not all men are the same. Some will do okay in the world that's coming. Some, maybe just a few of us, will not. You can see it in computers and robots and what they portend. In older worlds, there were things we could do, were designed to do, that nobody or no machine could do. We run fast, are strong and quick, aggressive and tough. We were given courage. We can throw spears long distances and fight in hand-to-hand combat.

"Eventually, computers and robots will run things. Humans will manage those machines, but that doesn't require courage or strength, or any characteristics like those. In fact, men are outliving their usefulness. All you need are sperm banks to keep the species going, and those are coming along now. Most men are rotten lovers, women say, so there's not much loss in replacing sex with science.

"We're giving up free range, getting organized, feathering our emotions. Efficiency and effectiveness and all those other pieces of intellectual artifice. And with the loss of free range, the cowboy disappears, along with the mountain lion and gray wolf. There's not much room left for travelers.

"I'm one of the last cowboys. My job gives me free range of a sort. As much as you can find nowadays. I'm not sad about it. Maybe a little wistful, I guess. But it's got to happen; it's the only way we'll keep from destroying ourselves. My contention is that male hormones are the ultimate cause of trouble on this planet. It was one thing to dominate another tribe or another warrior. It's quite another to have missiles. It's also quite another to have the power to destroy nature the way we're doing. Rachel Carson is right. So were John Muir and Aldo Leopold.

"The curse of modern times is the preponderance of male hormones in places where they can do long-term damage. Even if we're not talking about wars between nations or assaults on nature, there's still that aggressiveness that keeps us apart from each other and the problems we need to be working on. We have to somehow sublimate those male hormones, or at least get them under control.

"It's probably time to put away the things of childhood and grow up. Hell, I recognize it. I admit it. I'm just trying to make some good pictures and get out of life before I'm totally obsolete or do some serious damage."

Over the years, she had thought about what he'd said. It seemed right to her, somehow, on the surface of it. Yet the ways of him contradicted what he said. He had a certain plunging aggressiveness to him, but he seemed to be able to control it, to turn it on and then let go of it when he wanted. And that's what had both confused and attracted her—incredible intensity, but controlled, metered, arrowlike intensity that was mixed with warmth and no hint of meanness.

On that Tuesday night, gradually and without design, they had moved closer and closer together, dancing in the kitchen. Francesca was pressed close against his chest, and she wondered if he could feel her breasts through the dress and his shirt and was certain he could.

He felt so good to her. She wanted this to run forever. More old songs, more dancing, more of his body against hers. She had become a woman again. There was room to dance again. In a slow, unremitting way, she was turning for home, toward a place she'd never been.

It was hot. The humidity was up, and thunder rolled far in the southwest. Moths plastered themselves on the screens, looking in at the candles, chasing the fire.

He was falling into her now. And she into him. She moved her cheek away from his, looked up at him with dark eyes, and he kissed her, and she kissed back, longtime soft kissing, a river of it.

They gave up the pretense of dancing, and her arms went around his neck. His left hand was on her waist behind her back, the other brushing across her neck and her cheek and her hair. Thomas Wolfe talked about the "ghost of the old eagerness." The ghost had stirred in Francesca Johnson. In both of them.

Sitting by the window on her sixty-seventh birthday, Francesca watched the rain and remembered. She carried her brandy into the kitchen and stopped for a moment, staring at the exact spot where the two of them had stood. The feelings

Robert James Waller

inside of her were overwhelming, they always were. Strong enough that over the years she had dared do this in detail only once a year or her mind somehow would have disintegrated at the sheer emotional bludgeoning of it all.

Her abstinence from her recollections had been a matter of survival. Though in the last few years, the detail was coming back more and more often. She had ceased trying to stop him from coming into her. The images were clear, and real, and present. And so far back. Twenty-two years back. But slowly they were becoming her reality once again, the only one in which she cared to live.

She knew she was sixty-seven and accepted it, but she could not imagine Robert Kincaid being nearly seventy-five. Could not think of it, could not conceive of it or even conceive of the conceiving of it. He was here with her, right in this kitchen, in his white shirt, long gray hair, khaki slacks, brown sandals, silver bracelet, and silver chain around his neck. He was here with his arms around her.

She finally pulled back from him, from where they stood in the kitchen, and took his hand, leading him toward the stairs, up the stairs, past Carolyn's room, past Michael's room, and into her room, turning on a small reading lamp by the bed.

Now, all these years later, Francesca carried her brandy and walked slowly up the stairs, her right hand trailing behind her to bring along the memory of him up the stairs and down the hallway into the bedroom.

The physical images were inscribed in her mind so clearly that they might have been razor-edged photographs of his. She remembered the dreamlike sequence of clothes coming off and the two of them naked in bed. She remembered how he held himself just above her and moved his chest slowly against her belly and across her breasts. How he did this again and again, like some animal courting rite in an old zoology text. As he moved over her, he alternately kissed her lips or ears or ran his tongue along her neck, licking her as some fine leopard might do in long grass out on the veld.

He was an animal. A graceful, hard, male animal who did nothing overtly to dominate her yet dominated her completely, in the exact way she wanted that to happen at this moment.

But it was far beyond the physical, though the fact that he could make love for a long time without tiring was part of it. Loving him was—it sounded almost trite to her now, given the attention paid to such matters over the last two decades—spiritual. It was spiritual, but it wasn't trite.

In the midst of it, the lovemaking, she had whispered it to him, captured it in one sentence: "Robert, you're so powerful it's frightening." He _was_ powerful physically, but he used his strength carefully. It was more than that, however.

Sex was one thing. In the time since she'd met him, she had settled into the anticipation—the possibility, anyway—of something pleasurable, a breaking with a routine of hammering sameness. She hadn't counted on his curious power.

It was almost as if he had taken possession of her, in all of her dimensions. That's what was frightening. She never had doubted at the beginning that one part of her could remain aloof from whatever she and Robert Kincaid did, the part that belonged to her family and life in Madison County.

But he simply took it away, all of it. She should have known when he first stepped out of his truck to ask directions. He had seemed shamanlike then, and her original judgment was correct.

They would make love for an hour, maybe more, then he would pull slowly away and look at her, lighting a cigarette and one for her. Or sometimes he would just lie beside her, always with one hand moving on her body. Then he was inside her again, whispering soft words into her ear as he loved her, kissing her between phrases, between words, his arm around her waist, pulling her into him and him into her.

The Bridges of Madison County

And she would begin to turn in her mind, breathing heavier, letting him take her where he lived, and he lived in strange, haunted places, far back along the stems of Darwin's logic.

With her face buried in his neck and her skin against his, she could smell rivers and woodsmoke, could hear steaming trains chuffing out of winter stations in long-ago nighttimes, could see travelers in black robes moving steadily along frozen rivers and through summer meadows, beating their way toward the end of things. The leopard swept over her, again and again and yet again, like a long prairie wind, and rolling beneath him, she rode on that wind like some temple virgin toward the sweet, compliant fires marking the soft curve of oblivion.

And she murmured, softly, breathlessly, "Oh, Robert . . . Robert . . . I am losing myself."

She, who had ceased having orgasms years ago, had them in long sequences now with a half-man, half-something-else creature. She wondered about him and his endurance, and he told her that he could reach those places in his mind as well as physically, and that the orgasms of the mind had their own special character.

She had no idea what he meant. All she knew was that he had pulled in a tether of some kind and wound it around both of them so tightly she would have suffocated had it not been for the vaulting freedom from herself she felt.

The night went on, and the great spiral dance continued. Robert Kincaid discarded all sense of anything linear and moved to a part of himself that dealt only with shape and sound and shadow. Down the paths of the old ways he went, finding his direction by candles of sunlit frost melting upon the grass of summer and the red leaves of autumn.

And he heard the words he whispered to her, as if a voice other than his own were saying them. Fragments of a Rilke poem, "around the ancient tower . . . I have been circling for a thousand years." The lines to a Navajo sun chant. He whispered to her of the visions she brought to him— of blowing sand and magenta winds and brown pelicans riding the backs of dolphins moving north along the coast of Africa.

Sounds, small, unintelligible sounds, came from her mouth as she arched herself toward him. But it was a language he understood completely, and in this woman beneath him, with his belly against hers, deep inside her, Robert Kincaid's long search came to an end.

And he knew finally the meaning of all the small footprints on all the deserted beaches he had ever walked, of all the secret cargoes carried by ships that had never sailed, of all the curtained faces that had watched him pass down winding streets of twilight cities. And, like a great hunter of old who has traveled distant miles and now sees the light of his home campfires, his loneliness dissolved. At last. At last. He had come so far . . . so far. And he lay upon her, perfectly formed and unalterably complete in his love for her. At last.

Toward morning, he raised himself slightly and said, looking straight into her eyes, "This is why I'm here on this planet, at this time, Francesca. Not to travel or make pictures, but to love you. I know that now. I have been falling from the rim of a great, high place, somewhere back in time, for many more years than I have lived in this life. And through all of those years, I have been falling toward you."

When they came downstairs, the radio was still on. Dawn had come up, but the sun lay behind a thin cloud cover.

"Francesca, I have a favor to ask." He smiled at her as she fussed with the coffeepot.

"Yes?" She looked at him. Oh, God, I love him so, she thought, unsteady, wanting even more of him, never stopping.

"Slip on the jeans and T-shirt you wore last night, along with a pair of sandals. Nothing

Robert James Waller

else. I want to make a picture of you as you look this morning. A photograph just for the two of us."

She went upstairs, her legs weak from being wrapped around him all night, dressed, and went outside with him to the pasture. That's where he had made the photograph she looked at each year.

The Highway and the Peregrine

Robert Kincaid gave up photography
for the next few days. And except for
the necessary chores, which she min-
imized, Francesca Johnson gave up
farm life. The two of them spent all
their time together, either talking or
making love. Twice, when she asked,
he played the guitar and sang for her in a
voice somewhere between fair and good, a
little uncomfortable, telling her she was his
first audience. When he said that, she smiled

and kissed him, then lay back upon her feelings, listening to him sing of whaling ships and desert winds.

She rode with him in Harry to the Des Moines airport, where he shipped film to New York. He always sent the first few rolls ahead, when it was possible, so the editors could look at what he was getting and the technicians could check to make sure his camera shutters were functioning properly.

Afterward he took her to a fancy restaurant for lunch and held her hands across the table, looking at her in his intense way. And the waiter smiled, just watching them, hoping he would feel that way sometime.

She marveled at the sense Robert Kincaid had of his ways coming to a close and the ease with which he accepted it. He could see the approaching death of cowboys and others like them, including himself. And she began to understand what he meant when he said he was at the terminus of a branch of evolution and that it was a dead end. Once, in talking about what he called "last things," he whispered: " 'Never again,' cried the High-Desert Master. 'Never and never and never again.' " He saw nothing beyond himself along the branch. His kind was obsolete.

On Thursday they talked after making love in the afternoon. Both of them knew this conversation had to occur. Both of them had been avoiding it.

"What are we going to do?" he said.

She was silent, torn-apart silent. Then, "I don't know," softly.

"Look, I'll stay here if you want, or in town, or wherever. When your family comes home, I'll simply talk with your husband and explain how it lies. It won't be easy, but I'll get it done."

She shook her head. "Richard could never get his arms around this; he doesn't think in these terms. He doesn't understand magic and passion and all those other things we talk about and experience, and he never will. That doesn't necessarily make him an inferior person. It's just too far removed from anything he's ever felt or thought about. He has no way of dealing with it."

"Are we going to let all of this go, then?" He was serious, not smiling.

"I don't know that, either. Robert, in a curious way, you own me. I didn't want to be owned, didn't need it, and I know you didn't intend that, but that's what has happened. I'm no longer sitting next to you, here on the grass. You have me inside of you as a willing prisoner."

He replied, "I'm not sure you're inside of me, or that I am inside of you, or that I own you. At least I don't want to own you. I think we're both inside of another being we have created called 'us.'

"Well, we're really not inside of that being. We *are* that being. We have both lost ourselves and created something else, something that exists only as an interlacing of the two of us. Christ, we're in love. As deeply, as profoundly, as it's possible to be in love.

"Come travel with me, Francesca. That's not a problem. We'll make love in desert sand and drink brandy on balconies in Mombasa, watching dhows from Arabia run up their sails in the first wind of morning. I'll show you lion country and an old French city on the Bay of Bengal where there's a wonderful rooftop restaurant, and trains that climb through mountain passes and little inns run by Basques high in the Pyrenees. In a tiger preserve in south India, there's a special place on an island in the middle of a huge lake. If you don't like the road, I'll set up shop somewhere and shoot local stuff or portraits or whatever it takes to keep us going."

"Robert, when we were making love last night, you said something that I still remember. I kept whispering to you about your power—and, my God, you have that. You said, 'I am the highway and a peregrine and all the sails that ever went to sea.' You were right. That's what you feel; you feel the road inside of you. No, more than that, in a way that I'm not certain I can explain, you are the road. In the crack where illusion meets reality, that's where you are, out there on the road, and the road is you.

"You're old knapsacks and a truck named Harry and jet airplanes to Asia. And that's what I want you to be. If your evolutionary branch is a dead end, as you say it is, then I want you to hit that end at full speed. I'm not sure you can do that with me along. Don't you see, I love you so much that I cannot think of restraining you for a moment. To do that would be to kill the wild, magnificent animal that is you, and the power would die with it."

He started to speak, but Francesca stopped him.

"Robert, I'm not quite finished. If you took me in your arms and carried me to your truck and forced me to go with you, I wouldn't murmur a complaint. You could do the same thing just by talking to me. But I don't think you will. You're too sensitive, too aware of my feelings, for that. And I have feelings of responsibility here.

"Yes, it's boring in its way. My life, that is. It lacks romance, eroticism, dancing in the kitchen to candlelight, and the wonderful feel of a man who knows how to love a woman. Most of all, it lacks you. But there's this damn sense of responsibility I have. To Richard, to the children. Just my leaving, taking away my physical presence, would be hard enough for Richard. That alone might destroy him.

Robert James Waller

"On top of that, and this is even worse, he would have to live the rest of his life with the whispers of the people here. 'That's Richard Johnson. His hot little Italian wife ran off with some long-haired photographer a few years back.' Richard would have to suffer that, and the children would hear the snickering of Winterset for as long as they live here. They would suffer, too. And they would hate me for it.

"As much as I want you and want to be with you and part of you, I can't tear myself away from the realness of my responsibilities. If you force me, physically or mentally, to go with you, as I said earlier, I cannot fight that. I don't have the strength, given my feelings for you. In spite of what I said about not taking the road away from you, I'd go because of my own selfish wanting of you.

"But please don't make me. Don't make me give this up, my responsibilities. I cannot do that and live with the thought of it. If I did leave now, those thoughts would turn me into something other than the woman you have come to love."

Robert Kincaid was silent. He knew what she was saying about the road and responsibilities and how the guilt could transform her. He knew she was right, in a way. Looking out the window, he fought within himself, fought to understand her feelings. She began to cry.

Then they held each other for a long time. And he whispered to her, "I have one thing to say, one thing only, I'll never say it another time, to anyone, and I ask you to remember it: In a universe of ambiguity, this kind of certainty comes only once, and never again, no matter how many lifetimes you live."

They made love again that night, Thursday night, lying together until well after sunrise, touching and whispering. Francesca slept a little then, and when she awoke, the sun was high and already hot. She heard one of Harry's doors creaking and threw on some clothes.

He had made coffee and was sitting at the kitchen table, smoking, when she got there. He grinned at her. She moved across the room and buried her face in his neck, her hands in his hair, his arms around her waist. He turned her around and sat her on his lap, touching her.

Finally he stood. He had his old jeans on, with orange suspenders running over a clean khaki shirt, his Red Wing boots were laced tight, the Swiss Army knife was on his belt. His photo vest hung from the back of the chair, the cable release poking out of a pocket. The cowboy was saddled up.

"I'd better be going."

She nodded, beginning to cry. She saw the tears in his eyes, but he kept smiling that little smile of his.

"Is it okay if I write you sometime? I want to at least send a photo or two."

"It's all right," Francesca said, wiping her eyes on the towel hanging from the cupboard door. "I'll make some excuse for getting mail from a hippie photographer, as long as it's not too much."

"You have my Washington address and phone, right?" She nodded. "If I'm not there, call the *National Geographic* offices. Here, I'll write the number down for you." He wrote on the pad by the phone, tore off the sheet, and handed it to her.

"Or you can always find the number in the magazine. Ask for the editorial offices. They know where I am most of the time.

"Don't hesitate if you want to see me, or just to talk. Call me collect anywhere in the world, the charges won't appear on your bill that way. And I'll be around here for a few more days. Think about what I've said. I can be here, settle the matter in short order, and we could drive northwest together."

Francesca said nothing. She knew he could, indeed, settle the matter in short order. Richard was five years younger than him, but no match intellectually or physically for Robert Kincaid.

He slipped into his vest. Her mind was gone, empty, turning. "Don't leave, Robert Kincaid," she could hear herself crying out from somewhere inside.

Taking her hand, he walked through the back door toward the truck. He opened the driver's door, put his foot on the running board, then stepped off it and held her again for several minutes. Neither of them spoke; they simply stood there, sending, receiving, imprinting the feel of each on the other, indelibly. Reaffirming the existence of that special being he had talked about.

For the last time, he let her go and stepped into the truck, sitting there with the door open. Tears running down his cheeks. Tears running down her cheeks. Slowly he pulled the door shut, hinges creaking. Harry was reluctant to start, as usual, but she could hear his boot hitting the accelerator, and the old truck eventually relented.

He shifted into reverse and sat there with the clutch in. First serious, then with a little grin, pointing toward the lane. "The road, you know. I'll be in southeast India next month. Want a card from there?"

She couldn't speak but said no with a shake of her head. That would be too much for Richard to find in the mailbox. She knew Robert understood. He nodded.

The truck backed into the farmyard, crunching across the gravel, chickens scattering from under its wheels. Jack chased one of them into the machine shed, barking.

Robert Kincaid waved to her through the open

passenger-side window. She could see the sun flashing off his silver bracelet. The top two buttons of his shirt were open.

He moved into the lane and down it. Francesca kept wiping her eyes, trying to see, the sunlight making strange prisms from her tears. As she had done the first night they met, she hurried to the head of the lane and watched the old pickup bounce along. At the end of it, the truck stopped, the driver's door swung open, and he stepped out on the running board. He could see her a hundred yards back, looking small from this distance.

He stood there, with Harry turning over impatiently in the heat, and stared. Neither of them moved; they already had said good-bye. They just looked—the Iowa farm wife, the creature at the end of his evolutionary branch, one of the last cowboys. For thirty seconds he stood there, his photographer's eyes missing nothing, making their own image that he never would lose.

He closed the door, ground the gears, and was crying again as he turned left on the county road toward Winterset. He looked back just before a grove of trees on the northwest edge of the farm would block his view and saw her sitting cross-legged in the dust where the lane began, her head in her hands.

* * *

Richard and the children arrived in early evening with stories of the fair and a ribbon the steer had won before being sold for slaughter. Carolyn was on the phone immediately. It was Friday, and Michael took the pickup truck into town for the things that seventeen-year-old boys do on Friday nights—mostly hang around the square and talk or shout at girls going by in cars. Richard turned on the television, telling Francesca how good the corn bread was as he ate a piece with butter and maple syrup.

She sat on the front porch swing. Richard came out after his program was finished at ten o'clock. He stretched and said, "Sure is good to be home." Then, looking at her, "You okay, Frannie? You seem a little tired or dreamy or somethin'."

"Yes, I'm just fine, Richard. It's good to have you back safe and sound."

"Well, I'm turnin' in, it's been a long week at the fair, and I'm bushed. You comin', Frannie?"

"Not for a little bit. It's kind of nice out here, so I think I'll just sit awhile." She was tired, but she was also afraid Richard might have sex in mind. She just couldn't handle that tonight.

She could hear him walking around in their bedroom, above where she pushed back and forth on the swing, her bare feet on the porch floor. From the back of the house, she could hear Carolyn's radio playing.

She avoided going into town for the next few days, aware all the time that Robert Kincaid was only a few miles away. Frankly, she didn't think she could stop herself if she saw him. She might run to him and say, "Now! We must go now!" She had defied risk to see him at Cedar Bridge, now there was too much risk in seeing him again.

By Tuesday the groceries were running low and Richard needed a part for the corn picker he was getting back in shape. The day was low-slung, steady rain, light fog, cool for August.

Richard got his part and had coffee with the other men at the cafe while she shopped for groceries. He knew her schedule and was waiting out in front of the Super Value when she finished. He jumped out, wearing his Allis-Chalmers cap, and helped her load the bags into the Ford pickup, on the seat and around her knees. And she thought of tripods and knapsacks.

"I've got to run up to the implement place again. I forgot one more piece I might need."

They drove north on U.S. Route 169, which formed the main street of Winterset. A block south of the Texaco station, she saw Harry rolling away from the pumps, windshield wipers slapping, and out onto the road ahead of them.

Their momentum brought them up right behind the old pickup, and sitting high in the Ford, she could see a black tarpaulin lashed down tight in the back, outlining a suitcase and guitar case wedged in next to the spare tire lying flat. The back window was rain-spattered, but part of his head was visible. He leaned over as if to get something from the glove box; eight days ago he'd done that and his arm had brushed across her leg. A week ago she'd been in Des Moines buying a pink dress.

"That truck's a long way from home," remarked Richard. "Washington State. Looks like a woman driving it; long hair, anyway. On second thought, I'll bet it's that photographer they been talkin' about at the cafe."

They followed Robert Kincaid a few blocks north to where 169 intersected with 92 running east and west. It was a four-way stop, with heavy cross traffic in all directions, complicated by the rain and the fog, which had gotten heavier.

For maybe twenty seconds they sat there. He was up ahead, only thirty feet from her. She could still do it. Get out and run to Harry's right door, climb in over the knapsacks and cooler and tripods.

Since Robert Kincaid had driven away from her last Friday, she realized, in spite of how much she thought she'd cared for him then, she had nonetheless badly underestimated her feelings. That didn't seem possible, but it was true. She had begun to understand what he already understood.

But she sat frozen by her responsibilities, staring at that back window harder than she had ever looked at anything in her life. His left signal light came on. In a moment he'd be gone. Richard was fiddling with the Ford's radio.

She began to see things in slow motion, some curious trick of the mind. His turn came, and . . . slowly . . . slowly . . . he moved Harry into the intersection—she could visualize his long legs working the clutch and accelerator and the muscles in his right forearm flexing as he shifted gears—curling left now onto 92 toward Council Bluffs, the Black Hills, and the Northwest . . . slowly . . . slowly . . . the old pickup came around . . . so slowly it came around through the intersection, putting its nose to the west.

Squinting through tears and rain and fog, she could barely make out the faded red paint on the door: "Kincaid Photography—Bellingham, Washington."

He had lowered his window to help him get through the bad visibility as he turned. He made the corner, and she could see his hair blowing as he began to accelerate down 92, heading west, rolling up the window as he drove.

"Oh, Christ—oh, Jesus Christ Almighty . . . no!"

The words were inside of her. "I was wrong, Robert, I was wrong to stay . . . but I can't go. . . . Let me tell you again . . . why I can't go. . . . Tell me again why I should go."

And she heard his voice coming back down the highway. "In a universe of ambiguity, this kind of certainty comes only once, and never again, no matter how many lifetimes you live."

Richard took the truck across the intersection heading north. She looked for an instant past his face toward Harry's red taillights moving off into the fog and rain. The old Chevy pickup looked small beside a huge semitrailer rig roaring into Winterset, spraying a wave of road water over the last cowboy.

"Good-bye, Robert Kincaid," she whispered, and began to cry, openly.

Richard looked over at her. "What's wrong, Frannie? Will you _please_ tell me what's wrong with you?"

"Richard, I just need some time to myself. I'll be all right in a few minutes."

Richard tuned in the noon livestock reports, looked over at her, and shook his head.

Ashes

Night had come to Madison County. It was 1987, her sixty-seventh birthday. Francesca had been lying on her bed for two hours. She could see and touch and smell and hear all of it from twenty-two years ago.

She had remembered, then remembered again. The image of those red taillights moving west along Iowa 92 in the rain and fog had stalked her for more than two decades. She touched her breasts and could feel his chest muscles sweeping over them. God, she loved him so. Loved him then, more than she thought possible, loved him now even more. She would have done anything for him except destroy her family and maybe him as well.

She went down the stairs and sat at the old kitchen table with the yellow Formica top. Richard had bought a new one; he'd insisted on it. But she'd also asked that the old one be stored in a shed, and she had wrapped it carefully in plastic before it was put away.

"I don't see why you're so attached to this old table, anyway," he had complained while helping her move it. After Richard died, Michael had brought it back into the house for her and never asked why she wanted it in place of the newer one. He'd just looked at her in a questioning way. She'd said nothing.

Now she sat at the table. Then, going to the cupboard, she took down two white candles with small brass holders. She lit the candles and turned on the radio, slowly adjusting the dial until she found some quiet music.

She stood by the sink for a long time, her head tilted slightly upward, looking at his face, and whispered, "I remember you, Robert Kincaid. Maybe the High-Desert Master was right. Maybe you were the last one. Maybe the cowboys *are* all close to dying by now."

Before Richard died, she had never tried to call Kincaid or to write, either, though she had balanced on the knife edge of it every day for years. If she talked to him one more time, she would go to him. If she wrote him, she knew he would come for her. That's how close it was. Through the years he never called or wrote again, after sending her the one package with the photographs and the manuscript. She knew he understood how she felt and the complications he could cause in her life.

She subscribed to _National Geographic_ in September of 1965. The article on the covered bridges appeared the following year, and there was Roseman Bridge in warm first light, the morning he had found her note. The cover was his photo of a team pulling a wagon toward Hogback Bridge. He had written the text for the article as well.

On the back page of the magazine, the writers and photographers were featured, and occasionally there were photographs of them. He was there sometimes. The same long silver hair, the bracelet, jeans or khakis, cameras hanging off his shoulders, the veins standing out on his arms. In the Kalahari, at the walls of Jaipur in India, in a canoe in Guatemala, in northern Canada. The road and the cowboy.

She clipped these and kept them in the manila envelope with the covered-bridge issue of the magazine, the manuscript, the two photographs,

Robert James Waller

and his letter. She put the envelope beneath her underwear in the bureau, a place Richard would never look. And like some distant observer tracking him through the years, she watched Robert Kincaid grow older.

The grin was still there, even the long, lean body with the good muscles. But she could tell by the lines around his eyes,. the slight droop of the strong shoulders, the slowly sagging face. She could tell. She had studied that body more closely than anything else in her life, more closely than her own body. And his aging made her long even more for him, if that was possible. She suspected—no, she knew—he was by himself. And he was.

In the candlelight, at the table, she studied the clippings. He looked out at her from pláces far away. She came to the special picture from a 1967 issue. He was by a river in East Africa, facing the camera and up close to it, squatting down, getting ready to take a photograph of something.

When she had first looked at this clipping, years ago, she could see the silver chain around his neck now had a small medallion attached to it. Michael was away at college, and when Richard and Carolyn had gone to bed, she got out a powerful magnifying glass Michael had used for his stamp collection when he was young and brought it close to the photo.

The Bridges of Madison County

"My God," she breathed. The medallion said "Francesca" on it. That was his one small indiscretion, and she forgave him for it, smiling. In all of the photos after that, the medallion was always there on the silver chain.

After 1975 she never saw him again in the magazine. His byline was absent as well. She searched every issue but found nothing. He would have been sixty-two that year.

When Richard died in 1979, when the funeral was over and the children had gone back to their own homes, she thought about calling Robert Kincaid. He would be sixty-six, she was fifty-nine. There was still time, even with the loss of fourteen years. She thought hard about it for a week and finally took the number off his letterhead and dialed it.

Her heart nearly stopped when the phone began to ring. She heard the receiver being picked up and almost put the phone back on the hook. A woman's voice said, "McGregor Insurance." Francesca sank but recovered enough to ask the secretary if she had dialed the correct number. She had. Francesca thanked her and hung up.

Next she tried the Information operator in Bellingham, Washington. Nothing listed. She tried Seattle. Nothing. Then the Chamber of Commerce offices in Bellingham and Seattle. She asked if they would check the city directories. They did, and he was not listed. He could be anywhere, she thought.

She remembered the magazine; he had said to call there. The receptionist was polite but new, and had to get someone to help her with the request. Francesca's call was transferred three times before she talked with an associate editor who had been at the magazine for twenty years. She asked about Robert Kincaid.

Of course the editor remembered him. "Trying to locate him, huh? He was a hell of a photographer, if you'll excuse the language. He was cantankerous, not in a nasty way, but persistent. He was after art for art's sake, and that doesn't work very well with our readership. Our readership wants nice pictures, skillful pictures, but nothing too wild.

"We always said Kincaid was a little strange; none of us knew him well outside of the work he did for us. But he was a pro. We could send him anywhere, and he'd deliver, even though he disagreed with our editorial decisions most of the time. As for his whereabouts, I've been checking our files while we talked. He left the magazine in 1975. The address and phone number I have are . . ." He read off the same information Francesca already had. She stopped trying after that, mostly because she was afraid of what she might discover.

She drifted along, allowing herself to think

more and more about Robert Kincaid. She was still able to drive well enough, and several times a year she would go to Des Moines and have lunch in the restaurant where he had taken her. On one of those trips, she bought a leather-bound book of blank pages. And on those pages she began recording in neat handwriting the details of her love affair with him and her thoughts about him. It required nearly three volumes of the notebooks before she was satisfied she had completed her task.

Winterset was improving. There was an active art guild, mostly female, and talk of refurbishing the old bridges had been going on for some years. Interesting young folks were building houses in the hills. Things had loosened up, long hair was no longer cause for stares, though sandals on men were still pretty scarce and poets were few.

Yet except for a few women friends, she withdrew completely from the community. People remarked about it and how they often would see her standing by Roseman Bridge and sometimes by Cedar Bridge. Old folks frequently become strange, they said, and contented themselves with that explanation.

On the second of February 1982, a United Parcel Service truck trundled up her driveway. She hadn't ordered anything she could recall. Puzzled, she signed for the package and looked at the address: "Francesca Johnson, RR 2, Winterset, Iowa 50273." The return address was a law firm in Seattle.

The package was neatly wrapped and carried extra insurance. She placed it on the kitchen table and opened it carefully. Inside were three boxes, packed securely in Styrofoam peanuts. Taped to the top of one was a small padded envelope. To another was taped a business envelope addressed to her and carrying the law firm's return address.

She removed the tape from the business envelope and opened it, shaking.

January 25, 1982

Ms. Francesca Johnson
RR 2
Winterset, IA 50273

Dear Ms. Johnson:

We represent the estate of one Robert L. Kincaid, who recently passed away....

Francesca laid the letter on the table. Outside, snow blew across the fields of winter. She watched it skim the stubble, taking corn husks with it, piling them up in the corner of the wire. She read the words once more.

> *We represent the estate of one Robert L. Kincaid, who recently passed away. . . .*

"Oh, Robert . . . Robert . . . no." She said it softly and bowed her head.

An hour later she was able to continue reading. The straightforward language of the law, the precision of the words, angered her.

> *"We represent . . ."*

An attorney carrying out his duties to a client.

But the power, the leopard who came riding in on the tail of a comet, the shaman who was looking for Roseman Bridge on a hot August day, and the man who stood on the running board of a truck named Harry and looked back at her dying in the dust of an Iowa farm lane—where was he in those words?

The letter should have been a thousand pages long. It should have talked about the end of evolutionary chains and the loss of free range, about cowboys struggling with the corners of the wire, like the corn husks of winter.

Robert James Waller

The only will he left was dated July 8, 1967. His instructions about having the enclosed items delivered to you were explicit. If you could not be found, the materials were to be incinerated.

Also enclosed inside the box marked with the word "Letter" is a message for you he left with us in 1978. He sealed the envelope, and it has been left unopened.

Mr. Kincaid's remains were cremated. At his request, no marker was placed anywhere. His ashes were scattered, also at his request, near your home by an associate of ours. I believe the location was called Roseman Bridge.

If we may be of further service, please do not hesitate to contact us.

Sincerely yours,
Allen B. Quippen, Attorney at Law

She caught her breath, dried her eyes again, and began to examine the remaining contents of the box.

She knew what was in the small padded envelope. She knew it as surely as she knew spring would come again this year. She opened it carefully and reached in. Out came the silver chain. The medallion attached to it was scratched and read "Francesca." On the back, etched in the tiniest of letters, was: "If found, please send to Francesca Johnson, RR 2, Winterset, Iowa, USA."

His silver bracelet was wrapped in tissue paper at the bottom of the envelope. A slip of paper was included with the bracelet. It was her handwriting:

> *If you'd like supper again when "white moths are on the wing," come by tonight after you're finished.*

Her note from the Roseman Bridge. He'd kept even that for his memories.

Then she remembered that was the only thing he had of hers, his only evidence she existed, aside from elusive images on slowly decaying film emulsions. The little note from Roseman Bridge. It was stained and curved, as if it had been carried in a billfold for a long time.

She wondered how many times he had read it over the years, far from the hills along Middle River. She could imagine him holding the note before him in the thin light of a reading lamp on a nonstop jet to somewhere, sitting on the floor of a bamboo hut in tiger country and reading it by flashlight, folding and putting it away on a rainy night in Bellingham, then looking at photographs of a woman leaning against a fence post on a summer morning or coming out of a covered bridge at sundown.

The three boxes each contained a camera with a lens attached. They were battered, scarred. Turning one around, she could read "Nikon" on the viewfinder and, just to the upper left of the Nikon label, the letter *F*. It was the camera she had handed him at Cedar Bridge.

Finally she opened the letter from him. It was written in longhand on his stationery and dated August 16, 1978.

Dear Francesca,

I hope this finds you well. I don't know when you'll receive it. Sometime after I'm gone. I'm sixty-five now, and it's been thirteen years ago today that we met when I came up your lane looking for directions.

I'm gambling that this package won't upset your life in any way. I just couldn't bear to think of the cameras sitting in a secondhand case in a camera store or in some stranger's hands. They'll be in pretty rough shape by the time you get them. But, I have no one else to leave them to, and I apologize for putting you at risk by sending them to you.

I was on the road almost constantly from 1965 to 1975. Just to remove some of the temptation to call you or come for you, a temptation

I have virtually every waking moment of my life, I took all of the overseas assignments I could find. There have been times, many of them, when I've said, "The hell with it. I'm going to Winterset, Iowa, and, whatever the cost, take Francesca away with me."

But I remember your words, and I respect your feelings. Maybe you were right; I just don't know. I do know that driving out of your lane that hot Friday morning was the hardest thing I've ever done or will ever do. In fact, I doubt if few men have ever done anything more difficult than that.

I left *National Geographic* in 1975 and have been devoting the remainder of my shooting years mostly to things of my own choosing, picking up a little work where I can get it, local or regional stuff that keeps me away only a few days at a time. It's been tough financially, but I get along. I always do.

Much of my work is around Puget Sound. I like it that way. It seems as men get older they turn toward the water.

Oh, yes, I have a dog now, a golden retriever. I call him "Highway," and he travels with me most of the time, head hanging out the window, looking for good shots.

In 1972, I fell down a cliff in Maine, in Acadia National Park, and broke my ankle.

The chain and medallion got torn off in the fall. Fortunately they landed close by. I found them again, and a jeweler mended the chain.

I live with dust on my heart. That's about as well as I can put it. There were women before you, a few, but none after. I made no conscious pledge to celibacy; I'm just not interested.

I once watched a Canada goose whose mate had been shot by hunters. They mate for life, you know. The gander circled the pond for days, and more days after that. When I last saw him, he was swimming alone through the wild rice, still looking. I suppose that analogy is a little too obvious for literary tastes, but it's pretty much the way I feel.

In my imagination, on foggy mornings or afternoons with the sun bouncing off northwest water, I try to think of where you might be in your life and what you might be doing as I'm thinking of you. Nothing complicated—going out to your garden, sitting on your front porch swing, standing at the sink in your kitchen. Things like that.

I remember everything. How you smelled, how you tasted like the summer. The feel of your skin against mine, and the sound of your whispers as I loved you.

Robert Penn Warren once used the phrase

"a world that seems to be God-abandoned." Not bad, pretty close to how I feel some of the time. But I cannot live that way always. When those feelings become too strong, I load Harry and go down the road with Highway for a few days.

I don't like feeling sorry for myself. That's not who I am. And most of the time I don't feel that way. Instead, I am grateful for having at least found you. We could have flashed by one another like two pieces of cosmic dust.

God or the universe or whatever one chooses to label the great systems of balance and order does not recognize Earth-time. To the universe, four days is no different than four billion light years. I try to keep that in mind.

But, I am, after all, a man. And all the philosophic rationalizations I can conjure up do not keep me from wanting you, every day, every moment, the merciless wail of time, of time I can never spend with you, deep within my head.

I love you, profoundly and completely. And I always will.

The last cowboy,
Robert

P. S., I put another new engine in Harry last summer, and he's doing fine.

The package arrived five years ago. And looking at the contents had become part of her annual birthday ritual. She kept his cameras, bracelet, and the chain with the medallion in a special chest in the closet. A local carpenter had made the box to her design, out of walnut, with dust seals and padded interior sections. "Pretty fancy box," he had said. Francesca had only smiled.

The last part of the ritual was the manuscript. She always read it by candlelight, at the end of the day. She brought it from the living room and laid it carefully on the yellow Formica, near a candle, lit her one cigarette of the year, a Camel, took a sip of brandy, and began to read.

Falling from Dimension Z

ROBERT KINCAID

There are old winds I still do not understand, though I have been riding, forever it seems, along the curl of their spines. I move in Dimension Z; the world goes by somewhere else in another slice of things, parallel to me. As if, hands in my pockets and bending a little forward, I see it through a department store window, looking inward.

In Dimension Z, there are strange moments. Coming around a long, rainy, New Mexico curve west of Magdalena, the highway turns to a footpath and the path to an animal trail. A pass of my wiper blades, and the trail becomes a forest place where nothing has ever gone. Again the wiper blades and, again, something further back. Great ice, this time. I am moving through short grass, in furs, with matted hair and spear, thin and hard as the ice itself, all muscle and implacable cunning. Past the ice, still further back along the measure of things, deep salt water in which I swim, gilled and scaled. I cannot see more than that, except beyond plankton is the digit zero.

Euclid was not always right. He assumed parallelness, in constancy, right to the end of things; but a non-Euclidean way of being is also possible, where the lines come together, far out there. A vanishing point. The illusion of convergence.

Yet I know it's more than illusion. Sometimes a coming together is possible, a spilling of one reality into another. A kind of soft enlacing. Not prim intersections loomed in a world of precision, no sound of the shuttle. Just . . . well . . . breathing. Yes, that's the sound of it, maybe the feel of it, too. Breathing.

And I move slowly over this other reality, and beside it and underneath and around it, always with strength, always with power, yet always with a giving of myself to it. And the other senses this, coming forward with its own power, giving itself to me, in turn.

Somewhere, inside of the breathing, music sounds, and the curious spiral dance begins then, with a meter all its own that tempers the ice-man with spear and matted hair. And slowly—rolling and turning in adagio, in adagio always—ice-man falls . . . from Dimension Z . . . and into her.

The Bridges of Madison County

At the end of her sixty-seventh birthday, when the rain had stopped, Francesca put the manila envelope in the bottom drawer of the rolltop desk. She had decided to keep it in her safe deposit box at the bank after Richard died but brought it home for a few days each year at this time. The lid on the walnut chest was shut on the cameras, and the chest was placed on the closet shelf in her bedroom.

Earlier in the afternoon, she had visited Roseman Bridge. Now she walked out on the porch, dried off the swing with a towel, and sat down. It was cold, but she would stay for a few minutes, as she always did. Then she walked to the yard gate and stood. Then to the head of the lane. Twenty-two years later, she could see him stepping from his truck in the late afternoon, trying to find his way; she could see Harry bouncing toward the county road, then stopping, and Robert Kincaid standing on the running board, looking back up the lane.

A Letter from Francesca

Francesca Johnson died in January of 1989. She was sixty-nine years old at the time of her death. Robert Kincaid would have been seventy-six that year. The cause of death was listed as "natural." "She just died," the doctor told Michael and Carolyn. "Actually, we're a little perplexed. We can find no specific cause for her death. A neighbor found her slumped over the kitchen table."

In a 1982 letter to her attorney, she had

requested that her remains be cremated and her ashes scattered at Roseman Bridge. Cremation was an uncommon practice in Madison County— viewed as slightly radical in some undefined way —and her wish generated considerable discussion at the cafe, the Texaco station, and the implement dealership. The disposition of her ashes was not made public.

Following the memorial service, Michael and Carolyn drove slowly to Roseman Bridge and carried out Francesca's instructions. Though it was nearby, the bridge had never been special to the Johnson family, and they wondered, and wondered again, why their rather sensible mother would behave in such an enigmatic way and why she had not asked to be buried by their father, as was customary.

Following that, Michael and Carolyn began the long process of sorting through the house and brought home the materials from the safe deposit box after they were examined by the local attorney for estate purposes and released.

They divided the materials from the box and began looking through them. The manila envelope was in Carolyn's stack, about a third of the way down. She was puzzled when she opened it and removed the contents. She read Robert Kincaid's 1965 letter to Francesca. After that she read his

1978 letter, then the 1982 letter from the Seattle attorney. Finally she studied the magazine clippings.

"Michael."

He caught the mixture of surprise and pensiveness in her voice and looked up immediately. "What is it?"

Carolyn had tears in her eyes, and her voice became unsteady. "Mother was in love with a man named Robert Kincaid. He was a photographer. Remember when we all had to see the copy of _National Geographic_ with the bridge story in it? He was the one who took the pictures of the bridges here. And remember all the kids talking about the strange-looking guy with the cameras back then? That was him."

Michael sat across from her, his tie loosened, collar open. "Say that again, slowly. I can't believe I heard you correctly."

After reading the letters, Michael searched the downstairs closet, then went upstairs to Francesca's bedroom. He had never noticed the walnut box before and opened it. He carried it down to the kitchen table. "Carolyn, here are his cameras."

Tucked in one end of the box was a sealed envelope with "Carolyn or Michael" written on it in Francesca's script, and lying between the cameras were three leather-bound notebooks.

Robert James Waller

"I'm not sure I'm capable of reading what's in that envelope," said Michael. "Read it out loud to me, if you can handle it."

She opened the envelope and read aloud.

January 7, 1987

Dear Carolyn and Michael,

Though I'm feeling just fine, I think it's time for me to get my affairs in order (as they say). There is something, something very important, you need to know about. That's why I'm writing this.

After looking through the safe deposit box and finding the large manila envelope addressed to me with a 1965 postmark, I'm sure you'll eventually come to this letter. If possible, please sit at the old kitchen table to read it. You'll understand that request shortly.

It's hard for me to write this to my own children, but I must. There's something here that's too strong, too beautiful, to die with me. And if you are to know who your mother was, all the goods and bads, you need to know what I'm about to say. Brace yourself.

As you've already discovered, his name was Robert Kincaid. His middle initial was "L," but

I never knew what the L represented. He was a photographer, and he was here in 1965 photographing the covered bridges.

Remember how excited the town was when the pictures appeared in <u>National Geographic</u> You may also recall that I began receiving the magazine about that time. Now you know the reason for my sudden interest in it. By the way, I was with him (carrying one of his camera knapsacks) when the photo of Cedar Bridge was taken.

Understand, I loved your father in a quiet fashion. I knew it then, I know it now. He was good to me and gave me the two of you, who I treasure. Don't forget that.

But Robert Kincaid was something quite different, like nobody I've ever seen or heard or read about through my entire life. To make you understand him completely is impossible. First of all, you are not me. Second, you would have had to have been around him, to watch him move, to hear him talk about being on a dead-end branch of evolution. Maybe the notebooks and magazine clippings will help, but even those will not be enough.

In a way, he was not of this earth. That's about as clear as I can say it. I've always thought of him as a leopardlike creature who rode in on the tail of a comet. He moved that way, his body was like that. He somehow coupled enormous intensity with warmth and kindness, and there was a vague sense of tragedy about him. He felt he was becoming obsolete in a world of computers and robots and organized living in general. He saw himself as one of the last cowboys, as he put it, and called himself old-fangled.

The first time I ever saw him was when he stopped and asked directions to Roseman Bridge. The three of you were at the Illinois State Fair. Believe me, I was not scouting around for any adventure. That was the furthest thing from my mind. But I looked at him for less than five seconds, and I knew I wanted him, though not as much as I eventually came to want him.

And please don't think of him as some Casanova running around taking advantage of country girls. He wasn't like that at all. In fact, he was a little shy, and I had as much to do with what happened as he did. More, in fact. The note tucked in with his bracelet is one I posted on Roseman Bridge so he would see it the morning after we first met. Aside from his photographs of me, it's the only piece of evidence he had over the years that I actually existed, that I was not just some dream he had.

I know children have a tendency to think of their parents as rather asexual, so I hope what

I'm going to say won't shock you, and I certainly hope it won't destroy your memory of me.

In our old kitchen, Robert and I spent hours together. We talked and danced by candlelight. And, yes, we made love there and in the bedroom and in the pasture grass and just about anywhere else you can think of. It was incredible, powerful, transcending lovemaking, and it went on for days, almost without stopping. I always have used the word "powerful" a lot in thinking about him. For that's what he had become by the time we met.

He was like an arrow in his intensity. I simply was helpless when he made love to me. Not weak, that's not what I felt. Just, well, overwhelmed by his sheer emotional and physical power. Once when I whispered that to him, he simply said, "I am the highway and a peregrine and all the sails that ever went to sea."

I checked the dictionary later. The first thing people think of when they hear the word "peregrine" is a falcon. But there are other meanings of the word, and he would have been aware of that. One is "foreigner, alien." A second is "roving or wandering, migratory." The Latin peregrinus, which is one root of the word, means a stranger. He was all of those things—a stranger, a foreigner in the more general sense of the word, a wanderer, and he also was falconlike, now that I think of it.

Children, understand I am trying to express what cannot be put into words. I only wish that someday you each might have what I experienced; however, I'm beginning to think that's not likely. Though I suppose it's not fashionable to say such things in these more enlightened times, I don't think it's possible for a woman to possess the peculiar kind of power Robert Kincaid had. So, Michael, that lets you out. As for Carolyn, I'm afraid the bad news is that there was only one of him, and no more.

If not for your father and the two of you, I would have gone anywhere with him, instantly. He asked me to go, begged me to go. But I wouldn't, and he was too much of a sensitive and caring person to ever interfere in our lives after that.

The paradox is this: If it hadn't been for Robert Kincaid, I'm not sure I could have stayed on the farm all these years. In four days, he gave me a lifetime, a universe, and made the separate parts of me into a whole. I have never stopped thinking of him, not for a moment. Even when he was not in my conscious mind, I could feel him somewhere, always he was there.

But it never took away from anything I felt for the two of you or your father. Thinking only of myself for a moment, I'm not sure I made the right decision. But taking the family into account, I'm pretty sure I did.

Though I must be honest and tell you that, right from the outset, Robert understood better than I what it was the two of us formed with each other. I think I only began to grasp its significance over time, gradually. Had I truly understood that, when he was face to face with me and asking me to go, I probably would have left with him.

Robert believed the world had become too rational, had stopped trusting in magic as much as it should. I've often wondered if I was too rational in making my decision.

I'm sure you found my burial request incomprehensible, thinking perhaps it was the product of a confused old woman. After reading the 1982 Seattle attorney's letter and my notebooks, you'll understand why I made that request. I gave my family my life; I gave Robert Kincaid what was left of me.

I think Richard knew there was something in me he could not reach, and I sometimes wonder if he found the manila envelope when I kept it at home in the bureau. Just before he died, I was sitting by him in a Des Moines hospital, and he said this to me: "Francesca, I know you had your own dreams, too. I'm sorry I couldn't give them to you." That was the most touching moment of our lives together.

I don't want to make you feel guilt or pity or any of those things. That's not my purpose here. I only want you to know how much I loved Robert Kincaid. I dealt with it day by day, all these years, just as he did.

Though we never spoke again to one another, we remained bound together as tightly as it's possible for two people to be bound. I cannot find the words to express this adequately. He said it best when he told me we had ceased being separate beings and, instead, had become a third being formed by the two of us. Neither of us existed independent of that being. And that being was left to wander.

Carolyn, remember the horrible argument we had once about the light pink dress in my closet? You had seen it and wanted to wear it. You said you never remembered me wearing it, so why couldn't it be made over to fit you. That was the dress I wore the first night Robert and I made love. I've never looked as good in my entire life as I did that night. The dress was my small and foolish memory of that time. That's why I never wore it again and why I refused to let you wear it.

After Robert left here in 1965, I realized I knew very little about him, in terms of his family

history. Though I think I learned almost everything else about him—everything that really
counted—in those few short days. He was an
only child, both his parents were dead, and he
was born in a small town in Ohio.

I'm not even sure if he went to college or even
high school, but he had an intelligence that was
brilliant in a raw, primitive, almost mystical
fashion. Oh yes, he was a combat photographer
with the marines in the South Pacific during
World War II.

He was married once and divorced, a long
time before he met me. There were no children.
His wife had been a musician of some kind, a
folksinger I think he said, and his long absences
on photographic expeditions were just too hard
on the marriage. He took the blame for the
breakup.

Other than that, Robert had no family, as
far as I know. I am asking you to make him
part of ours, however difficult that may seem to
you at first. At least I had a family, a life with
others. Robert was alone. That was not fair,
and I knew it.

I prefer, at least I think I do, because of
Richard's memory and the way people talk, that
all of this be kept within the Johnson family,
somehow. I'll leave it to your judgment, though.

In any case, I'm certainly not ashamed of

what Robert Kincaid and I had together. On the contrary. I loved him desperately throughout all these years, though, for my own reasons, I tried to contact him only once. That was after your father died. The attempt failed, and I was afraid something had happened to him, so I never tried again out of that fear. I simply couldn't face that reality. So you can imagine how I felt when the package with the attorney's letter arrived in 1982.

As I said, I hope you understand and don't think ill of me. If you love me, then you must love what I have done.

Robert Kincaid taught me what it was like to be a woman in a way that few women, maybe none, will ever experience. He was fine and warm, and he deserves, certainly, your respect and maybe your love. I hope you can give him both of those. In his own way, through me, he was good to you.

Go well, my children.
Mother

There was silence in the old kitchen. Michael took a deep breath and looked out the window. Carolyn looked around her, at the sink, the floor, at the table, at everything.

When she spoke, her voice was almost a whisper. "Oh, Michael, Michael, think of them all those years, wanting each other so desperately. She gave him up for us and for Dad. And Robert Kincaid stayed away out of respect for her feelings about us. Michael, I can hardly deal with the thought of it. We treat our marriages so casually, and we were part of the reason that an incredible love affair ended the way it did.

"They had four days together, just four. Out of a lifetime. It was when we went to that ridiculous state fair in Illinois. Look at the picture of Mom. I never saw her like that. She's so beautiful, and it's not the photograph. It's what he did for her. Just look at her; she's wild and free. Her hair's blowing in the wind, her face is alive. She just looks wonderful."

"Jesus," was all Michael could say, wiping his forehead with the kitchen towel and dabbing at his eyes when Carolyn wasn't looking.

Carolyn spoke again. "Apparently he never tried to contact her all these years. And he must have died alone; that's why he had the cameras sent to her.

"I remember the fight Mom and I had over the pink dress. It went on for days. I whined and asked why. Then I refused to speak to her. All she ever said was, 'No, Carolyn, not that one.' "

And Michael remembered the old table at which

they were sitting. That's why Francesca had asked him to bring it back into the kitchen after their father died.

Carolyn opened the small padded envelope. "Here's his bracelet and his silver chain and medallion. And here's the note Mother mentioned in her letter, the one she put on Roseman Bridge. That's why the photo he sent of the bridge shows the piece of paper tacked to it.

"Michael, what are we going to do? Think about it for a moment, I'll be right back."

She ran up the stairs and returned in a few minutes carrying the pink dress folded carefully in plastic. She shook it out and held it up for Michael to see.

"Just imagine her wearing this and dancing with him here in the kitchen. Think of all the time we've spent here and the images she must have seen while cooking and sitting here with us, talking about our problems, about where to go to college, about how hard it is to have a successful marriage. God, we're so innocent and immature compared to her."

Michael nodded and turned to the cupboards above the sink. "Do you suppose Mother kept anything to drink around here? Lord knows I can use it. And, to answer your question, I don't know what we're going to do."

He rummaged through the cupboards and

found a bottle of brandy, almost empty. "There's enough for two drinks here, Carolyn. Want one?"

"Yes."

Michael took the only two brandy glasses from the cupboard and set them on the yellow Formica table. He emptied Francesca's last bottle of brandy into them, while Carolyn silently began reading volume one of the notebooks. "Robert Kincaid came to me on the sixteenth of August, a Monday, in 1965. He was trying to find Roseman Bridge. It was late afternoon, hot, and he was driving a pickup truck he called Harry. . . ."

Postscript: The Tacoma Nighthawk

As I wrote the story of Robert Kincaid and Francesca Johnson, I became more and more intrigued with Kincaid and how little any of us knew about him and his life. Only a few weeks before the book went to the printer's, I flew to Seattle and tried again to uncover additional information about him.

I had an idea that since he liked music, and was an artist himself, there might have been someone in the music and art culture of the Puget Sound area who knew him. The arts editor of the *Seattle Times* was helpful. Though he did not know of Kincaid, he provided me access to pertinent sections of the newspaper from 1975 through 1982, the period in which I was most interested.

Working through the 1980 editions, I came across a photo of a black jazz musician, a tenor saxophone player named John "Nighthawk" Cummings. And beside the photo was the credit line *Robert Kincaid.* The local musician's union provided me with Cummings's address, advising me that he had not played actively for some years. The address was on a side street near an industrial section of Tacoma, just off Highway 5 running down from Seattle.

It took several visits to his apartment before I found him at home. He was wary, initially, of my inquiries. But I convinced him I had a serious and benign interest in Kincaid, and he became cordial and open after that. What follows is a slightly edited transcript of my interview with Cummings, who was seventy at the time I talked with him. I simply turned on my tape recorder and let him tell me about Robert Kincaid.

Interview with "Nighthawk" Cummings

I was doin' a gig at Shorty's, up in Seattle where I was livin' at the time, and I needed a good black-and-white glossy of myself for publicity. The bass player told me there was a guy livin' out on one of the islands who did some good work. He didn't have a phone, so I sent him a postcard.

He came by, a real strange-lookin' old dude in jeans and boots and orange suspenders, takes out these old beat-up cameras that didn't even look like they'd work, and I thought, Uh-oh. He put me up against a light-colored wall with my horn and told me to play and keep on playing. So I played. For the first three minutes or so, the guy just stood there and looked at me hard, real hard, with the coolest blue eyes you've ever seen.

After a little while, he starts takin' pictures. Then he asks if I'll play "Autumn Leaves." And I do that. I play the tune for maybe ten minutes straight while he keeps banging away with his cameras, takin' one shot after another. Then he says, "Fine, I've got it. I'll have them for you tomorrow."

Next day he brings them by, and I'm knocked over. I've had a lot of pictures taken of me, but these were the best, by far. He charged me fifty dollars, which seemed pretty cheap to me. He thanks me, leaves, and on his way out asks where I'm playin'. So I tell him, "Shorty's."

A few nights later, I look out at the audience and see him sittin' at a table off in the corner, listenin' real hard. Well, he started comin' in once a week, always on a Tuesday, always drank beer, but not much of it.

I sometimes went over on breaks and talked with him for a few minutes. He was quiet, didn't say a lot, but real pleasant, always asked politely if I'd mind playin' "Autumn Leaves."

After a while we got to know each other a little I used to like to go down to the harbor and watch the water and ships, turns out, so did he. So we got to the point we'd sit on a bench for whole afternoons and talk. Just a couple of old guys winding it down, starting to feel a little irrelevant, a little obsolete.

Used to bring his dog along. Nice dog. Called him Highway.

He understood magic. Jazz musicians understand it, too. That's probably why we got along. You're playing some tune you've played a thousand times before, and suddenly there's a whole new set of ideas coming straight out of your horn without ever going through your conscious mind. He said photography and life in general were a lot like that. Then he added, "So is making love to a woman you love."

He was workin' on somethin' where he was tryin' to convert music into visual images. He said to me, "John, you know that riff you almost always play in the fourth measure of 'Sophisticated Lady'? Well, I think I got that on film the other morning. The light came across the water just right and a blue heron kind of looped through my viewfinder all at the same time. I could actually _see_ your riff while I was hearing it and hit the shutter."

He spent all his time on this music-into-images thing. Was obsessed by it. Don't know how he made a living.

He never said much about his own life. I knew he'd traveled a lot doing photography, but not much more until one day I asked him about the little silver thing he had on a chain around his neck. Up close, I could see the name _Francesca_ on it. So I asked him, "Anything special about that?"

He didn't say anything for a while, just stared out at the water. Then he said, "How much time do you have?" Well, it was a Monday, my night off, so I told him I had as much as it took.

He started talkin'. It was like a faucet got turned on. Talked all afternoon and most of the night. I had the feelin' he'd kept this all inside of him for a long time.

Never mentioned the woman's last name, never said where it all took place. But, man, this Robert

Robert James Waller

Kincaid was a poet when he talked about her. She must've really been something, one incredible lady. Started quotin' from a piece he'd written for her—something about Dimension Z, as I recall. I remember thinking it sounded like one of Ornette Coleman's free-form improvisations.

And, man, he cried while he talked. He cried *big* tears, the kind it takes an old man to cry, the kind it takes a saxophone to play. Afterward, I understood why he always requested "Autumn Leaves." And, man, I started to love this guy. Anyone who can feel that way about a woman is worth lovin' himself.

So I got to thinkin' about it, about the power of this thing he and the woman had. About what he called the "old ways." And I said to myself, "I've got to play that power, that love affair, make those old ways come out of my horn." There was somethin' so damn lyrical about it.

So I wrote this tune—took me three months. I wanted to keep it simple, elegant. Complex things are easy to do. Simplicity's the real challenge. I worked on it every day until I began to get it right. Then I worked on it some more and wrote out some lead sheets for the piano and bass. Finally, one night I played it.

He was out there in the audience, Tuesday night, as usual. Anyway, it's a slow night, maybe twenty people in the place, nobody payin' much attention to the group.

He's sittin' there, quietly, listenin' hard like he always did, and I say over the microphone, "I'm gonna play a tune I wrote for a friend of mine. It's called 'Francesca.' "

I watched him when I said it. He's starin' at his bottle of beer, but when I said "Francesca," he slowly looked up at me, brushed back his long gray hair with both hands, lit a Camel, and those blue eyes came right at me.

I made that horn sound like it never had before; I made it cry for all the miles and years that separated them. There was a little melodic figure in the first measure that sort of pronounced her name—"Fran . . . ces . . . ca."

When I finished, he stood real straight by his table, smiled and nodded, paid his bill, and left. After that I always played it when he came by. He framed a photograph of an old covered bridge and gave it to me for writin' the song. It's hangin' right over there. Never told me where he took it, but it says "Roseman Bridge" right below his signature.

One Tuesday night, seven, maybe eight years ago, he doesn't show. He's not there the next week, either. I think maybe he's sick or somethin'. I start to worry, go down to the harbor, ask around.

Nobody knows nothin' about him. Finally, I take a boat over to the island where he lived. It was an old cabin—shack, really—down by the water.

While I'm pokin' around, a neighbor comes over and asks what I'm doin'. So I tell him. Neighbor says he died about ten days ago. Man, I hurt when I heard that. Still do. I liked that guy a lot. There was somethin' about that cat, somethin'. I had the feelin' there were things he knew that the rest of us don't.

I asked this neighbor about the dog. He doesn't know. Said he didn't know Kincaid, either. So I call the pound, and sure enough they've got old Highway down there. I go down and get him out and gave him to my nephew. The last I saw of him, he and the kid were having a love affair. I felt good about that.

Anyway, that's about it. Not long after I found out what happened to Kincaid, my left arm started going numb when I play for more than twenty minutes. Something to do with a vertebra problem. So I don't work anymore.

But, man, I'm haunted by that story he told me about him and the woman. So, every Tuesday night I get out my horn, and I play that tune I wrote for him. I play it here, all by myself.

And for some reason I always look at that picture he gave me while I play it. Somethin' about it, don't know what it is, but I can't take my eyes off that picture when I play the tune.

I just stand here, about twilight, makin' that ol' horn weep, and I play that tune for a man named Robert Kincaid and a woman he called Francesca.